DEATH OF
THE DUCHESS

DEATH OF
THE DUCHESS

ELIZABETH EYRE

HARCOURT BRACE JOVANOVICH, PUBLISHERS

NEW YORK   SAN DIEGO   LONDON

Requests for permission to make copies of any part
of the work should be mailed to: Permissions,
Harcourt Brace Jovanovich, Publishers,
8th Floor, Orlando, Florida 32887.

First published in 1991 by Headline Book Publishing

Library of Congress Cataloging-in-Publication Data
Eyre, Elizabeth.
Death of the duchess/by Elizabeth Eyre.—1st ed.
p.   cm.
ISBN 0-15-124102-3
I. Title.
PR6009.Y74D4   1992
823'.914—dc20   91-25927

Designed by Camilla Filancia
Printed in the United States of America
First edition
A B C D E

To

NICCOLÒ MACHIAVELLI

in fond memory

CONTENTS

1. "So the Dog Barked, After All"   *1*
2. "They're Not Her Hands"   *8*
3. "Whose Colours?"   *20*
4. Dark as the Grave   *29*
5. "It Was Missing"   *44*
6. "Did I Kill the Duchess?"   *57*
7. "My Mistress Wishes to Sell This Ring"   *66*
8. "She Owed Me . . ."   *77*
9. "I Release You of Your Task"   *93*
10. "The Omens Are Excellent"   *104*
11. "Call Me Madam"   *116*
12. No Time to Waste   *124*
13. Cousin Caterina   *137*
14. "You've Lost Your Hair!"   *144*
15. "Like Grasping a Cloud"   *158*
16. "What Sort of Money?"   *169*
17. A Friend to True Love   *174*

18. "Escape, Would You?"   *184*

19. "You Want My Father
to Commit Treason?"   *192*

20. "There Is Her Murderer!"   *202*

21. "My Son, What Have You Done?"   *210*

22. After the Devil, the Dead Man   *215*

23. No One Is What They Seem   *224*

24. The Promise of Venus   *231*

DEATH of
the DUCHESS

1. "So the Dog Barked, After All"

"From this very bed she was snatched!"

The Lord Jacopo di Torre's long sleeve followed his dramatic gesture and swept a scent bottle from the bedside chest. The Duke's emissary, with an agility unexpected in one of his strong build, caught it and stood turning it as if to admire the carved onyx and gold. Jacopo waited for a comment about the bed, whose sheets had been wrenched back, pillows tossed abroad with every sign of a violent struggle. There could be no doubt that he was right. This had been the very bed.

"You heard nothing?" asked the deep foreign voice.

Jacopo's hands, waiting for the next gesture, balled themselves and struck at his forehead. "Nothing. Dear Mother of God, I sleep like the dead!"

The emissary's dark eyes genially surveyed the doorful of servants who gaped and manoeuvred for a better view. "And no one else heard anything?"

Heads were shaken. An elderly woman in an extinguishing headkerchief kept up a low wail amid her linen. Jacopo glanced at her with irritation. "Even my sister slept. No one heard anything. In this whole household, every living soul slept!"

Not one of the servants seemed ready to oppose this. To sleep soundly at a legitimate hour was, after all, the mark not of laziness but of exhaustion brought on by virtuous toil.

The emissary replaced the scent bottle, pushed askew with a finger the other objects on the chest—a pair of silver tweezers, an ivory comb, a Book of Hours in a red velvet cover, a carved ivory mirror with a bronze nymph for handle—and picked up the silver posset cup, removed the lid, and sniffed at it. The servants followed every action with the acute interest they would have given to a mime.

"You think she was drugged?" Jacopo pounced on the idea. "Was that why we did not hear her?" He seemed relieved that his daughter had not suffered the frustration of crying out unheard. "Ah. No. No one in this household . . ." Indignant agreement from the servants drowned out what promised to be an inconclusive remark in any case. A drug must be introduced by some hostile hand.

The heavy shoulders shrugged, and the emissary indicated, with a movement more economical than Jacopo's, the bed. A drugged girl might scarcely be capable of putting up such a fight. Brocade bed-curtains of green and gold sagged at the far side, ripped from the half-tester.

"The dogs slept too?"

Some agitation started among the servants; faces turned in question. "In the yard . . . other side the house . . . her little dog—"

The emissary caught the words. "Her little dog?"

"My daughter's dog." Jacopo gazed about, as though it should have the manners to come out and apologise. "It must have run away. Terrified."

"Too terrified to bark." The emissary nodded as if it were axiomatic that a wise dog would stifle noise for fear of harm. He asked no further about yard dogs that might be expected to sense an intruder where the righteously slumbering household did not.

"How did they get in?"

Jacopo chivvied him to the window with darting motions of the hands that failed of actually touching the fine black leather of the man's jerkin. He duly examined the forced shutters and stepped out onto the small loggia. He had a habit, which Jacopo found as irritating as his sister's wailing, of humming deep in his chest when he was shown anything. It was not a tune, but a sound like a satisfied bee. It conveyed the disturbing impression that all he saw was what he expected to see. He leant over the stone balustrade and, narrowing his eyes, surveyed the ground below. Jacopo snapped, "The roof. They came over the *roof*."

At his leisure, the large man reversed, sat on the balustrade, and, with a hand round the Ionic pillar, leant out to look along the roof, at the ridged tiles and the houseleeks.

"It is possible, just possible, to leap onto our roof from the next house. It is the only way they could have come. My walls are high; the gates to the courtyard are of course barred at night."

"But they did not leave this way, carrying the girl."

Certainly the roof did not look negotiable for anyone laden with a struggling girl, and even less so would be the leap to the neighbouring tiles.

"Of course not. Of course not. They left by a side door that gives onto the street. A servant found it unbarred this morning."

"Who found it?"

A man thrust forward, apple red with importance and, taking permission from a wave of his master's hand, spoke, while the others nodded in confirmation of a tale no longer fresh to them.

"It being my duty to fetch wood to the kitchens from the yard store of a morning, and going along past this door, I saw the bar was down, which it never is, us not using that door, and then I saw . . ." He paused, clearly expecting to be asked what it was he saw. As the emissary watched him in silence, he hurried on with his drama. "I saw—this!"

He produced what had been crumpled between his hands, a piece of torn cloth, yellow and red. Jacopo snatched it from him and held it out, quivering, to the emissary, close enough for him to sniff it, had he so required.

"You see! You see?"

The emissary would have had some difficulty not seeing the cloth thrust at his face, but he did not stir.

"You see? I told the Duke I had proof. It is the noble, the esteemed Lord Ugo Bandini who has abducted my daughter! These are his colours!"

The emissary took the piece of cloth and pulled it about, inspecting it idly. He hummed.

"Where was this found?"

"Caught on a nail, sir, just by the door."

"The villain must be brought to justice!" Jacopo twitched the cloth from the emissary's fingers. His indignation had a respectful echo, a groundswell of agreement from the servants. The stranger's eyes lifted to examine them again.

"Is your daughter, only, missing?"

That *only* made Jacopo draw himself up. "Her maid, it is true, is also gone. She slept here, of course. A Circassian slave." The straw mattress against the wall was indicated by a slight move of the hand. "They must have taken her for fear she would discover their appearance to us."

"She made no noise either."

Jacopo's eyes stared from widened circles of white. "Gagged! They were both, then, gagged! Snatched from their beds, carried off from under my roof. Who but Ugo Bandini would treat the Duke's command with such contumely? He has done this to prevent my daughter's marriage to his wretched son. I freely own"—he flung out his arms, as one revealing even his faults— "that I want the marriage no more than he does, but I am obedient to the Duke. The Duke must force Ugo Bandini to confess the crime. Who but he would perpetrate such a deed?"

"Bandits, for a ransom?"

"*Bandits!*" Jacopo's voice cracked; then he seemed to consider this idea for the first time and not to like it. The servants whispered, arguing, while the aunt renewed her moan and the emissary waited, head on one side.

"You think it unlikely, my lord. Yet it is said that you are the richest man in the city. Except for the Lord Ugo."

4

At the aspersion, Jacopo broke out once more, brandishing the coloured cloth. "Bandits? *He* is the bandit. This is my proof! My motherless daughter is in his hands. Let him look to her safety! The Duke must order that she be restored!"

"Excuse me, my lord." The emissary extended a hand, brown and powerful, took the piece of red and yellow, and stowed it in the bosom of his jerkin. "As you say, it is a witness. And now"—he bowed—"may I see the door which was found open?"

He saw it, after scrutinising the wall to the side of the stairs on the way down (a fresco obliterated by the grease of years of passage) and the nail which had held the cloth. He saw even the street outside the door, a side-lane, narrow and dark, with no inhabitant but an old man walking away with fragile slowness in the rutted mud, and a cur tormenting his heels. The emissary was minutely interested in a pile of horse dung near the door, and by the information, delivered with emphasis and repetition and by several voices, that the nightsoil of the household was conveyed away every week on this very day to the master's farm in the country, by a dung-cart left in this very lane the night before, to be collected this very morning. Farm men brought the clean cart, hitched the horse to the full one, and took it away. The clean cart, he was informed, that would prove the truth of what they told him stood in the kitchen yard just round the corner. It had been dragged in there the moment the house was awake, as the master liked, they added, discovering Jacopo's presence among them and bobbing their heads zealously.

Jacopo, seeing that the Duke's emissary was not content with observing horse dung in the lane but was now strolling up the lane towards the corner, the street and the yard gates, parted the servants after the manner of Moses with the Red Sea and bustled into the lane, grabbing up his velvet skirts and giving the dung all the room it needed.

"You think they went this way?"

"All possibilities are to be examined, my lord. The Duke was insistent."

Jacopo's mouth, opened for perhaps a protest, snapped shut. He adapted his step to the emissary's. A cat, eating something fascinating in the dust, lifted its head, sped across the lane and vanished into a dark doorway whence came a sound of clattering pots and yawning.

Round the corner they found the tall gates of the kitchen courtyard open to the street beneath the brick arch of the wall and a trio of burly men delivering jars of oil from a handcart. A smallish, vacant-looking man, not in livery but comprehensively clad in grime, stood watching, cradling and fondling a little woolly white dog in his arms. Jacopo speeded up and approached this man with pointing finger.

"Where did you get him? Where?"

The man looked up in innocent surprise, his mouth falling open with the ease of long practice. There was straw and dust in his black beard.

"It's m'lady's dog. Biondello."

"I know what it is. Where did you *find* it?"

The emissary, now at Jacopo's side, extended a finger to scratch the top of the dog's head, and withdrew it, nodding as though someone had made a useful statement.

"Where did you find him?" Jacopo spoke as one would address a large crowd in, say, an arena, and everyone except the small man and the emissary jumped. The small man did not actually jump, because he was being shaken by Jacopo.

"Foot of the wall, out there." He nodded at the street. He showed no resentment at the shaking and perhaps was grateful for the stimulus. Jacopo was the one now stunned and speechless.

The emissary said, "So the dog barked, after all."

The lack-wit had large round eyes. He looked up at the broad-shouldered man in black.

"Yes. Biondello had a good try."

He rocked the dog in his arms, bending his head over it and crooning as a girl might do to her doll. The movement allowed the dog's head to fall back and showed the gash across its throat. Blood dabbled the fluff of the white chest, and there was blood on its teeth.

"Who's a good little dog, then?"

A strange sound erupted from Jacopo, now rigid at the emissary's side.

"She's been abducted! *My daughter has been abducted!*"

Patently, it had needed the sight of the little dead dog to bring home to him the fact he had been trumpeting since dawn. Howling and weeping, he had to be led indoors by his sister and a knot of house servants. No sooner had the knot crammed itself in at the door than it burst out again and Jacopo appeared on the threshold, pointing.

"You! Benno! Out! Get out! Don't show your face near my doors again!"

As he bundled himself back into the house, it was obvious that someone had made a blunder: the dog, the dismissed servant or the master himself.

2. "THEY'RE NOT HER HANDS"

The emissary, undisturbed by the disturbance, continued to look about him in the street and the courtyard, watched, from a prudent position outside the gates, by Benno caressing the dead dog. He examined the dung-cart, its shafts up on a trestle, its lining of pitch far from clean, and finally he prepared to depart. He sent a message, by one of those who still found time to stare at him over the kitchen half-door, to present his compliments to their master and to tell him that a full report would be made to the Duke. At the courtyard entrance, Benno stood cuddling the dog so that its head was under his chin. He offered to fetch the emissary's horse.

"I have no horse."

Nothing but incomprehension in the large, mud-brown eyes.

"You're the Duke's man."

"I am, for the moment, the Duke's man."

"Where's your horse? Where's your servants?"

"I came on foot. You see more on foot. No servant. Servants talk too much." The deep voice was neutrally informative, neither kind nor unkind. The half-wit came closer, the dog seeming to squirm in his hands as he pressed it to him.

"I'll be your servant."

The emissary considered this piece of opportunism.

"I don't talk too much."

After a moment the emissary said, "Show me where you found the dog."

He quartered the ground in this vicinity, watched by Benno. The life of the street was now well established. People passed to and fro. An urchin offered to help look for the missing object and moved about on his hunkers like a busy frog for as long as the large man searched. This willingness earned him a ruffle of the louse-encumbered mat that was his hair, and a small coin. The emissary then set off at a brisk stride, Benno trotting to keep up. They climbed the steep streets towards the Palace, whose bleak defensible walls rose like cliffs above the town. The emissary's good clothes incited various sellers to importune him with offers of bread, water, olives, wine, dishes, knives, cloth, braid, jewellery, spices, confectionery and their bodies. As the two came to the long ramp circling the castle wall up to the gate, Benno paused at the sight in understandable discouragement; the emissary stopped too.

"What do you intend to do with the dog?"

Benno put his head on one side. "I could bury it somewhere nice. Under a rosebush. She'd like that."

The emissary hummed. It might have betokened approval. They set off up the ramp.

The Duke was in his chapel hearing Mass. He was also dictating to his secretary and looking over an architect's drawing held up by a page. He turned his head at the moment the tall figure in black lifted the curtain at the chapel doorway. The secretary was dispatched to bring him to the Duke, who extended a hand to be kissed and said, "So?"

The bell at the altar tinkled, rung by a round-faced child who was picking his nose. The priest, aglitter with silk and gold in the candlelight, raised the Host. The Duke, his secretary, the page and Sigismondo touched knee to the marble floor and crossed themselves. After a few minutes with eyes closed, the Duke came abruptly to his feet and made for the door, his spurs jangling on the stone. A page waited outside with a cup; the

Duke disencumbered himself of the brocade curtain, which had clung affectionately to his shoulder, and drank the cup off at one draught, filling the anteroom with a head-spinning smell of spiced wine.

The Duke was a lean man in his early forties. His French mother had bequeathed him blue eyes, but the force of their glance was his own addition. His mouth was wide, the nose short but with flared nostrils. It was a face, haggardly handsome and instinct with energy, of a man it might be rewarding to amuse but deeply unfortunate to provoke. At the moment, latent temper drew down his brows.

"Has Lord Ugo stolen his enemy's daughter?" He thrust the the cup towards the page and walked off swiftly along a high-vaulted passage ornamented with biblical frescoes. "I offer those two my own arbitration of their dispute and arrange its solution by the marriage of their children, and *they insult me.*"

"To the foolishness of man there is no end," Sigismondo answered. They came out on a long loggia above a great sloping courtyard where horses waited. Farther down, near the gates, an ungainly bonfire was being constructed. The Duchess's favourite, her mistress of the robes, a widow, was to marry today, and the Duchess had chosen to give the feast this evening—which probably accounted also for a thunderous argument for five voices going on somewhere indoors.

The Duke leant over the balustrade and shouted, "Walk the horses. *Walk* them!"—upsetting the grooms out of a cosy chat. He wheeled to face Sigismondo.

"Is Ugo Bandini to blame?"

"Shall I tell Your Grace what I found?"

The Duke fixed Sigismondo with the blue stare and waited.

"The abductors entered, I am told, over a roof. The roof in question is well made and without flaw. The houseleeks flourish on it unharmed. I was shown where the lady's chamber shutters had been forced. The servants keep the lady's loggia spotless. Her room was disordered, very much so. She, and her maid, were gone. Some of the servants sleep in the kitchen, some up under the roof. None of them heard a sound; they were not roused by the yard dogs. No one heard them bark. Nor did the lady's lapdog bark."

The Duke's face was intent.

"A side door to the lane was found unbarred. The lady and her maid, a Circassian slave, had been taken down a staircase. They may have been unconscious, but at all events there was no damage to the painted walls, no marks of scratching or the kick of a shoe. On a nail near the unbarred door was found this."

He offered the particoloured rag to the Duke, who glanced and exclaimed, "So it *was* Bandini! I'll have his head for it—"

The cloth was offered closer. The ducal head bent to examine the stitching. Sigismondo pointed to buckled threads on the yellow piece where the nail had caught. The Duke fingered the frayed edges of the piece.

"And this was torn from, one supposes, a sleeve, with force enough to rip it clean away—and without its owner knowing." The Duke's gaze now had reached incandescence. "Jacopo di Torre has done it himself! *He* has spirited his daughter away with pretence of an abduction, and placed this rag to put the blame on Bandini—to avoid marrying the girl to Bandini's son. To avoid reconciliation. To disparage *my command*." The distant grooms turned their heads.

"So far, the dumb witnesses say as much, Your Grace."

"So far. Ah." He was at once quiet. "Go on."

"Outside in the alley, horses had waited, well-fed country horses, my lord Duke, not mere dung-cart pullers. These, one supposes, belonged to Jacopo's men, with whom the docile daughter was to go with her slave-girl and her little dog. Then turn the corner into the road, and we find four things: plaster fresh kicked from a wall; the wheel-spokes of a dung-cart that had stood in the road, kicked to raw wood; a trample of hoof-marks, even close to the wall; and, beneath a splash of blood on the plaster, a dead lapdog."

The Duke was almost vibrant with attention.

"During all this time, while I searched, the Lord Jacopo's demeanour had been full of indignation, of fury against the Lord Ugo. When he saw the body of the dog, he cried out with great despair, '*My daughter has been abducted!*' and he had to be led into the house, stumbling."

The Duke's head went back. Something not pleasant enough to be called a smile moved his lips. "The biter bit? The girl *was* stolen? Taken from Jacopo's men in the street?"

"Which suggests that Jacopo's plan to hide his daughter was known by someone who took advantage of it to steal her."

"Ugo Bandini?"

Sigismondo shrugged. The Duke turned restlessly away and wheeled back. "This feud is costing me the peace of my city, and its prosperity. Jacopo has ruined a cousin of Bandini; there was a fire in a warehouse of di Torre's that burnt a street down, that he swore was set by Bandini, and may well have been. They fight in the street, destroying goods and endangering innocent citizens. Trade is neglected to pursue this battle."

"Is it of recent birth, this feud?"

"They have been rivals before, but the death of Matteo di Torre at a civic banquet started the worst of it. And all this time I am threatened by my neighbour, Francesco of Castelnuova—and there is the girl Cosima di Torre, the boy Leandro Bandini, to unite the families . . . *They insult me!* I shall see these warring parents before the feast tonight. Can you find the girl?"

"I can try."

"Tomorrow. I want you there at the meeting with these two tonight." The Duke clicked his fingers and extended his hands to a page who came hurrying with gloves. As these were being put on, Sigismondo spoke.

"With respect, Your Grace."

"With respect, Sigismondo? You have other thoughts?"

"The scent will be warm still."

"You are free until the feast. I do not suppose that in the few years since first we met you have learnt to move more slowly." He strode off. Sigismondo, straightening from his bow, watched the Duke join the horses. A girl, her gold hair in a gold net, herself furled in a sable cloak, was talking to the gentlemen who waited, and caressed the big dun whose green-and-white trappings declared it to be the Duke's. She curtsied as the Duke arrived, and he kissed her—his daughter Violante, child of an adored mistress who enjoyed the unfair advantage over all other mistresses of being dead and thereby faultless. Recently widowed, she had come back to her father, much to his delight.

As he left the loggia, Sigismondo drew back deferentially before another nobleman. His entourage and dress showed his importance—he wore the furs and embroidered velvets of rank—and he had a strong likeness to the Duke, both in face and in a slenderness that showed even in their long hands, alike right to the shape of the nails. They shared that flare of nostril that spoke of a harsh temper, but this man must be the Lord Paolo, the Duke's half-brother, whose reputation was of gentleness. Where he differed from the Duke was in the shape and colour of his eyes, dark eyes made melancholy by a curious downward fold of the upper lid, and in his olive complexion and dark hair. This, receding though partly hidden by the fur of his hat, made him look older than the Duke by more than his two years of seniority.

He paused and said, "Sigismondo?"

"My lord."

"I thought you must be he." Lord Paolo smiled. It was a smile that did not reach the sad eyes. "I am glad to have the chance to thank you."

"My lord?"

"You saved my brother's life. All Rocca owes you thanks. You choose to be modest, but it can't have slipped your mind. I understand he employs you now as his agent?" He gestured his entourage to stand away out of hearing. "It must be about this bitter affair of the feud."

"His Grace mentioned the death of Matteo di Torre?"

If the Lord Paolo noticed that his question had been answered with another, he merely laughed. "Alas. I seem heartless, I know, but I was next to him at the banquet. The trumpets sounded for the toast to His Grace, and poor Matteo, instead of rising to his feet with us, fell straight forward into his dish of scallops. Of course, his cousin Jacopo thought of poison, with a Bandini on Matteo's other hand, but I—I thought of shellfish, and did not finish my excellent scallops."

This time the eyes had smiled, and Sigismondo's face, by nature sombre, responded.

"What about the missing girl? I suppose it is the Bandini, although how they could have got hold of her is a mystery. Girls of good family are kept so close. What have you discovered?"

Sigismondo smiled again, shrugged, and spread his hands. "Nothing of use, my lord."

"What, then, that is of no use?"

A page in green and white came running in, saw the Lord Paolo, and approached him, bowing.

"I'm waited for." Lord Paolo retreated towards the door. "His Grace isn't patient. We must speak later."

———

Sigismondo found Benno where he had left him, but dogless. "You found a rosebush?"

"There was ever such a nice young gentleman that was being carried in a chair, and he stopped them when I was being thrown out and he asked me about the dog and he made his servant take me to the gardener with orders about the rosebush. He's the Duke's nephew that's a cripple, the Lord Paolo's son. I never saw him before; he don't go about the streets."

Sigismondo gave a hum of general assent. They walked down the wide cobbled ramp, and Benno began to speak, but, looking up at the dark, somewhat monumental face, he stopped and trotted alongside in silence. They left the Castello, coming out from the gatehouse tunnel and looking over the coral-and-gold patchwork, higgledy-piggledy, of tiled roofs punctuated by the tall spires of churches and the towers of minor palaces. Beyond these were fields and the great encircling wall with its gates and turrets; beyond that lay farmland, brown patches of woods and the rising undulations of the hills. The river, which through the centuries had sliced through the hills to the north, had come up against the outcrop of Rocca in the course of its meanderings through the valley and, recognising an immovable object when it saw it, took a respectful loop around its base and dawdled off into the distance where, just visible, lay the sea.

After a walk through the town, Benno found the answer to the question he had not asked. They reached the town's east gate, not far from di Torre's house, and Sigismondo fell into conversation with the guard.

Benno might, on experience so far, believe geniality to be well beyond Sigismondo's capability or even his wishes. Now, in easy conversation with the guard, he flowered into smiles. He told jokes. It could be observed that he had good teeth. In twelve minutes he had established that the guard indeed kept good watch, for they were accountable to the Duke's marshal, a man in whom the milk of human kindness had long ago curdled. Because of the interest being shown in Rocca by the Duke Francesco of Castelnuova, they kept tally of who went in and out. No strangers this morning, no riders, only market people and the charcoal men, and the di Torre dung-cart that went out as usual.

"That one's too mean to pay the city scavengers. All his shit has to go back on his own fields."

"Nothing unusual about that cart, eh? No escort of angels."

This went down so well that they almost neglected to tally in a pigeon seller and a dwarf from up in the hills.

Sigismondo left them and asked Benno for the handiest way to the next gate. Benno closed his mouth and led Sigismondo through alleys and courts; down arched twittens between houses; through a church, two market gardens, a carpenter's yard and a square full of washerwomen full of interesting suggestions as to their relationship as the linen was smacked on the troughs; and out onto a main street where he halted to smile up proudly. He received an approving hum on three descending major notes, and a grip on the shoulder.

This gate was busy. It took longer, but Sigismondo leant on the wall in the sun, and bought almonds of a passing seller, and handed them round, and commented on the passersby, the succulence of two girls who went up the street, and the ancestry of the Duke's marshal. Before long he was conversing.

Out of this gate, which gave onto the road to another of the Duke's towns, a good many went. In the early morning, yes, it was easier to notice people. The only outgoers that were unusual and therefore noticeable this morning, for instance, had been a closed litter escorted by a Dominican. It was decrepit, the curtains shabby, and both their laces and the horse's harness mended with twisted tow. The monk was taking his aunt to her family to die among her kin, and the litter-driver was not being paid enough to make him good-tempered.

At the third gate was Benno's cousin Nardo, gifted from birth with an enormous curiosity and a tongue hinged in the middle. He wanted to know what Benno did strolling the streets. Benno claimed to be looking for a job, since he rather thought he was out of one. Nardo told him, taking some trouble about it, why his own job would be beyond Benno's intellectual grasp, and Benno listened, wide-eyed and agape, to a description of what it entailed.

"Do you have to *remember* things like who went in and out?"

Nardo not only had to remember any influx of unknown people but was gifted with total recall. In face of Benno's amazed incredulity, he recited the day's traffic. Sigismondo once again leant his shoulders on the wall and listened. Once more he had found a patch of sun that gilded his face and threw the surprising shadow of his eyelashes on his cheekbones. Nardo's list had some of the properties of infinity, but Benno's expression did not change. The sole item of interest, a grain of rice in an interminable trickle of sand, was that a party of horsemen had left the town not long after the gates were opened, one man with a girl wearing a fine cloak huddled in his arm. This rider, arranging his own cloak, had lost hold of it just as he rode under the flambeau on the wall and had shown the Bandini yellow and red beneath.

The great bell in the clock tower gave the town its accustomed nasty shock at last, and Sigismondo heaved his shoulders from the wall, told Benno that he hadn't got all day, and set off up the street. When Benno caught up with him, he said, "Nicely done. Now we need a horse."

The track they rode out on spread across a hundred yards of countryside. Wagons had made mudholes and deep ruts, and had driven wide to avoid former mudholes and deep ruts, and riders had ridden either side of this to avoid the mess, and those on foot had plodded on either side of this to avoid the parched hoof-tracks and manure.

Where any path led off this highway to left or right, Sigismondo rode to look at it, and Benno, up behind him on the big bay, would lean to see if what Sigismondo was looking at would tell him what it was. He had no idea why one such path held such appeal for the Duke's emissary that he turned the horse along it. They rode into trees at the edge of a sizeable wood.

He gazed in the direction of Sigismondo's pointing finger, where a thin line of smoke waved upwards through the trees ahead. He thought he understood, for anyone tending a fire might of course have noticed horsemen passing with a girl. Sigismondo moved his heels and the horse quickened pace. The riders ducked beneath bare winter branches of the oaks as they went farther into the wood. At length they came upon a small clearing and the fire.

Benno writhed round and dropped from the horse, stumbled, as his ankles hurt, and ran forward towards the white-dressed figure lying half in the fire. Sigismondo's feet thudded to the ground, and together they lifted the girl from the embers. There was a choking smell of burnt meat, burnt cloth and burnt hair. Benno coughed, a sound very like someone who might vomit.

She had been lying on her face and there was very little left of it. Her small skull was blistered and scorched, the frizzled roots of her hair across it.

Benno ducked from the sight. He was weeping. He picked up a fold of her skirt and thrust it at Sigismondo.

"My lady. My lady." Gold thread glittered in arabesques on the cream satin. A small pink embroidered flower had a crystal in its centre that winked in the light as Benno's hand trembled. "They killed her. *The devils . . .*"

Sigismondo released her hands, which had been tied behind her, with one sweep of his knife, and Benno possessed himself of one of them and kissed it, weeping. Sigismondo sat back on his heels and waited. After a minute Benno made a questioning sound, blinked, and scrubbed at his eyes. He stared at the hand he grasped. Then he looked up and met the steady brown gaze of Sigismondo, who hummed thoughtfully.

"You're right, Benno," he agreed. "They're not her hands."

3. "WHOSE COLOURS?"

Benno said, "Sascha." He lowered the hand he held, gently, to the girl's breast, as if to hide the rough, short nails, the needle-frayed fingers, a callus from some routine work she would not ever do again.

"Her maid, Benno?"

Once more picking up the embroidered hem of the dress, and holding it out to the brooding face opposite, Benno asked, "Why is she wearing my lady's dress?"

"A disguise. To fool people. To make any who saw her, such as your cousin Nardo, believe it was a lady riding away with horsemen."

"They only saw her cloak, not her dress." Benno stood up and glanced about.

"No cloak." Sigismondo had seen that already. "The dress *might* have shown; they might have seen it, as they saw the horseman's livery."

Benno, reminded of the Bandini, clenched his fists, but before he could speak, Sigismondo leant forward and began to undo the girl's dress.

"What are you doing?"

"If you're my servant, you'll not question what I do. In this instance, I'll tell you. We're looking for injuries."

Benno scrambled nearer and helped to pull off the dress and the shift. He looked at the bruised throat and bloodied thighs, and said, "Bandini devils. But I mean, she was only a slave. That's what servants get, isn't it?"

Sigismondo began to put the dress on again, wrapping the

terrible head in her shift. Then he crossed the girl's hands on her breast and, kneeling up, pulled off his hood. Benno, once again startled by the totally shaven head, only automatically knelt, and as Sigismondo spoke phrases of Latin, Benno stared and failed to say "Amen." Sigismondo looked at him and he hastily shut his mouth. However, his face had asked the question, and Sigismondo, humming amusement, rubbed a hand over his bare brown scalp.

"I'm not a priest, no."

He said no more. They returned to the city with the girl in Sigismondo's embrace under his cloak, Benno at his stirrup, unaware of the stripes of tears down the grime of his face.

Sigismondo commandeered a blanket from the inn where they had hired the horse and rode on up to the Palace, where he asked for a private audience of the Duke. That he was at once granted it made Benno's jaw drop once more. He trotted after his master, turning his head constantly to admire painted columns, friezes, statues and tapestries, and coming up suddenly against Sigismondo's back when they stopped at a door. While his master was admitted, Benno gaped at the marble door-casing and, it being suggested forcefully by the guard that he should remove his person somewhat, he stood back. He felt in his pocket for an old sweetmeat stuck to the lining, prised it out and put it in his mouth. He sucked at it loudly and revolved slowly on his heels to take in the coved ceiling with its gold leaf gleaming in the torches' light. There were decorated pillars with painted oak garlands twining up, and tapestries of the hunt that rippled in the draughts and made the figures seem to move. There were garlands of bay, tied with scarlet ribbons, that servants were busy hanging along the front of the gallery above; the work was done without the argument and shouting he was used to in the di Torre household. He was admiring the smooth black and white lozenges of the floor when he heard a familiar voice and slid prudently into the nearest shadows.

Jacopo di Torre had arrived, supported by his secretary, a man who would have looked at home in a weasel's den and who had once deliberately stuck the point of his quill into Benno's hand when he interrupted him at work, and by his steward, who habitually kicked Benno whenever he saw him. Benno became one with the shadows.

His former master was, in these few hours, a changed man. Grief had dealt rather badly with his face, hollowing the cheeks and swelling the eyes and nose. Even the hair straggling from under the velvet cap seemed greyer than before. Now the swollen lids lifted and rage succeeded grief; secretary and steward changed their grasp desperately from support to restraint: Ugo Bandini approached with contemptuous slowness, furred gown dragging on the marble, pages in red and yellow two paces behind.

"*Where is she?* I will have justice of the Duke! You shall be forced to give her up!"

Ugo Bandini chose the most infuriating response. He said nothing. A man of late middle age, he had a lugubrious face, all downward folds like that of a hound, and an expression managing to combine exhaustion with superiority. Benno, ingrained by the years of being partisan, could perfectly understand anyone wanting to kill him just for looking like that, let alone for stealing their daughter. Steward and secretary were having a time of it preventing Jacopo from surging forward to hammer Ugo into the black-and-white marble. Benno decided he would look rather well as the centrepiece to one of the bay garlands, his neck encircled by the scarlet ribbon.

Others were arriving now; the servants were being bustled to finish with the garlands by a man with a gold-tipped white wand, who used it to point out the bits they had not got straight. A page ran up the steps of the dais to brush the red velvet seat and carved back and arms of the chair of state, and to tidy its fringes of gold bullion. He ran lightly down again, his curled hair bobbing at each step.

Men and women had already collected in gossiping groups near the dais. There was an impression of rich jewel-sewn cloth sweeping in sleeves and skirts, of fur and brocade, gold-woven gauze twisted round the women's heads, great ornate brooches and pendants. Benno's loyal eyes saw no woman as lovely as the Lady Cosima, though several were as young—appearing in public only because they were married. Jacopo had turned away from the crowd, his cramped shoulders eloquent of the feelings barely under control. Most of the crowd glanced at the two men continually, isolated on either side of the hall.

The curtains of gold brocade over the door that had admitted Sigismondo now parted. The two pages in green and white with bannered trumpets swept them to their lips and blew, the sound hushing the crowd and turning them all like puppets to face the man who entered.

He stood for a moment magnificent, in an open gown, green lined with ermine, and a high-collared cloak, observing the bent heads, doffed caps and curtseys, and then he strode to the chair. When he sat, pages arranged the great spread of fur that draped three steps beneath him. A small movement of one of his hands made all rise from their reverences; a second movement brought Sigismondo's dark figure to stand on the lowest step at one side. Benno was aware of a whispering in the crowd. His master, standing there, one foot on the next stair, with lowered eyes and bared head, his face grave, hands at his sides, produced an extraordinary sense of strength.

As the Duke seemed about to speak, a figure detached itself from a small group and approached to whisper in the Duke's ear. Benno identified him, the Duke's bastard half-brother, the Lord Paolo, much loved at Court as a peacemaker and in the city as a giver of charity.

The Duke's brother stepped back; the Duke raised a hand and spoke. "We will hear the Lords di Torre and Bandini in private."

Benno shared the feeling of acute disappointment obvious among the withdrawing courtiers. Unlike them, however, he had no intention of leaving, and a strong confidence born of experience that, having made himself invisible, he would not be seen. Indeed, two ladies, discontentedly murmuring to each other as they passed, brushed his face with their gauzy head-veils without seeing him in the pillar's dark embrasure.

Finally, all had left except the Duke's brother, a man with a clerk's face Benno supposed to be the Duke's secretary, the enemy lords and Sigismondo. Pages and guards retired, closing the doors. Benno, for the moment holding his breath, had a strong and curious feeling that Sigismondo, though he had not turned his head towards him at all, knew that he was there.

"My lords."

Formally, the Duke bent his head to both; both bowed to him. Jacopo, deprived of supporters, looked oddly frail, but his energy returned in a rush when the Duke turned to him and said only, "Your daughter—"

"*Stolen!* I accuse Ugo Bandini! There stands the man who has snatched my daughter from me! I demand justice from my Duke!"

The Duke, who could scarcely be accustomed to interruption, frowned. His tone sharpened.

"There are questions to be put to you, di Torre: why, if your daughter was snatched from her chamber, did she have time to dress and to take with her the slave-girl and the dog?"

Di Torre started an answer, failed in it and began a protest, stopped, and glared at Sigismondo.

"You told our agent that her abductors must have come over the roof, yet there was no sign of disturbance, no tiles cracked, no plants broken. Nor did any dogs bark, so the men you say came either were no strangers to the household, or they never entered."

Protest bubbled now on Jacopo's lips, but the Duke went relentlessly on, his voice ringing harshly in the room's emptiness. "You yourself, di Torre, arranged for your daughter to go. You sought to disobey our decree that she marry Leandro Bandini. *You sought to deceive us.* And you have been terribly repaid."

He nodded to Sigismondo, who went out through the gold-hung doorway and reappeared bearing a blanket-wrapped form. At the foot of the dais he laid it down and pulled the blanket away. The white-clad body with its swathed head rolled free, a hand hitting the floor, and the swathing fell partly aside, disclosing a burnt cheek and ear.

Sigismondo had let fall the blanket and moved straight to di Torre so that he was behind him, catching him, as he dropped. The Lord Paolo was almost as quick, hurrying to a side table out of sight behind the dais curtains and returning with a cup of wine. The clerk, on the Duke's orders, laid the blanket over the girl's body once more, turning his face from the sight.

Di Torre gasped and groaned, drank wine, and was helped upright. Lord Paolo was the only one showing concern. Bandini evinced a most dislikeable righteous distaste. The Duke looked as merciless as a wild animal before the jump that sets its teeth in your throat.

"That is not your daughter, di Torre. It is her slave-girl, who, either in fear or in complicity, put on her clothes."

Jacopo was still working on some form of reply when the Duke turned his blue stare on Bandini.

"And you, my lord. To maintain the feud between your two families, the feud that threatens our state, you have been ready to kill."

Benno had once seen a man walk off the edge of a mounting block expecting a stair; the same change happened now to Bandini's face. "Your Grace, I swear—"

The Duke's hand, flashing light from its rings, silenced him. "You took di Torre's daughter from outside his house. There were signs of struggle in the road, our agent tells us, and blood upon the wall. You had her conveyed out of the city at dawn."

The words gave Jacopo his strength, if not his senses. His hand fell to his dagger and he began to draw it. Sigismondo's hand clamped down and rammed the weapon back in its sheath before it had showed its steel in the Duke's very presence. Ignoring him, the Duke continued, "You had the slave-girl murdered and left in the fire to destroy any chance of identifying her face; you wished it thought that the lady Cosima di Torre had perished there, dishonoured."

Bandini, flinging his arms wide, answered, "Not by me, Your Grace. Not by me or my orders. I am innocent of all this. The Lord di Torre seeks as always to discredit me in your eyes, and by what a vile trick he has done it this time. What proof can there be that any of this is my doing? Robbers have taken the girl and murdered the maid."

"Why should robbers leave a valuable dress on the dead girl, a dress sewn with gold thread and ornamented with gems? Do robbers behave so?" The Duke's voice was cool now, as if he debated an ordinary question. "There was design to deceive."

"To put Your Grace's justice off their track, perhaps. Who can tell what may be in the minds of thieves? To honest men, the intentions of rogues are not to be fathomed." A raised arm jabbed a finger towards di Torre. "He has fastened this abduction upon me to deceive Your Grace. He, *he* has had the poor girl slaughtered to further his deception."

Jacopo turned on Sigismondo with sudden energy and scrabbled at the breast of his jerkin. "The cloth, man, the cloth!" He was busy trying to undress Sigismondo, who looked down at his efforts with grave interest and then produced the rag of yellow and red from the pocket on his belt. Jacopo snatched at it, but Sigismondo had swung it overhead from his grasp and, at the Duke's beckoning finger, brought it to him. Di Torre's voice cried like a daw, "Your Grace sees! Tell His Grace . . ."

The Duke's hand and glance silenced his tongue, but his hands continued to make urging movements as if to a dog. Sigismondo showed him the cloth. "Is this the one you mean, sir?"

"Of course, of course it is."

"It is the piece found on the nail by the door? The door by which the Lady Cosima seems to have left your house?"

"Yes, yes. See, that is the mark of the nail."

Ugo Bandini watched with close-shut mouth and eyes of fury, a hound on a tight leash. Sigismondo approached the Duke, and, going down on one knee, showed him the cloth. "Your Grace will see here the pucker where the nail held the cloth." His deep voice might be that of a priest teaching. "The seam is well stitched and close."

"We observe." The plural at this juncture might be supposed to mean not the Duke himself only but his brother too, who had come forward with quick interest.

Sigismondo stepped to a pillar near the dais, and his fingers found what he must have noted, a nail for hanging garlands. He fitted the cloth over this and, after a moment's pause, gave it a sharp wrench. Returning, he held out the rag between his hands. The nail had dragged a hole in it, and every stitch in the seam was frayed.

Lord Paolo spoke. "Then this was not torn before? Surely, it could not have been manufactured to implicate . . ." He drew back, averse to saying out loud what he thought, but his eyes went towards Bandini.

His distaste was magnified a thousandfold in the whole person of Ugo Bandini. He seemed to swell with indignation, but his outburst and di Torre's violent denial rang together. They turned on each other but discovered Sigismondo between them. This silenced them for the moment it took Lord Paolo to say, "If I may ask a question of Your Grace's agent?"

The Duke still watched the antagonists. He gave permission, as before, with a hand.

"Was it you who found—this poor girl?"

"Yes, my lord."

"How did you trace her?"

"I asked at the gates, my lord."

"The guards at the gates, they must know the household servants of the great houses, do they not? They could surely have identified any of them leaving the city. You have not said that those who went out with the girl were of di Torre's or Bandini's house. If the guards did not know them, then surely they must be robbers."

"They were hooded, my lord, and this was at cocklight; but they did see the colours of one rider by the flambeaux."

"Colours?" said the Duke. "Whose colours?"

Sigismondo held out the scrap of cloth. "Bandini, Your Grace."

4. DARK AS THE GRAVE

The Duke was on his feet as the two men launched into howling oratory. His handclap, like a musket shot, silenced them and brought an eruption of men-at-arms through the doors. He held up his hand to still his men and ordered the doors closed. In the resumed quiet, he nodded to his secretary, who went to stand at his desk. Di Torre was once more sagging, Bandini working his hands inside his sleeves in frustration.

"When I last called you before me," said the Duke, and his voice cracked with anger, "I warned you that one single act more in this feud from either of you would be punished. The fine I threatened then is now exacted. You are both now confined to your houses, you and your families."

As both men began to speak, he strode to the front of the dais and there, towering above them, said, "Silence!" The secretary's quill skittered and squeaked, recording his decree. Sigismondo had stepped back from between the men and stood with hands clasped before him. The Duke's surge of movement was a tangible force that stilled the antagonists.

"You would speak? You would object? Protest at my mercy? I tell you now—do you mark me, Bandini? do you hear, di Torre?—that this is the last of my mercy to you. If either lifts hand or causes hand to be lifted against the other, their kind, goods, chattels, servants or lands, that man forfeits his possessions to the state, his household goods and merchandise, moneys and bonds, clothing and chattels, and his very life shall be at our mercy. I will have these wars no more. Bandini, you will restore the girl. This is our decree this day and shall not be revoked."

He turned on his heel and strode from the chamber, the great cloak swirling behind him. The secretary still wrote, the guards opened the doors, and the Duke's marshal entered. Both men seemed stricken to stone. Di Torre recovered first, hurrying to meet his secretary and steward, talking to them frenetically as they followed him to the door, and paying no heed to the slave-girl's shrouded form. Bandini spoke to Sigismondo, who bowed slightly, before he went out by another door. The girl's body was lifted and taken away. Courtiers entered, crowding round the great fireplace, speculating loudly and with animation on what might have passed, guessing and making bets. Sigismondo turned and came down the length of the room. With one hand he collected Benno from his niche and propelled him past the men-at-arms at the side door into an anteroom of plain, unadorned stone. He gave Benno's head a slight cuff that set it ringing.

Benno followed him down a stair and into an unexpected small room in a bend of the flight. A leather curtain shut it off from the stair; a lantern burnt on the floor beside a pallet. There was a decided lack of space for anything else. Sigismondo lifted a corner of the bed and pulled out a roll from below it, which undid into a cloak resembling the Duke's only in size, being plain dark wool. He lent Benno a corner of it, furled himself in the rest, and said, "We have time to sleep before the feast. If you can make yourself cleaner you may stand behind me at table and get a share."

Benno, who had long ceased to smell his own odours and who had been smelling the feast for some time, felt cheerful. He had not given any thought to how he might eat; that was Sigismondo's responsibility as his master, and he felt well catered-for in the prospect. He curled up on the end of the pallet.

"I've never been to a feast before," he said.

"Make the most of it. Tomorrow may be well occupied."

"What—," Benno said, and stopped.

"M'm-m'm. Well done . . . I'm far from sure that Bandini will be able to restore your lady to her father."

"What's he done with her, then?" Benno straightened up, alarmed, and the bed's ropes creaked.

"I'm far from sure that he ever did anything with her."

"But his colours, that Nardo saw?"

"His colours, like the ones di Torre hung on a nail in his house? We may be looking farther than Bandini. Perhaps even beyond Rocca."

"Beyond?" Beyond the city itself was far enough for Benno to envisage. He knew the road to Jacopo di Torre's country villa, and some of the rides round it where Cosima was allowed out as she could not be in the city, but it had not occurred to him that there was more. The Lady Cosima was very learned and had told him there were places called Rome and France, and her explanations had placed these for him in the sky beyond Rocca's wide valley.

"The Duke Francesco has an interest in causing trouble."

"I thought the Duke was called Ludovico," Benno said.

Sigismondo suddenly hummed in a sound like laughter. "Our Duke Ludovico is Duca di Rocca. All the world is made up of states like Rocca. To the east is the Duke Francisco. His duchy is mountainous, and he'd like the rich farmland and the sea coast of Rocca. Like the di Torre and the Bandini, these Dukes have their rivalries."

A vast and terrifying horizon opened to Benno, a world of confusion, distance and the unknown. He took breath.

"How . . ."

"M'm. Ask."

"Does it go far?" Benno asked uncertainly.

"Does what?"

"The world."

There was a silence in the near-dark. Sigismondo's voice

came at last. "I've travelled over some of it. It's much the same everywhere: rocks, fields, hills, streams, cities, farms. I've been to places where they speak other tongues—Muscovy, the Holy Land, Hispania, England, the Low Countries."

Benno sighed. He could make out Sigismondo's head propped against the wall with the square shape of the leather pillow behind. His eyes were shut. The smell of cooking distracted Benno's mind, and he evaded the thought of all that strangeness by homely imagination of the feast.

The night was a cold one. Even the Duchess, giving the feast for the Lady Cecilia, could not command it otherwise; a wind with ice on its breath came down from the snow-sprinkled hills to the north to investigate the preparations. The bonfire in the Palace courtyard that was to burn all evening flamed more brightly to its gusts, and sparks blew away to the cold stars; round the courtyard were the windows and balconies where spectators, waiting for the feast, leant out to admire the conflagration and to throw down sweetmeats at the crowd below. They held their furs and velvets close round their throats.

The wind was less kind to the beggars crowding outside the walls, trying to cram into what shelter they could find, waiting patiently enough for what would come their way when the feast was over. The wind at its keenest brought the sound of drums, tabors and the confused roar of people enjoying themselves inside.

As there must always be those who starve while others gorge, so there must be those who work while others benefit in idleness. The kitchens were ablaze with fires and quarrels; sweat fell into the dishes as cooks bent to arrange the last touches, to press the last bit of gold leaf that kept falling off, to spread the peacock's feathers behind the roasted bird so that it could sail in its glory on the golden dish and make the guests applaud. They would be less pleased when they came to eat it, but they knew that.

Already goosefat had been smeared on burns, kitchen boys rubbed their kicked bottoms or the bruises from ladles, one cook was so drunk his knives had been taken from him; and the cage of small birds, waiting to be popped into the baked pastry coffin and later to entertain the company by flying out when it was cut open, had been knocked over onto the floor and burst, filling the pastry-kitchen with the hustle of wings. Birds flew into the fires, banged against the shutters, tried to escape up the chimneys, knocked linen caps askew, were panicked by flying aprons, and muted into everything. A tart of little jellies, in almond-milk, in the shape of various animals was luckily already coloured with saffron. There was otherwise a great wiping, scraping and covering with sauces.

In another part of the castle, a white palfrey was still having its mane and tail plaited with ribbons by grumbling grooms. It was well used to the process and did no more than step sideways on someone's foot. Out in the yard, painters put the last touches of silver to the azure cut-outs of wooden waves, harassed by the carpenter anxious to fix the waves to a boat whose wooden wheels they were meant to hide. The boat had already capsized twice, and a boy with a stinking gluepot was aboard fixing sails again. In a room near Sigismondo's a number of dwarves were putting on gaudy costumes, posing in feathered hats and squabbling *à l'outrance* as to who should wear the one with plumes dyed superbly scarlet. Two dwarves sat in peaccable silence in a corner, mending long chains of iron-grey paper, rustling like a nest of mice as they worked.

These and other preparations were given terminal urgency by the news that the Duke and Duchess had entered the hall and taken their places under the canopy. Halfway down one wall, the musicians' gallery jutted out. The players operated under difficulty, for they must play loudly enough to be heard but not so loud as to interfere with conversation, and besides, the Duke's reputation as a patron of the arts absolutely required that as well as a harp, a cittern, several lutes and trumpets, and a horn, his orchestra should be modern enough to possess a clavicembalo, which many thought surpassed the organ for its variety of notes; in consequence they were so cramped that a trumpet player had caught his instrument in a garland during the prolonged fanfare that heralded and accompanied the Duke's entrance. He was having trouble freeing it from a young thicket of bay and a number of loops of ribbon.

Trailing ribbons were a constant feature this evening. In an anteroom off the great hall, seven girls were twining green, silver and blue ribbons round their bare arms and, in spite of the fire blazing in the hearth, were delaying the moment when they would have to strip to the layer of gauze that provided the minimum of decency. At a wedding feast for a lady who had been married before, no one expected more than the minimum of decency, and before the evening would be over, a good deal of indecency was confidently expected.

Rumours of the Duke's anger and its consequences for the di Torre and Bandini families had reached everyone there, and indeed the absence of some of the kinsfolk of the two parties meant that some guests sat at higher places than they could have hoped for. Speculation about the fate of Cosima di Torre was a hushed undercurrent in the talk. No one among friends of the two enemies dared make partisan remarks in the presence of the Duke. Heads were perpetually being turned to study his expression, although it disappointingly maintained a steady amiability. He sat, after all, next to the bride. Heads turned also to stare at the Duke's agent, the man from nowhere, so hard to place socially that it had taken a directive from the Duke himself for his steward to find him room at one of the long side tables. Courtiers nearby eyed him as if an executioner sat at meat beside them, though he wore good velvet and linen and bore himself in modest quiet. An uncouth servant stood behind him, but it was the man himself who held the eye. Mysteries might amuse, but secrets were made to be investigated. Someone had heard he was a soldier who had saved the Duke's life a good few years ago, before he inherited his present rank. Ladies pointed out, in support of this tale, the breadth of this man's shoulders. He was clearly a man of the sword. Others objected. His shaven head made him resemble a man of the cloth. One lady was visited by the conviction that he was a Templar, and this gained credence: there was very little, after all, that could not be believed of the Templars.

The Lady Cecilia, in whose honour the Duchess gave this feast, was thought a little vivacious for a new bride, even one who was bride for the third time. Her first husband, as Sigismondo could gather from talk along the table, had been an elderly lord believed to have died of ecstasy in her arms. The second, younger, had had the ineptitude to break his neck in a boar hunt. The third, middle-aged and heavily built, florid, had black eyebrows bristling over small black eyes, and devotedly watched his wife's face and other parts of her that were exposed to view. When enough wine had been drunk to lower the moral tone of the talk, speculation began on how long he would last before going the way of the first husband. The Lady Cecilia glanced at him often with arch promise and would turn again to the Duke with a warmth that implied a generosity with such promises.

The Duchess did not notice, or did not mind, or did not wish it to be thought that she minded. Her wedding celebrations had been far gaudier than this and were fondly remembered by the citizens of Rocca, or by such who could remember anything after three days and nights of the fountain in the great square of Saint Agnes running wine. She had had better luck than the Duke's first wife, too, presenting him with a son only last summer, who looked in a fair way to survive; the other two, girls, having died shortly after their births, had thus saved her husband a great deal of money in dowries in the years to come.

Lady Cecilia had presented neither former husband with children. The lady on Sigismondo's left ascribed this to bad luck, and the lady on his right, to a sponge dipped in vinegar.

All this time the servers had been hurrying in the space before the tables, bringing dishes, pouring wine, carving from the platters of roast swan; opening great pies of capons, hens and wildfowl baked with marrow, egg yolks, prunes, figs and spices; offering baskets of manchet bread; and now the trumpeters received their signal from the wand of the steward below and launched into another fanfare. A boy with an ivy garland on his hair managed to get to the front of the gallery and, as the trumpets were lowered and the diners hushed, he began a somewhat shrill, piercingly sweet solo. Pages drew back the curtains at the end of the hall for the entrance of the nymphs; stripped at last to their gauze, they rippled before them long scarves of silk, also in blue, green and silver, sufficiently like the undulating waves now being described in the song. The curtains were drawn apart again as the nymphs processed up the hall, and it was seen that they were whifflers for Venus Anadyomene herself, in a long tunic of white silk with a broad, jewelled girdle. Her hair, white as her tunic and probably also of silk, flowed to her knees. She was leading a white palfrey, and a small flock of doves was released, or rather thrown, into the air after her. The palfrey, its mane glittering with gold and silver ribbons, bore on its back a boy of about six, in a wig of gold curls and nothing else but a quiver of gold arrows and a gold-painted bow, which he pretended to aim at the guests. After him came more nymphs strewing silk rose petals from gilt baskets.

The solo, in Latin, praised the generosity of the Queen of Love in giving her favours to those who truly worshipped her, the Lady Cecilia evidently qualifying; when the procession reached the high table, the boy Cupid, fiercely concentrating, took aim. The Lady Cecilia's husband received one dart, a gilt reed fledged with rose-dyed feathers, full on his broad chest, where it hung, caught in the braid. The applause made the palfrey sidle, spoiling Cupid's aim. The Lady Cecilia's dart failed to reach her and, to the accompaniment of her amused cry, dropped into the Duke's goblet, spattering his hand with wine. Later this would be regarded as full of omen, but now the Duke wiped the red drops away with the napkin his page at once offered, and he laughed and clapped with the rest, making some joke to Cupid that none could hear.

The procession of Venus withdrew, while the doves flapped in the roof or landed among the food and were impounded by servers. The next course came in, to a burst of music: heron; a cockatrice compounded of the rear of a pig and the front half of an immense capon, sewn meticulously together and nestled in vegetables; large fish so ornamented with rosettes of sauce that their disguise was absolute; hens that were mere chicken skins moulded over the boned meat and stuffing; and game pies and hares in wine.

The next entertainment arrived to a roll of drums and a continued clash of tambourines. The Florentine hired by the Duchess was still concerned with classical or nuptial allusions but had also used what came to hand. The curtains, hoisted high this time, admitted a ship, the height of a man and the length of two, with curved, monstrous prow, turrets either end and a sail of white silk. The clash and roll and the martial trumpets covered the trundling of its wheels as a team of Tritons, green-wigged and in tunics sewn with shells, nets and weed, propelled it forward. The welcome this got was doubled when a second ship appeared, and when it was happily perceived that both were manned by dwarves and there was to be a battle at sea.

The Florentine had suffered no lack of material. Duke Ludovico's father had collected avidly in two categories: Greek manuscripts and dwarves. He had collected them until the city very likely contained more than any in Italy, save perhaps Ferrara. The old Duke had enviously eyed the tiny apartments custom-built for the Ferrarese dwarves at the top of the palace, and had put in hand a copy of this at Rocca, with improvements, just before his death. His son, although proud of his dwarf collection, was more interested in building a new library to house his books.

This interlude proved a *succès fou*. The Lady Cecilia's husband had to be rescued from choking on his wine when a dwarf, hurling a gilt spear at the opposing ship, fell out of the turret and damaged himself on a Triton. There were explosions from minute guns, which set the alarmed doves clattering about in the roof. The diners participated warmly, not only urging on the warriors but throwing chicken legs and bread or scoring with a well-aimed jelly. It was thought high time to trundle the ships out again, the bespattered dwarves still shrieking, bellowing and posing martially upon the decks, some working off a grudge or two by getting down to some serious fighting, others bowing thanks for the food, eating it off their or others' persons and searching the planks for the coins that had also been thrown.

The smell of gunpowder was dispersed by a short visit from the nymphs scattering scent. The doves in the roof slowly settled again, peering from the painted beams and once more risking descent to the tables.

The next course contained more sweetmeats than before— white gingerbread of marzipan ginger-flavoured and gilded, red gingerbread spiced with cinnamon and coloured with wine and sandalwood. The roar of talk by now almost obliterated the musicians' efforts, and only a reedy sound came down. Cups were filled and refilled. There were dishes of spiced cream; of ground almonds jellied and variously tinted, with whole nuts and a sauce of wine; and candied fruits. There were jelly ponds with orange fish and angelica reeds; eggs in hens' nests of shredded lemon peel, lambs of whipped cream upon little hills of jelly.

A dove made the error of descending in front of Sigismondo and was impounded so instantly that his neighbours jumped and cried out. He offered it to a server hurrying by with an empty dish, but the boy made a difficulty over taking hold of it. From behind, Benno said, "Let me, sir," and took the dove in willing wine-stained hands.

At this stage of the feast, the guests had all but forgotten the shadows of the Duke's anger that had lowered over the start. They were reminded of the savage nature that lurks in all humankind by the next diversion. To a discordant squeal of music, two lines of dwarves, possibly those from the sea-battle, possibly spares, burst through the curtains, getting tangled on purpose in their folds, and fanned out, carrying with exaggerated effort two long chains ending in a collar round the neck of a Wild Man, whose mask was more sad than savage. Shaking shaggy arms and making a dismal roar, he capered at the centre, pretending to wrestle with his collar and shrinking in mock terror when dwarves at the rear cracked whips at him.

A moment's hesitation came, when some of the dwarves were seen to glance at one another, nudge and argue, the next move uncertain, or as if the dwarf responsible for it was absent. The Wild Man solved the problem by falling on his knees before the Duke, grovelling in tribute and holding out his furry hands for pardon. The Duke, smiling, signalled to him to rise and he, springing to his feet, tore at his collar and broke it apart in triumph. The dwarves, apparently pulling on the chains to control him, now fell over. One line managed to keep the domino effect; the other failed and tumbled in shrieking heaps. One of the guests laughed part of his dinner onto his plate.

The Wild Man, now free, crouched and stared round. He made little rushes here and there, the dwarves getting to their feet and running from him, shedding whips, hats and bits of chain, taking refuge behind the servers, behind curtains and under the tables, where they caused havoc among the ladies' skirts.

The Wild Man now heard the music for the first time, cupping his paw behind his ear. The dwarves hushed; the diners hushed. The harp rippled; the clavicembalo's sweetest tones charmed. His movements became gentle. The dwarves emerged and danced, and he made humble efforts to copy them, became increasingly confident and leapt about. In his happy dance he appeared of a sudden to see the Duchess. He pressed his hands to his eyes as though blinded, then with a bound of dreadful agility he was poised on the high table itself among the cups and dishes. The Lady Cecilia, either frightened or offended that the Wild Man's head was turned towards the Duchess and not the bride, shrieked so loudly that she could be heard above the dwarves' renewed clamour.

The Duchess, on the contrary, applauded, and the Wild Man began to curvet among the plates with delicate skill, touching nothing, keeping time to the music. The dwarves, reassured as to his tameness, crept closer to watch. Bending low before the Duchess and putting his head wistfully to one side, the Wild Man drew from the bosom of his costume a heart of red satin, which he held out to her. The Duchess, with an amused smile, took it, and as he sprang up in joy his furred foot—alas—struck the Duchess' goblet, sending it flying. Wine flooded across the cloth and onto her silver brocade. There was a general gasp; the harpist stopped; the Duchess was on her feet.

All the guests of course rose, a bench overturned and stewards ran forward with their wands to deal with the Wild Man. He had already sprung backwards from the table and now cowered and howled, his arms over his head. The Duchess could be heard commanding the stewards not to beat the poor savage, and she was laughing. She asked the guests to be seated, and a rustle all through the hall followed her order. She spoke to the Duke and to the Lady Cecilia, and withdrew. While she was going to change her dress, the bride was not to wait on her this evening.

The Wild Man ran from the hall, still desolately howling and followed by the dwarves, hurling after him their hats and whips and entering into the improvisation with gusto. Music picked up again; servers quickly mopped and put fresh linen cloth at the Duchess' place; her goblet was wiped, restored and refilled. Some tumblers ran in. The Lord Paolo now, after a word with the Duke, helped his son from his chair among his cushions and, refusing help from the servants, took him up in his arms. The Lady Violante leant across to enquire after her cousin and was reassured as the boy sm led at her. He was carried out amid a perfunctory murmur of concern, and admiration of the careful father. One of Sigismondo's neighbours became maudlin on the subject.

The tumblers were interrupted by a man-at-arms thudding the butt of a halberd thrice to the floor. The music ceased, save for a flute that tootled on a few bars; the curtains parted to reveal an over-smiling, fashionably dressed man who raised his arms and, after a flourishing bow to the Duke, turned in the centre of the room, announcing: "Noble lords, lovely ladies! By command of Her Grace, in the great court—fireworks! A display of unprecedented artistry. It may be seen from the great loggia also. A deer hunt . . ."

What other wonders were to appear went unheard, because the Duke rose, offering his hand to the Lady Cecilia. Her husband managed to get to his feet but made an exit more remarkable for urgent speed than grace, ushered skilfully to a side door by pages. The Lady Violante followed her father, handed by a cavalier who bent obsequiously to listen as she spoke.

The festaiuolo was still announcing further wonders while the company made for the doors. Pages waited there with cloaks, for the loggia would be cold. Some kept their seats, and the servers still came with trays of small sweetmeats or dishes of sorbets while the tumblers and the music resumed.

Sigismondo, perhaps aware of Benno's urgent wishes, got up and accompanied one of his neighbours out, taking a hooded cloak at the door. Benno (the dove, still warm, in his bosom) was ignored by the pages, but outside, a servitor gave him a blanket wrap. He found a bench at the back of the loggia where a trio of gentlemen's servants gave him three inches to stand on. Once he had placed where his master was, against a pillar towards the end, where he could see the company by the bonfire light, Benno gave his mind and soul to the entertainment.

He forgot everything for the next space of time. He gaped at the whirling lights, the moving figures, the fountains, the coloured explosions, the stars that burst in the night sky; his breath steamed on the air before his face but he noticed no cold. He came down to earth, literally, as somebody pushed past the bench and disturbed his precarious balance. He heard the question—"Signore Sigismondo?"—and he wormed through the crowd after him. Sigismondo bent his head to hear the messenger, nodded and started for the nearest door. Benno slid after him. They made their way through a room full of knights in exotic pasteboard armour and some allegorical figures with towering headdresses, one an outsize skull, one green with iron-grey teeth. Benno, bewildered, kept Sigismondo's shoulders in view, followed him out and up a spiral staircase, along a blank stone corridor unlike the ornate public rooms, where the music and the pops of fireworks became distant and then louder as they emerged at a stairhead. Sigismondo crossed to a highly decorated doorway where a curiously pallid man-at-arms stood aside and opened one of the carved doors. Benno, prevented, sighed and waited where he was. Sigismondo entered. He saw, first of all, the Duke, who leant on the wall past the curtained foot of a bed. In a looking-glass with a frame of carved gilt, his reflection in profile stared, the brooch on his cap winking. Sigismondo rounded the curtains.

The Duchess, in her shift, lay upon the bed; two fat wax candles showed her spread body, the hand drooping over the edge, the open mouth dark as the grave.

5. "IT WAS MISSING"

The prevalent smell was of blood. As the small winter airs shifted in the room the smells shifted: blood, candlewax and smoke, scent and sweat, blood. Her shift was crumpled at the waist round the dark stem of a knife-hilt; her thighs gleamed pale.

The Duke, his voice hardly more than a whisper, said, "I found her so."

Sigismondo stepped forward. His hand flowed, from crossing himself, to touch the Duchess at the neck below the ear. He laid the back of his hand against the cheek, hummed and brooded over the body without disturbing the knife. Next, he pushed open a jib door that stood ajar near the bedhead and glanced into the small closet there, where a light burned. A crackle of the fireworks the Duchess had paid for came through the closet window. The bedroom was close-shuttered and the smell of death was strong, alien to human sense.

Sigismondo stood with his head on one side as though he listened, and then moved with a pounce that brought the Duke out of his daze. From under the waterfall of brocade curtains at the foot of the bed, Sigismondo dragged out an inert figure. The head lolled back, showing a red graze on the brow. Dark hair lay on Sigismondo's sleeve. Here, too, the mouth was open, but he breathed.

"Leandro Bandini?" The Duke was puzzled. He pointed at the tow-like hair that seemed to clothe the body like an animal's hide. "The Wild Man?"

"So it would appear, Your Grace."

Sigismondo bent and sniffed at the young man's breath; he

stayed, nostrils flared and mouth parted, like a cat that tastes a scent. He sniffed again. The Duke put a hand to the dressing table as though to prevent himself falling.

"Drunk! He comes here drunk, forces my lady and kills her to save his skin."

Sigismondo was examining the young man's hands and did not point out that, if this had been Leandro Bandini's intention, it had gone essentially wrong.

"Not drunk, my lord. It's a drug I can smell. There's no blood on his hands or the Wild Man's skin." He stood up. "Your Grace, this is a Bandini. We have not had reason to trust the words of di Torre or Bandini; nor should we trust what appear to be their deeds."

The Duke looked at Sigismondo. He said, "Let him be committed to the dungeons, no one to have access to him unless by my order."

Sigismondo bent to take hold of the young man, but the Duke continued, "Wait."

He drew from his finger a heavy intaglio ring, a sardonyx with the arms of Rocca, and held it out to Sigismondo.

"Question whom you choose."

The first person Sigismondo chose was the festaiuolo hired by the Duchess to stage-manage the masques at dinner. He had received the Duke's message cancelling the rest of the entertainment, and Sigismondo found him in the anteroom to the hall, a small man in a highly mobile state of apprehension and annoyance, trying to deal with the performers cheated of their display. They stood about, grumbling, reluctant to remove the clothes they had lost the chance of showing, while Niccolo Sanseverino tried to collect headdresses and useful accessories such as Envy's iron teeth and Fortune's wig with its forelock, bald at the back. A wicker basket held Orpheus' gilded harp; a horn of plenty, also gilded and spilling out its contents of green silk leaves, wax apples and peaches and grapes; piles of ribbons; Cupid's gilt bow and quiver. He was not at all inclined to spare time for Sigismondo, until he saw the Duke's ring.

"But of course. Anything I can do, sir. The Duke can command me at any time. But you must know the Duchess commands me this evening." His small black eyes glanced from Sigismondo's face to the ring again, while with one hand he waved away an insistent Bacchante. "Is she very displeased with what occurred?"

Sigismondo's hum could have signified anything. He said, "Where can we talk unheard?" and Niccolo, taking a belt of ivy leaves out of the hands of a boy in a leopard pelt who had scarcely undone it, towed his property basket and led the way into an alcove as tiny as the room off the Duchess' bedroom, also with a single candle burning. He offered Sigismondo a stool and took one himself. Between them, a carpet-covered table was crowded with little pots of coloured lard and dishes of white skin-paint. A slate on the wall, written in almost illegible script, bore a list ticked, half-erased and written over.

"It's the Wild Man, isn't it? He finished it for us."

Niccolo, sagging with sudden weariness, poured wine into a horn cup and offered it to Sigismondo, who bowed his head, lifted the cup to him, drank and handed it back after wiping the rim.

"What can you tell me about the Wild Man?"

"Drunk. He must have been drunk. There's no accounting for what he did in any other way. I should never have taken him on. All my instincts warned me." He shook his head again and poured more wine. "A vagabond." He drank it back, his greasy black curls brushing the costumes hanging in a bunch behind him.

"This mistake. Tell me about it."

A hulking form filled the entrance, its arms embracing a huge bundle of white silk. "Where you want this?"

"There." He pointed behind Sigismondo, who rose, took the bundle and put it into a lined basket against the wall. He sat, reaching to pull the curtain across the alcove, and repeated, "This mistake. Tell me."

"You saw!" Niccolo flung his arms wide. A costume painted with ears and open mouths fell off the bundle. He pushed it aside. "He made a complete wreck of the reference to Saint Cecilia. He'd been rehearsed. He couldn't pretend he'd confused them. He'd been shown where they'd sit. The Lady Cecilia was the other side of the Duke, yes, but how could he mistake the Duchess for her? And—"

"A vagabond might not have seen the Duchess before?"

Niccolo snorted. "The Lady Cecilia is a blonde. He was told, the *blonde*. How could anyone mistake? But he gives the heart to the dark lady and ignores the bride." He sank his head into his hands but forbore to tear his hair—already thin in front as if the victim of past disasters.

"Where did you hire him?"

"He came off the streets from a travelling troupe. All manner came. He showed that he could dance. When I arrive in a city"—he preened himself a little and arranged some of the greasepaint pots in an orderly line—"it becomes known. People present themselves. And it was true that for this conception of mine I looked for a mime and dancer out of the ordinary." He made his fingers prance on the table among the pots. "You saw him upon the table? When he rehearsed, I scattered dishes everywhere, different places every time, and he never touched one. He must have been drunk."

"Did you see him before he went into the hall?"

"I put the costume on him myself. No detail is beneath my notice when my art is concerned."

"Did you think then that he was drunk?"

"He was the same as ever he was. Cool. Quiet. He talked to no one."

"What did he look like?"

"Very pale. He had the face of an angel except when he opened his mouth, when he revealed crooked teeth and a gutter accent. Otherwise, one could have used him for Gabriel in a mime of the Annunciation. In a gold wig, of course. His red hair would have made any audience take him for Judas Iscariot."

Sigismondo nodded and hummed. "Where is he now?"

"Vanished."

"Vanished?"

"I suppose he feared a beating. *Which* he deserved, but the Duchess ordered he should be spared. The kindest lady!"

"Had he received his pay?"

"I was to get their pay after the feast. Money for costumes and carpentry I had been given. All my performers knew they could not be paid yet."

Sigismondo silently shook his head at the proffered cup and studied his hands folded before him on the table. The Duke's ring gleamed in the candlelight.

"Did you see him go into the hall?"

"Certainly. I watch everyone in, to make sure every detail is correct. Even so"—and he frowned at the memory, refilling the cup—"with Poggio missing, there were mistakes."

"Poggio?"

"The dwarf. He should have run to push the Wild Man down to kneel before the Duke. I'd told one of the rest to do it in his place, but"—he shrugged and flung out his hands—"they were excited."

Sigismondo gave a descending hum of appreciation of this certain fact. There was no doubt of the vivacity displayed by the dwarves.

"Poggio was the Duke's dwarf. I'd rehearsed with him."

Niccolo's tone was that of the aggrieved professional. "He was very apt. Then"—once more the spread arms—"the Duke is angry. Some joke Poggio told that he should not, against the dignity of Her Grace, they say; and Poggio is dismissed. Banned from the city! And I have no time to rehearse another properly. Yet they expect a performance without faults."

"The Wild Man. Did he wear his mask when you saw him into the hall?"

"Naturally."

"When did you last see his face?"

Niccolo, surprised, put down the cup and half closed his eyes, considering. He opened them to look round the alcove.

"Why, here." He turned his gaze on Sigismondo with deep curiosity. "What has happened, then? Does the Duke wish to punish him?"

The curtain was wrenched aside, and the boy last seen surrendering his ivy-leaf belt stood there, panting, still in his leopard skin. He paused on seeing Sigismondo but he was too full of his news not to spill it.

"The Duchess! The Duchess is dead! Murdered!"

Niccolo sprang to his feet. "The Duchess? Who did it? The poor lady! Dear God! Who would do such a thing? A terrible— *Who'll pay me?*"

Sigismondo had risen more slowly, and as Niccolo was about to launch himself into the crowd outside he took him by the arm so that he whirled round with the force of his own impetus.

"The Wild Man's costume."

A dozen hands reached for Niccolo. Half-dressed, patchily painted grotesques were clamouring, and he was rocked by dwarves round his legs pulling different ways at his jerkin. Some informed him that the Duchess was dead; the rest cried out for their pay.

"Wait, wait, only be patient—"

"Money—"

49

"—promised—"

"—the Duchess—"

"—how we eat?"

"—all the way from Venice—"

A hush spread from the far side of the room. Attendants in slate blue and ochre had come in, Paolo's men, and after them, the Lord Paolo himself. Niccolo pushed forward to bow, apologising for the dishevelment and disorder, offering his condolences—a perfunctory murmur from the troupe—and asking what they were to do. Sigismondo leant on the wall, arms folded, to wait.

The Lord Paolo was wan and grave, but spoke with his accustomed gentleness. He was sorry they had been left in ignorance of events, but he had been speaking to the noble guests. Was there some trouble about money that he had heard just now? He would pay the Duchess' debt to them, of course, himself. Let them be easy. There would be food and lodging in his quarters, and his steward would give them their money.

"You were to have been lodged here? But the Duke will not wish you to be here. I would not have him reminded, you understand. Pack everything up. My men will help you."

"Is it known who killed the poor lady?" someone asked. Lord Paolo shook his head. "I fear it is the son of Ugo Bandini."

Instant shouts and vituperation arose among the dwarves; di Torre and Bandini had their factions even here. The Lord Paolo reminded them of the Duke's decree about disturbances of the peace, and the voices died to a rumble. His men were seizing the hampers. The troupe pulled off the remains of the costumes in a hurry and searched for their clothes. Cupid, asleep on a pile of them, was roused, had his hose pulled on, was shaken, kissed and carried away. Niccolo cried, "Wait, wait; I must make sure of the costumes. Wait, wait," and tried to halt the men. A dwarf under the scarlet plumed hat ran by and he turned to catch him.

Sigismondo's right hand was holding his chin, a forefinger over his mouth. His left hand nursed his elbow. In the hubbub he was still. The gold shank of the ring glowed in the torchlight.

The Lord Paolo beckoned. Sigismondo detached himself from the wall and came through the excited throng.

"We see the outcome of this morning's sad affair."

Sigismondo bowed.

"There will be no need now for further search on your part. Bandini will have to yield up the Lady Cosima—but I fear that will not save his son. The Duke's mercy must be tempered with strength."

Sigismondo bowed again.

"Though I have always counselled mercy," said the Lord Paolo, as he turned away. The crowd made room for him to go.

"Sir. Sir."

A tiny child, smaller than the Cupid and with a head of curls not unlike the gilded wig, but wearing a page's tabard, tugged at Sigismondo's tunic and looked up at him with huge brown eyes.

"Sir. My lady wants you."

Sigismondo crouched to child level. "My lady?"

"Follow me." The infant, having secured Sigismondo's attention, assumed his obedience and set off, weaving smartly among the legs of the crowd in the entrance hall, through guests remaining to churn over the unbelievable news and the rumour that Ugo Bandini, hearing of his son's dreadful deed, had taken refuge with the Cardinal Pontano in fear of the Duke. In the great hall, servants, clearing tables and filling their mouths, were busy with the same subject. Sigismondo followed, as deft in avoiding shoulders as the page in avoiding legs. Anyone who saw him coming, however, instinctively made way; he was used to this and, in battle, appreciative.

The Castello Rocca might have been constructed by giant rabbits: passages of every kind, rough stone or painted plaster, narrow or wide, some apparently leading nowhere but saved from frustration by a curtain and an eel-like twist by the tiny page, who had picked up a flambeau once they were beyond the standing lights—a rabbit of experience. Sigismondo followed in perfect trust, a man who knew when to commit himself to the unknown, and who knew himself less at danger than many in so doing.

The apartments of Agnolo de Villani, master of the Duke's horse and, since earlier in the day, husband and presumably also master of the Lady Cecilia, were reached at last. The infant page opened a door, drew aside the last curtain and announced, "The Lord Sigismondo."

Sigismondo, suddenly and flatteringly ennobled, bowed low. He had seen the Lady Cecilia at the banquet when she was in an hour of exaltation, the fair bride in whose honour it was all taking place. One might expect conventional signs of grief, such as an effort at tears, gracefully disordered hair. What he saw was swollen eyelids and a composure that spoke of discipline. The gold net still held the golden hair, she had not changed the gown of yellow velvet, but the Lady Cecilia of that time was not the one he saw now.

"You are in the Duke's confidence, I believe."

Sigismondo held out his hand, the sardonyx with the arms of Rocca now uppermost again. She nodded and clapped her hands. Another page, with more muscle at his command than the infant, appeared with a folding stool upholstered in red velvet, which he set up for the guest with a flourish. At a gesture from the lady, Sigismondo sat and was offered a goblet of wine by the page, who withdrew the moment Sigismondo's hand took the silvergilt stem.

"You saw Her Grace?" Her eyes showed the memory of that figure.

"Yes, my lady. The Duke sent for me at that time."

"He sent for me, too." She looked down at her hands, long

and white, laced in her lap. "He knew she would have wished it. We'd always been friends; as children we played together in her father's house. I came with her to Rocca when she married. I married a man of Rocca so that I might stay near her. It was right that I should do the last things for her." She unlaced her hands, took her cup from the carved chest at her side and drank. A log burning on the big hearth collapsed in a shower of sparks, and she started and set down the cup with a rattle.

"Do you know who killed her?" She turned once again towards Sigismondo, the gold net grating softly on her jewelled collar. "Was it not Bandini? Why is he not dead?"

Sigismondo shook his head, a slight, slow movement. "His Grace wishes me to make sure that justice is done. There are no certainties at this moment."

"Leandro Bandini is in prison."

An equally slight shrug. "Leandro Bandini is unconscious. When he can speak, we'll learn more."

"But he was found, His Grace tells me, at the foot of the bed. He had been struck on the brow, and a candlestick was lying beneath Her Grace's hand. Who else could have done it?" She stared at the fire now, not glancing at the man who sat before her. "A man had lain with her before she died."

Sigismondo hummed in assent. His silence was interrogative. She began to speak and stopped. The fire, consuming the log greedily, gave a hot glow to her face. "The Duke was with her when you came there."

Her statement, which he did not deny, was left in the silence between them, its implication too dangerous to be put into words: if the last man to lie with the Duchess were the Duke, might he not be her murderer? If the last man to lie with the Duchess were not the Duke, if he had found her as they had seen her, might he not have killed an adulterous wife?

Sigismondo's question was delicate, a great cat tapping a mouse with its paw to see if it would run.

"Do you know of any who loved the Duchess?" There was no harm in being loved, only in loving.

"Many loved the Duchess."

The mouse would not run.

"Men can be reckless. Did Leandro Bandini show his love?"

"That one." She turned her long neck scornfully, with the net's sibilant little sound. "He paid court to all. Handsome, rich, he believed the world lay at his feet."

Now he had been thrown on the straw of a dungeon somewhere below them.

"If he paid court to one more than another, it was to the Lady Violante. He made eyes at her, wrote her poems, rode by her side when he could. But it is fashionable to court her, and men also will do such things to draw eyes away from their true love." Especially, she did not say, if the true love were a married woman, the wife of their Duke.

A draught strengthened, flattening a candle-flame. Wax spilled down the candle, over the dish of the holder, and onto the dark oak beneath. "The knife"—her voice was choked, reluctant—"it was a wound made by a knife. . . . Is it known whose knife it was?"

Sigismondo, whose hand had removed it, shook his head once more. "A knife such as anyone might carry."

"Not the knife of a rich young man."

He acknowledged her sharpness with the lift of an eyebrow. Unspoken, again, that a knife not likely to be carried by a rich young man would be less likely to be carried by the Duke. The idea of sudden murder in a fit of rage receded, yet, as the lady had said, men were given to ruses. The Duke, had he intended to kill the Duchess, would be most likely to bring an anonymous weapon.

As they sat, contemplating the fire without speaking, an angry voice sounded outside, demanding. A mouse-like squeak protested in reply. The door was opened, the curtain dragged aside, and Agnolo di Villani stood there in a night gown of purple-black velvet, his face suggesting unmistakably that his wedding night completely failed his expectations. He glared at Sigismondo, who had risen and bowed, and at his wife.

"You did not send to say you had returned. Who is this man?" His interest in Sigismondo's name seemed less acute than his interest in the colour of his entrails. The Lady Cecilia, however, was perfect in charming brute suspicions, an art she might have learned with her first two husbands; she stood up, hurried to him and twined her fingers in the velvet of his bulky sleeves. She arched her long neck to rub her face along his chest like a cat that caresses itself on another. For this moment she was a different woman.

"My lord. It is the Duke's man. He has authority to enquire into the matter of the Duchess."

Di Villani looked over his wife's head at the Duke's man, his dislike complicated by the need to show compliance. He spoke in a growl, a bear waiting for a long-delayed dinner.

"What is to be known? The Bandini boy's taken."

"The Duke has instructed me to find out all that can be found concerning the deed."

"Why employ you? There are his own men here." Of whom I am not the least, he might have said.

"For the same reason that he first employed me to enquire into the disappearance of the Lady Cosima: that I belong, and am known to belong, to neither faction, sir."

"The Lady Cecilia is tired. It is late." It would have been later, had the feast continued as planned, before the bridal pair were bedded, but the happy exhaustion brought on by an excess of merrymaking is very different from that caused by laying out the murdered body of your closest friend. Sigismondo bowed and made to withdraw. Agnolo di Villani acknowledged the bow with an uncouth jerk of the head and turned quickly towards the tall curtained bed in the room's shadows.

The tiny page stood at his post outside, apparently unwearied and ready to escort Sigismondo back through the Palace warren. He had scarcely picked up the flambeau when the Lady Cecilia appeared, lifting the curtain and glancing back over her shoulder. She came so close to Sigismondo that he could smell the musky scent she wore, heavy with civet as well as jasmine, and she whispered, "Her ring."

"Her ring?"

"Her ring, Her Grace's ring that never leaves her finger. It was missing."

6. "DID I KILL THE DUCHESS?"

There could be no doubt whatsoever that the truly happy people in the duchy that night were the beggars. Outside the gate they feasted, with handfuls of venison pie, hatfuls of jellies; faces dripped pepper-and-vinegar sauce. Children gorged on gingerbread, tench, spiced veal. They tasted strange, unknown mixtures of saffron, nutmeg, cinnamon, ginger. A vast upturned pie had been eaten in seconds, its pork and eggs, almonds and dates stuffed into ecstatic mouths, the pastry cleaned from the stones. Over and over, the name of the Lord Paolo was spoken in blessing; the men who had brought the feast out to them had not said who had thought of them out in the cold, but that livery was well known.

In the Palace, Sigismondo and the small page exchanged bows, and the page accepted a coin given for his services with the flambeau. Sigismondo strode on towards the tiny room allotted him. Knots of servants still whispered in corners, drawing out their tasks to give time to gossip. They watched as he passed, and more than one crossed himself as if seeing an ill omen.

Benno had somehow obtained a small box brazier and a bundle of wood. The room glowed with comfort, and Sigismondo paused inside the curtain to smile. Benno had wound himself into the cloak as well and now struggled to rise, but Sigismondo, pausing only to feed the brazier and to push the bedding farther from its sparks, folded himself down on the pallet beside him.

"That's a good find."

"No one wanted it. It was where the players were to eat."

"Have you eaten?" There was a smell of roasting meat, and

Benno's nod and look of satisfaction were not surprising. Grease shone on his beard.

"There was a lot of food going."

Sigismondo nodded. "And what have you heard?"

"Some think the Duke killed her because of a lover and put Leandro Bandini there to be blamed. There had to be someone to blame although she'd been unfaithful, because of the alliance with her brother. Her brother's a Duke, too; I didn't know. Duke Ippolyto. They say our Duke couldn't risk just killing her; there had to be a scapegoat."

Sigismondo hummed. "And?"

Benno took up willingly, interrupted only by an almost negligible belch. "Well then, one of the Duke's guard said young Bandini forced her and then killed her so she wouldn't tell, and knocked himself out in his hurry to escape." Benno produced a quill and began picking his teeth.

"The simplistic view."

Benno looked up with unquestioning confidence. He said, "After all, there was blood on the Duke's hand. At dinner, you remember. The wine. So they say it was the Duke, that he caught her with the Wild Man making love, and he killed her, and he's got Leandro Bandini in prison waiting to be unmanned and drawn and quartered to please the Duke Ippolyto."

He reached to the floor by his bundled-up feet, found a leather bottle, upended it so vigorously over his mouth that he tipped backwards and all but kicked the brazier. Sigismondo's swift hand righted him.

"Ta. There's been another omen, too," he went on, getting to work on his teeth once more, which gave his narrative something the effect of a cleft palate. "The statue of Saint Agnes groaned this morning at Mass. Half the congregation heard it. And the Duke's new chapel in the Cathedral, they're digging the foundations still just beyond the Innocents' chapel and they dug up a nun's body and it was the holy sister Annunciata that died in the old Duke's time. They say it's bad she was disturbed."

Sigismondo reached under the bedding, produced a pack and, feeling inside, drew out a small flask in a straw case. They each drank, and Benno mopped his deplorable beard and went on. "There's another story. The Lord Paolo's page said he didn't believe it, but he told us. He said it's the sort of thing that people will say. The story goes that my—my old master the Lord Jacopo had lured Bandini to the palace, for a wager like, that he could get away with going there in disguise. If Leandro Bandini could get in, then the Lord Jacopo or his men could be here disguised as entertainers too; then they killed the Duchess and left him there to be guilty. People said that would be a great revenge if it was true, a really good payment for abducting my Lady Cosima—except for the Duchess. Some said that spoiled the skill of it, murdering the Duchess. Others said a feud doesn't have boundaries; anything is permissible."

"I hear that Bandini himself has taken refuge with the Cardinal Pontano." Sigismondo was not niggardly with gossip in return.

"Bandini's lent the Cardinal money. Some say he's lent money to the Pope. So the Church will look after him. Do you want some of this cloak?"

"If I do, I'll take it."

Benno nodded, believing this. "What did you get to hear besides?" He looked up hopefully.

"There's a ring missing from the Duchess' hand, one she always wore."

Benno gazed at the glowing wood. "If anyone took it they're stone mad. It'd be known. Did you see her body?"

"Yes."

Benno waited, then realised he was getting no more. Sigismondo passed him the flask, as either consolation or a reward for asking nothing. He drank, sighed, and kicked his bundled legs.

"You know, my life's really got interesting."

There had been footsteps, rapid or slow, up and down the stone stairway, but now someone stopped and said, "Master Sigismondo."

The bed creaked as Sigismondo leant and raised the curtain.

"You asked to be told when the prisoner came round. He's conscious and moaning."

Leandro's memories of what had led to this lying on the disgusting straw in the Duke's dungeon were blurred, but his immediate perceptions, as he swam up to consciousness, were too sharp. His head throbbed like a huckster's drum. The straw had odd rustlings where, he thought, rats must be at work. He imagined them on the remains of a former prisoner. Something dripped in the near-dark. He could see at all only by courtesy of a narrow slit high above his head, and clouds obscured the moon. He was very, very cold. He did not think he had ever been so cold, and it was also evident that someone, perhaps himself, had recently been sick in the straw.

He wondered if it would be worthwhile or even possible to drag himself away from the smell, though nearer to the rats. Some other sound made itself heard, voices muttering. At first he thought the rats were becoming vocal, but then the grate of heavy bolts being drawn back produced a clarity in his mind. The grating groan was like the voice of imprisonment itself. A dark-lantern shone at him across the straw, and as it was not easy to raise an arm, he merely shut his eyes. The door closed with a hollow finality, but he thought that someone was in the cell with him.

Leandro thought it was possible, even likely, that the Duke had sent someone to strangle him. Justice, even in this modern age, bent to expediency and caprice. He was accused of the murder of the Duchess. He remembered seeing her body, he remembered the Duke's remote, unreal face with eyes wide and blue as a winter sky, a nightmare face. Had he dreamt her body, a knife? He knew that criminals of any sense perished decently, in prison, before anyone could suspect they might be innocent. His father, his father's friends, had made such things clear in their talk ever since he could remember.

The Duke was said to be merciful. Strangulation here and now would be merciful, compared to being tortured in the usual way.

Nevertheless he was unable to look forward to it.

The lantern was placed on the floor not far from him, and the light fell on the man who sat there on one heel, looking at him.

Leandro knew he was definitely going to die very soon. The Duke, whose mercy was greater than he had suspected until now, had sent a priest to confess him. The strong features were thrown into relief boldly by the golden light, the features of some antique Roman emperor, sensual and commanding. The shaven head, however, that rose from the cowl, convinced Leandro that his death was near. His thoughts again drifted into confusion; he felt regret that he was still young and had always thought of his life as before him; he felt fear that he might forget some of his sins in this dreadful hour. He hoped that God might be even more merciful than the Duke, yet there was no way to God except through His church, His priests. The big priest was murmuring again, loud enough to be heard above the resumed rustling of the rats, long indifferent to any invasion of their privacy. He did not speak loud enough to be heard by anyone outside the door; confession was a sacrament not for the ears of others. Leandro tried to raise himself, to wipe a horrid incrustation from his chin, make himself respectable for his last quarter hour of bodily peace on this earth. A strong arm helped him up, and Leandro for the first time made sense of the murmur, for it was not Latin but the vernacular.

"I say I am come from the Duke. He has given me powers to question you."

Leandro sprawled back in the straw again, his limbs failing. The man was not a priest after all. He was a torturer.

The strong arm supported him up again. He felt like a puppet moved by a master hand. He understood of a sudden the phrase heard in church: *his bowels turned to water*. Desperately, he hoped not to disgrace himself, but he imagined his body's sinews cracking under that dispassionate gaze.

The prospect of strangulation was suddenly quite desirable.

"What happened before the Duke came? Tell me from the start. How did you come to be in the Palace?"

The voice might be low, speaking in his ear, but it had authority. Leandro, still suffering from the drum in his head, wondered weakly where the instruments of torture were, where the assistants? He had heard of the rack—one had to be fastened to it. Then someone wrote down the confession, a clerk. All was so unorthodox that he did not answer.

The question was repeated while a hand felt carefully over his scalp. It found an area that made him flinch.

"You've been struck more than once. A light blow on the brow, that shows. Perhaps you hit something as you fell. And now, sir,"—and the man reached for the lantern and, turning its light on Leandro, looked his face over, moving it by the chin as one might an animal's—"you were going to tell me how you came to be in the Palace although it's forbidden to you."

Of course this was the preliminary enquiry. The interrogation would come later. He would have to confirm all he now said, under torture—or say what he was told to say, his limbs broken to confirm each painful lie. The deep, patient voice in his ear reiterated the question: how did he come to be in the Duke's Palace?

Slowly, he began to tell. It was not, he supposed, what they wished to hear, but he began, still among waves of nausea that heaved in his stomach almost in time with the throb in his head. With the prospect of torture, he was aware of an immense fondness for his body, of pity for it to be treated so.

The man had come closer, so close that Leandro feared the foulness of his breath would reach him. Indeed, it must have done so, for the man, after a sniff that must have confirmed this, drew back a little and squatted on one heel, listening. There was a quality about this listening that made Leandro anxious to be exact, to convince him of the truth, whatever was to happen later.

"I never meant to disobey the Duke—would that I never had—but for the message."

"The message?"

Leandro recalled the man who had brought the message and his insistence on secrecy, the cowl hood pulled forward over a face he could hardly see. Once he had heard who sent the message, of course, secrecy was understood.

"From the Lady Violante. She sent to say she wished to see me during the feast. I was to come to the Cathedral door of the Palace at—I'll remember the hour. . . ."

"No matter the hour, sir. Continue."

Leandro held his forehead. "I can't remember. But a disguise would be given me. This one. I didn't care for it, but then, the lady . . ."

A low humming told him that the niceties of the situation were understood, were being weighed. Confidences about the Duke's young widowed daughter, apple of his choleric eye, were almost as dangerous to receive as to make.

"Did you expect such a message?"

The question really asked what terms he was on with the

lady. It was a question he would expect to be asked in an ambiance of red-hot pincers, not merely an enquiring tilt of the head.

"The lady has scarcely spoken to me. I didn't think she cared what I did. Of course I've paid her attentions. One does. I wrote poems—it's the proper thing to do. It means nothing. I never went beyond—I expected nothing. But when the message came, it was amazing. I felt . . . I don't know. I never thought she had taken me seriously. But even if it was only a caprice of hers, it was my courtly duty to go, and I hoped that she really meant . . ." Leandro's stomach heaved. He thought he might be about to vomit again. The strain of thinking was more than he could manage. "She has the choice of the nobility. I'm only a rich banker's son." The rich banker's son, dressed in his canvas-and-tow suit, stained with vomit, shivered in the filthy straw, contemplating his short future.

"Would you know again the man who gave you the disguise? Was it the man who also brought the first message?"

Leandro held his head once more, because it seemed to prevent the drum inside from bursting through his temples. "I did not really see either of them. This messenger had a hood; the other was in the shadows. I think they were much of a height. And there's such—confusion. But he wore a very small skull on a neck chain."

"The wine," prompted the deep voice. "The man who gave the disguise, did he give you the wine?"

"Wine?" Even the thought made his stomach shift queasily.

"You took wine." The voice was quietly sure, and he found himself remembering.

"Why, yes. He gave me a cup before I put on the mask. It was mulled wine, to warm me—from the Lady Violante, he said. She had thought I would be cold."

There was a rustle in the straw more purposeful than the

rats' scurryings. "Here is a clean shirt and hose. They may not fit, but they'll be preferable to that garment."

Leandro was not capable of much surprise at this juncture. He could feel only puzzlement. He tried, however, to co-operate in ridding himself of the unpleasant costume. As he found his way into the woollen shirt, which smelt pleasantly of lavender, his interrogator gravely examined the costume, humming in a disparaging manner, and then turned the lantern to enable Leandro to see to tie his points. That done, he picked up the lantern and once again came closer, took Leandro firmly by the chin and turned his face towards the light. As Leandro flinched from it, he was told, "Look at me," and he tried to obey. The shutter was instantly put across the light and the deep voice in a darkness full of fiery parabolas said:

"What exactly do you remember since the mulled wine?"

"Walking. Then . . . the next thing is someone holding me up and making me look at the Duchess." He stopped. The picture seen so clearly was the Duchess' body, but from a different angle. He was beside her on the bed, alone, aware of horror. He had tried to escape, had fallen; he could remember falling into darkness.

He turned away from the man as his stomach heaved, and he desperately tried to vomit nothing. Only bitter liquid came.

He clung on to the arm that had held him up during this. His lips were trembling, but he turned urgently and demanded:

"Did I do it? *Did* I kill the Duchess?"

7. "MY MISTRESS WISHES TO SELL THIS RING"

In the night, or what remained of it, while Sigismondo and Benno slept in their tiny room, the Duke lay awake in his great bed in his own room, alone, and Agnolo di Villani enjoyed his rights, someone was busy outside the Palace. In the grudging light of a winter dawn, those whose business took them out so early into the great square began to collect round the huge doors that kept the main entrance to the Castello. The paving-stones held no trace of the beggars' banquet, the dogs having cleaned what the beggars could not scrape up. The crowd stared at the doors and moved on as more came. Some signed themselves, few risked a word. They stared at blood, dried now, that had run in streams down the oak as though some giant hand had flung it there in accusation. No one needed to interpret. The news about the Duchess' death was common throughout the city already. The people of Rocca, although they had cause for both their love and their fear of their Duke, were human enough to be ready to think the worst.

By the time the Duke sent for Sigismondo, he had heard Mass in his chapel, where priests had been saying prayers for the dead all night by the body of the Duchess, lying in state under a black velvet pall sewn with the Rocca arms in gold. Tall wax candles burnt in torchères around her. The Duke had knelt at the foot of the catafalque before Mass, joining the priests' prayers, and he had stood to look at the pale face. It was beautiful in death, not as he had last seen it and had seen it before his eyes during the night, but composed to serenity by loving fingers. The little crease in her cheek which had always been there, even when she was not smiling, gave her still that air of being secretly, remotely, amused.

Sigismondo found the Duke in his study pacing restlessly to and fro. His secretary, a dark man with a thin, apprehensive face, stood at the lectern-desk, fair-copying from his tablets onto parchment. The Duke's great seal, and wax and ribbons, waited ready on the marble table. The Duke's hound, uneasy at his master's unease, sat near the hearth, swinging his head to follow the Duke's pacing. An enormous fire burnt in the cavern of the hearth, now and then a gust of wind from the mountains sending an eddy of apple-wood smoke into the room.

"You see this?"

The Duke pointed towards the secretary's work. Sigismondo, who could not be expected to know what was being written, acquiesced to seeing it, and the Duke continued. "I have a messenger waiting to carry this to the Duke Ippolyto. It invites him to come himself, or to send those who may represent him, to witness the execution of his sister's murderer. In a week's time, on the Feast of Saint Benedict." He reached the tall window in his pacing and, framed against the pale blue of the winter sky, stared at Sigismondo and asked, "Is the one to be executed Leandro Bandini?"

"That is for Your Grace to say. There are certain things in the matter Your Grace would wish to know." Sigismondo's eyes flickered towards the pages and secretary. The Duke banished them with a word, then beckoned Sigismondo, and for a moment they stood together looking down on the square below, its patterned pavement sloping a little down from the Castello and the Cathedral. People passed to and fro and gathered in knots by the fountain. Stalls were there as usual, and those who bought and those who sold had leisure, even on this chill day, to linger and talk. An arm was outflung towards the Palace gates. Some watched the Duke's men supervising the scrubbing away of the blood. The splash of water as well as a cry of voices came up through the glass.

"What can you tell me?"

"He was drugged, Your Grace."

The Duke's eyes fixed on him in concentration.

"Drugged. Who drugged him?"

"He would not know the man again."

"You have only his word for it?"

"I could tell he had drunk valerian, its smell concealed by verbena, in a draught of spiced wine which would disguise any strange taste; it would cause him to lose control of his senses, perhaps to see visions."

"Would it lead him to force Her Grace?" The question was delivered coolly, but the Duke's voice was harsher than ever.

Sigismondo watched the square below, the small figures moving beyond the distorting glass; then he said, "There was no sign of forcing. Her Grace's wrists were unmarked; there was no trace of violence other than her wound. There were no scratches on Bandini's face, neck or hands."

"Yet she struck him with her mirror or the candlestick."

"Someone did."

"Or he fell, fleeing?"

"It is possible, Your Grace." Sigismondo's tone all but dismissed the theory. "He was also struck, harder, on the *back* of the head." His hand indicated the place on his own smooth scalp.

The Duke put long fingers to his own forehead and massaged the creases between the fierce brows. He returned as if in despair to the thought that would not let him rest.

"She lay with him by consent."

The deep voice was firm. "With him, or with another."

The Duke's hands flew together, fist into palm. "*Find him. I shall not have peace until his death.*" He swung to look at the square as if he could see the scaffold and the moment that would set him free.

"Did Your Grace take a ring from the Duchess' hand last night?"

Sigismondo, broad hand splayed on the brocade curtain, pressing back its folds, looked down at the square as though his question had little significance. The Duke grasped its importance at once.

"What ring? I did not touch her."

His vehemence sounded as though he answered all the voices in the city who accused him.

"The ring Her Grace always wore."

"The emerald her brother gave her? Is that gone?"

"Was Your Grace with the Duchess until the Lady Cecilia came? You did not leave her until that time?"

The Duke shook his head.

"Then we conclude that the ring was taken before you discovered the Duchess."

"The murderer. There was no ring found on Leandro Bandini?"

It was Sigismondo's turn to shake his head. The Duke clasped his hands and, steepling the forefingers, struck them lightly against his lips. He frowned still. "We are dealing with a *thief*? Nothing else was taken?"

"The Lady Cecilia spoke of the ring only." The Duchess' honour, which was also the Duke's, had vanished during that time before her death.

"You will enquire further, no doubt, of the Lady Cecilia, the mistress of the robes." He paused. "A week. I cannot give you more than a week. I cannot delay the message to Ippolyto; he will come here at once and must be answered."

They looked down at the Duke's messenger, in green and white over total black, walking a great black horse in the inner

69

court to and fro, as the Duke had paced above. Man and beast walked in a cloud of their breath in the chill air.

"In a week my justice must be seen to be done."

If Sigismondo could find no more likely candidate for the scaffold, Leandro Bandini had not a long time left in which to regret coming to the assignation last night.

"Her cross is gone too."

The Lady Cecilia raised her eyes to Sigismondo with a look of dismay. Her gold hair was confined in a black silk net, her white skin ghostly in her black velvet gown against the dark panelling.

"What was it like?"

"It was of diamonds and pearls. It had belonged to the Duke's first wife, the Duchess Maria. My lady seldom wore it, being of the opinion that it did not become her. But everything became her."

Sigismondo brooded over the marquetry jewel case. Its crimson velvet was a voluptuous nest for engraved gems of sardonyx and crystal; brooches of balas rubies, table-cut diamonds, strange-shaped pearls that were the bodies of nereids or unicorns; a cluster of amethyst grapes with golden leaves; clasps of jade; a set of diamond buttons; rings of all kinds, the mount of one a pair of gold hands delicately presenting a large sapphire; a rose of rubies; filigree earrings; chains of gold and enamel work, heavy chains with links of twisted gold; ropes of pearls, in soft colours or the true pearl; a small lion lay on the velvet, a lion rampant, of gold, a gold collar attaching him to a chain, his eyes rubies, in his mouth a pearl the shape of a heart. The case was perfumed. Its musky scent lingered in the air of this empty room.

"You can be sure that is all that's gone?"

"I know her jewels."

"Did you alone know of this hiding place?"

"I alone, save for Her Grace. An old gentlewoman of the Duchess Maria's showed it to me, and she has since died."

Sigismondo made no comment on this; it was likely enough that in a palace full of servants, most of whom had been here before the Duke's second marriage, any of them might have seen either Duchess go to the wall and press the panel.

"When did you last fasten the case with all the jewels in?"

"When I dressed her for the feast. She did not wish me to dress her because I was the bride. But who else should do so? Who else could have proper manage of the maids? They are all very well . . ." She caught herself back, perhaps in realisation that she, like the despised maids, had no place now. She drew from under the lawn at her long throat a gold chain of ruby flowers. "She gave me this as a bridal gift. It is the only other thing not in here." Her face crumpled. She closed the box, and looked at that moment more like an unhappy child than a woman thrice married. She turned away, putting the box down on the table; her head made graceful bird-like movements as she dried her eyes. She said abruptly, "These jewels had better be given into the Duke's keeping. He has a strong-room and I—I cannot, it seems, keep them safe."

Outside the door there came voices, an infant pipe and a boy's. The small page entered, a wren of a child, already in the Duke's gift of a mourning tabard. He advanced round the bed and his eyes widened as he suddenly saw Sigismondo looming there, but schooling held; he fixed his gaze on his mistress' back and spoke rapidly.

"My lady, His Grace requires your presence in his library, with the Master Sigismondo."

The Duke, among the shelves and stands of books, the pigeon-holes of encased scrolls and documents, was at a table where the plans for his new library were spread. The architect, crow-like with his mourning gown over his brown working clothes, was in exposition, hands and arms at work as he spoke, conjuring distances, airy bays, galleries, columns. The Duke stopped him with raised hand and came towards them at his usual headlong stride.

"The ring is found." The blue eyes fixed, and Cecilia di Villani curtseyed deep. "A goldsmith has brought it to us."

"A goldsmith?" From her tone, the whole guild of goldsmiths was as foreign to her understanding as so many giraffes.

"A dwarf brought it to him for sale."

The lady made an attempt at this. The words *a dwarf* were formed by her lips.

"When the man asked the provenance of the ring, the dwarf said that her mistress had lost her post at Court because of the Duchess' death and would need money."

The Lady Cecilia closed her mouth with precision. Her eyes turned upward and her lids fluttered. She put out a hand for support in the general direction of Sigismondo, a wise choice, for as her knees gave way and her head fell back he was behind her. Her head lolled helplessly against his chest, loosening the black net, which slid away. A surprising quantity of soft golden hair cascaded over her drooping face and over the soft, black turned-leather of his jerkin. He gazed gravely over her head at the Duke, who looked morose.

"It is of course ridiculous," the Duke said. "The Lady Cecilia cannot be said to need money. She is overwrought. I don't suppose di Villani spared her. He's the man to ride his mares to death. He has the sensibilities *of a neatherd*," he finished.

Sigismondo appeared to have no difficulty in supporting her, and both men looked down at her head.

"I've ordered all the dwarves to attend in the west guard-room. My steward is in charge of it, and the goldsmith is to identify the one he saw. I will leave that in your hands. I am waiting to receive His Eminence, Pontano—who is going to tell me, I trust, why Bandini hasn't restored the di Torre girl, and to ask whether the death of his son is negotiable."

Cecilia di Villani now stirred in Sigismondo's arms and made small lost moans. The Duke gave her a blue glare, like a critic marking down an actor's performance, and left them.

Sigismondo changed his grip, bent to package the lady's considerable skirts together and get an arm round them, straightened up and walked out. She was emitting words of confusion and had got her head onto his shoulder by the time he reached the anteroom and put her down on a tapestry-covered bench there. The small page, aghast, was instantly at her side.

"I leave you in good hands, my lady," Sigismondo said. "You will excuse me. I have to see some dwarv s."

The small page resourcefully picked up the fan that hung at her girdle, and fanned her face with such vigour that her hair flew in all directions.

The goldsmith had put on a gown of dark blue stuff to come to the Palace, and he kept his hands in his sleeves as if for warmth; a working goldsmith's hands are apt to be unattractively stained. He was conscious of where he was, and the quite sudden arrival of Sigismondo failed to reassure him.

The Duke's steward had his back to the guardroom door, an impressive affair of oak. He was attended by two of the guard, in black-sleeved livery and carrying halberds. On seeing Sigismondo he opened the door, with a caution that showed apprehension.

While it was probably known to the steward how many dwarves there were, the immediate view suggested an illimitable number. They filled the floor, were standing on benches around the walls and sat in a row on the table. They were of both sexes, all ages and, within limits, of all sizes. None of them was pleased, and most were saying so.

All of them were in black and all wore, or were waving, even the males, headkerchiefs.

They pressed back from the door and enquired of the steward why they were there. Sigismondo's entrance produced a comparative quiet, but it did not last. It took the grounding of a guard's halberd, repeatedly, on the flagstones to produce a silence, sibilant with complaint.

"Had you all been quiet before, I would have explained—" The steward achieved no more. Babel supervened. Sigismondo had been watching, and now he leant across to speak to an elderly dwarf who had been relatively silent. This one accordingly stood up on the bench and raised his arms. As the rest saw him, they bit by bit stopped their clamour.

"That's better!" said the steward. "Now. What has happened is that a ring belonging to the Duchess, God rest her soul—"

A respectful "Amen" was the only interruption as yet, but there had come upon the gathering a watchfulness.

"—is missing. Or rather, was missing. As it happens, it was offered for sale to this worthy person this morning, and a colleague of his having identified it—"

"Is this to do with us?" enquired an ominous voice. There was now all the quiet anyone could want, a quiet of utter stillness. Hardly an eye blinked.

"I cannot be expected to tell you if I am continually—"

Sigismondo said, "The person who presented the ring for sale was of your stature."

Only the raised arms of the elderly dwarf prevented an outraged and chaotic explosion.

"This person was dressed as a woman, in a headkerchief. The Master Goldsmith, whom you see here, believes that it might have been a man. The Duke therefore commands that every one of you should be inspected by Master Goldsmith."

One of the row on the table, rapidly tying on his headkerchief, scrambled to his feet and said in a falsetto, "Ring for sale. Who'll buy my ring?" with out-thrust rear and a dance step.

The outrage this time was from the women, and he was pulled off the table, but the tone of the assembly had changed. Linen flew as heads were covered, kerchiefs adjusted; a commotion of simpering was hushed only by a scandalised "Remember the Duchess!" from somewhere. The inspection, now conceived as a turn of theatre, was accepted. Nothing could make it orderly. Sigismondo, whether recognising a *force majeure* or in dispassionate relish, did not try, but sat on a stone bench vacated by a line of dwarves as they precipitated themselves into the throng.

The steward and the guards organised something of a parade before the goldsmith. Kerchiefed faces were raised to his in turn, some bearded. Many came round for a second or a third time. They began to march.

Seeing panic burgeon in the goldsmith's complexion, Sigismondo suggested that to hear a voice might be of use; but it is open to doubt whether the repetition of "My mistress wishes to sell this ring," in every conceivable pitch, was truly an improvement. The goldsmith flung up his hands.

All he could be got to say was that *most of them* looked like the seller, which caused umbrage. The steward asked whether a further parade would not enable him to be certain, and the goldsmith, shaking his head very decidedly, said that, though he was afflicted to confess it, he could not, he really *could not*, identify the person.

The dwarves were permitted to disperse. Sigismondo, watching the steward trying to collect the kerchiefs he had issued, and being not only unable to halt those going out but faced with an elderly matron wearing, she coldly informed him, her own coif, and trying to placate the distressed goldsmith, was addressed by the dwarf he had first spoken to, who leant patiently on the table as his companions boiled out of the room.

"The Duchess had a great number of rings."

"This was one she always wore."

"That green one? A rich emerald, I suppose."

"Yes."

"Shortly they'll seize some of us to be tortured until they find one who'll confess." He was matter-of-fact.

"Very likely. Were all of you present? What about the missing one?"

He received a very sharp glance. "Poggio? He'd been banished. In the fashion, along with di Torre and Bandini. It didn't keep Leandro Bandini out."

"No."

The man nodded significantly.

"You are saying that banishment is ineffective."

Another nod.

"Where does Poggio live?"

Pushing himself away from the table, he passed Sigismondo on his way out. He said, "He was born in Altosta."

8. "SHE OWED ME . . ."

The bitter wind from the mountains had been amusing itself all day, plucking at the roofs of stalls and women's skirts and coifs, blowing hoods and hats off heads, rattling shutters as though keen to come in by the fire and thaw the ice from its breath, sidling under doors to worry people's ankles, and driving straw and dust everywhere. Now, rejoicing, it met Sigismondo and Benno on the road outside the city walls. As they bent before it, furling cloaks over their mouths, urging the horses on, the wind threw in a sprinkle of snow as an added caress, token of what lay ahead in the hills they rode towards.

Benno bore the journey with his habitual philosophy. His stomach was fuller than when he fed in Jacopo di Torre's kitchens; there were provisions and wine in the saddlebags, together with the nicely maturing dove; the horse under him was a good one from the Duke's stables, better than any he had been allowed to ride in di Torre's employment. He just had to remember to keep his mouth shut when his master was thinking, as the wind now was helping him to do. The only pain in his existence was worry about the Lady Cosima; Sigismondo had assured him that it was in the interest of anyone who was holding her to ensure her welfare, and he was willing to believe it, yet still he worried; to distract himself, he went over the various things he had eaten the night before, savouring them again in imagination and paying little heed to the rising track over the bare fields. After all, his master would certainly find the Lady Cosima, and God would protect her.

Altosta, as they wound up the hillside towards it, their horses slipping now and again on the great exposed slabs of rock powdered with snow, did not look much like a village. It more resembled a collection of ruins at which someone had flung birds' nests. Roofs constructed of branches, turf, straw, anything which might keep out the weather, and weighted with slabs of rock, crouched low and welcomed the snow as an extra layer of warmth. Huts perched on unlikely slopes or crammed themselves among boulders as if hiding, the spaces between them rutted with cart-tracks or blocked by frozen dung-heaps.

A donkey's bray rang out loud, on a gust of wind, from some ramshackle stable. Nobody stirred, although smoke seeped grudgingly from more than one thatch. Benno had a conviction, located at the back of his neck, that they had not arrived unnoticed.

His master had dismounted and stood, so shrouded and sinister in his black cloak that Benno thought no one could be blamed for fancying he carried a scythe at his saddle-bow, that Death was come. He got off his own horse, stumbled because his legs were so cold and waited hopefully.

What came to greet them in the end was a dog, a small dog whose ribs showed through the dirty wool of its coat, who had but one ear but bore it bravely aloft, whose tail slapped its flanks as it twisted from side to side in an ecstasy of welcome. Benno thought at once of his mistress' beloved Biondello, but this dog had seen no more food than its own fleas for a week. It went to Sigismondo as a saint might go to Death, with joy and trust.

It received earthly reward in the shape of a lump of sausage from the saddlebags, which disappeared into its stomach in a gulp. Benno, watching this, said, "I thought there'd be more. Villages like this send out dogs to eat strangers."

The dog now lay on its chin before Sigismondo, its rump in the air and its tail threatening to hurl it off balance.

"Perhaps there haven't been enough strangers," said Sigismondo, "or perhaps they've eaten the dogs."

Whether or not he was the only dog left, this one was grateful to be alive. Sigismondo's warning hand prevented Benno from giving him more to eat. "D'you want to kill him? His stomach has to learn what food is."

The sausage brought the child. Tied into dirty rags from head to foot, it came steadily towards them and stood at Sigismondo's feet by the dog, looking up with much the same expression. Sausages that came from the sky were worth such risk. Benno could hear a cautious unbarring of doors. A face appeared momentarily at a gap in a wall which a gross misuse of language might term a window. Another gust of wind brought wreathing, acrid smoke as though the village had been holding its breath and now let it out. A hen flapped over a hurdle fence and began to peck, staring wisely sidelong at grain it imagined.

"What do you want?"

Impossible to tell from where the voice came. It was the village speaking. Benno stopped in the act of handing a bit of sausage to the child, and it snatched and ran, diving into a hut. The dog barked. Sigismondo spoke from under his cowl and, despite the efforts of the wind to carry it away, his voice rang out clearly to their invisible audience.

"I come from the Duke to Altosta."

Benno was not surprised at the ensuing silence; even the hen stopped pecking. Dukes were bad news in villages; anyone in power always wanted more of what villages were short of: money, food, men to fight for them. Dukes didn't send free pigs to villages.

"Is it known here that the Duchess is dead? Murdered by an unknown hand?"

The silence continued. Duchesses, alive or dead, were no better news than Dukes. Murder was not news at all. They had some of their own, from time to time, and felt entirely no need for more. If Sigismondo had not been sent by the Duke, who therefore knew where he had got to and might presumably send soldiers along if he didn't come back, and if he had not sounded like a man who knew what to do with an axe, the village would have swallowed him up, servant, saddlebags, horses and all.

"The Duke has commanded me to seek out the dwarf Poggio. The first who tells me where he lives will get a reward."

The silence changed quality; perhaps a speculative mutter almost below the limit of sound showed that various factors were being weighed. Matters beyond the visitors' ken tipped the balance: the airs Poggio's mother had given herself since her son had been taken on at the Palace, the pig she'd bought herself with the money he sent. Yet many would get a share when she killed the pig, whether a cheek or half a trotter. Then there was the fact, awkward at the least, that she was a witch.

The tall man in the black cloak was tossing a coin up and again. It shone brighter than the harvest most of them never saw. There came the crab-like scampering, across the ruts and the blowing snow, of a larger bundle of rags. The hen squawked and flew; the dog cowered. The bundle extruded a hand like a root and pointed at the farthest hut in the village, retrieved the thrown coin and scuttled from sight. Sigismondo, followed by Benno leading the horses, and by the dog, picked his way to the Poggio residence.

It was tilted at a debauched angle in a nook of the hillside. Poggio's mother let Sigismondo in by hoisting the door open. Like all the village, she had been closely observing until now, and she had formed her plan and now carried it out. She denied not Poggio's existence, but his presence. She had not seen him since last summer. He was too busy to visit his poor mother. It was a pity he was not here when the gentlemen had come to see him, but his poor mother—

She was a large woman, a woman whose bulk in a village such as this showed a source of food denied to the others. Food was the only currency they had with which to pay for her skills as midwife, as layer-out of the dead, as mixer of potions for enemies and lovers, for wives, to endow fertility or to check it. Bunches of herbs hung in the half-dark round her head like suspended bats; a fire of twigs and rubbish gave off an unpleasant smell, to which a tallow lamp and Poggio's mother contributed. A snuffling grunt in the shadows told that a pig shared her accommodation.

Sigismondo heard out her excuses and lamentations without further question. He pushed back his cowl and hood, and her eyes took in the shaven head.

"A priest? Oh, Father, I'm telling the truth. I'll swear it on your cross. My Poggio isn't here, I've not seen . . ."

The priest produced not a cross convenient for her to perjure herself on, but a sword. She screamed. Three hens which had been quiescent in the rafters launched themselves into the room. The pig squealed. Benno, outside with the horses, on guard over beasts and saddlebags with a cudgel in hand, wondered if Poggio had been found.

He was not, at first, but as the sword enquired into the corners, somewhere halfway up one of the wattle-and-daub walls a quantity of straw plugging a hole fell out and a face appeared. It was a large, intelligent face with a wide mouth, turned-up nose and very bright eyes that examined Sigismondo with care. The next minute, the large face was followed out of the hole by a small body in a green jerkin and red hose. With the agility of a stoat he put his foot on one projection of the wall, his hand on another, and dropped to the floor. He flourished a Court bow.

"Poggio, and your servant, lord."

Poggio's mother, infected by these courtesies and unembarrassed by her son's proving her a liar, fetched, and wiped clean with the filthy sacking of her apron, a coppy-stool. When Sigismondo was seated, she put a cake of dung on the fire and poured a brew smelling of tansy into an earthenware cup, which she offered him, showing several teeth in an ingratiating smile. Poggio dumped himself on a pack of straw, presumably the bed, and seemed surprisingly ready to talk.

He was sorry to hear of the death of the Duchess. She had been kind to him. Yes, he had made a foolish joke about her, and the Duke had been angry. The Duke was often angry. All the dwarves had to be careful. Poggio had been hoping to be summoned back from exile at any time, but now that Her Grace was dead the Duke was not likely to want jokes.

Sigismondo drank his thin ale and smiled comfortably at him.

"On the contrary, His Grace has sent for you." He held out the hand on which the Duke's heavy ring gleamed. "As you hoped."

Poggio's face contorted into what he probably would have liked to express surprise and pleasure. To his mother, who was skilled in reading his face, and to Sigismondo, skilled in reading faces, it was plain he was terrified. Sigismondo's smile widened.

"He wants to question you about Her Grace's ring."

It was not particularly warm in front of the meagre fire, but Poggio's face shone with sweat.

"I know nothing of Her Grace's ring. I cannot. I was not there."

"You were not there—when?"

Poggio glanced desperately at his mother, who, quick on cue, bent to fold him in her arms, where he all but vanished.

"My child! Of what do you accuse my child? He has been with me all this time. What could he have done?"

Sigismondo rose, genial still. "That's what the Duke's torturers will discover. That's their task. Mine is but to escort your son to the city."

A wail from Poggio's mother, a convulsive wriggle from Poggio, and he was free from her and heading for the door. Sigismondo's sword across the door had the speed of him. Had Poggio been able to think, he might have preferred a quick death then to a slow one later, but a sword can be an eloquent object in the hand of a man with Sigismondo's face. He stopped. He was gestured back to the bed, and Sigismondo sat down again, holding out his cup to be refilled. Once full, it was handed to Poggio.

"Now you will answer my questions. Tell me the truth, and I shall know if it is the truth; and you will be spared the torture."

It was not a complete surprise that Poggio did not know where to begin when the end was so clearly in sight: a gallows. To confess to stealing the Duchess' ring was to ask for death, which would be likely to arrive in a quite complicated way. Poggio drank his ale and was silent.

The pig found something in a corner and ate it, loudly.

"Did you see Her Grace dead?"

It was a brutal question asked brutally. It startled Poggio into a reply.

"I didn't know she was dead, at first. Thought she was asleep." He was aggrieved. The Duchess had imposed on him, had put him in a difficult position.

"How did you come to be there?"

"In her room?"

"In the Palace at all. The Duke had forbidden you. How did you get in?"

Poggio could not resist a smile. It made his eyes crease and his nose turn up even more. He had a face made for telling jokes.

"There were plenty of us about. The big folk never know one from another. I know all the ways in and out of the Palace. . . . There's a little room just off the Duchess'—"

"By the bedhead, with a jib door."

Poggio nodded. "I waited there to see if I could talk to Her Grace, alone. To ask her to speak to the Duke for me. She had a kind heart." He crossed himself; the kind heart beat no more. "I thought I'd have to wait until the feast ended, but I'd hardly dozed off when I heard her voice coming nearer. That's a bit of luck, I thought." Poggio's voice had almost a cajoling note, the note of innocence hard done by. "Thought it all the more when I heard her sending the maids off. No Lady Cecilia either, which is a lady I'd avoid if I could, so I was coming out of my corner and ready to slip through the jib door and go down on my knees, not a trick I find easy, when I heard Her Grace talking again."

"You heard what she said?"

"It was nothing but a mumble, from either of them. Like you'd use to a lover. Lover it was, too, on account of the noise they were making not that long after. Gave that bed a beating." His eyes disappeared in their creases, but either memory, or the gravity of his listener, made him serious. "Oh, you can believe I kept quiet—that was a tight corner to be in. I couldn't hope for any favours from her if she found I'd been watching."

"Watching?" The word was a pounce, and Poggio nearly dropped the cup.

"Listening! I meant *listening!* I couldn't see anything, I tell you. I had the door a little open, yes, but it opens away from the bed, as Your Honour will have seen."

Sigismondo bent his head a little in agreement. "And then?"

"He must have left. I couldn't hear anything after they'd finished. The fireworks were going off. She'll be lying there resting, I thought, and doesn't she need to after that bout of Venus. Lying there with a smile on her face, shouldn't wonder, and drowsy. Just the mood to grant a favour to poor Poggio. So I pushed the door a bit and peeked round the arras to see could I get out without her seeing where I'd been, and then I saw—" He stopped and looked into the cup as if wondering where the ale had gone. His mother was quick to fill it. In the pause, Benno could be heard walking the horses round before the hut.

"And then you saw?"

"I saw her hand. It was over the edge of the bed and it didn't move, and I thought, She's asleep. I didn't dare waste more time, her maids might come back, anyone might—so I crept out, then I made a bit of noise so she'd wake up."

"And she didn't?"

Poggio looked round at his mother, who had come close, listening clearly for the first time to this tale, her sacking apron bunched in her hands.

"She was as dead as Noah's wife, wasn't she?" Poggio went treble with stress. "Lying there like that. I didn't need to touch her to know she was dead."

"But you did."

"Did what?" Poggio put down the cup.

"Touch her. When you took the ring."

"Well"—Poggio flung his arms wide, exasperated—"what could I do? She'd have done me a favour if I'd asked her. She'd got me sent away in the first place. She owed me."

"To the tune of two thousand ducats?"

Poggio's mother drew in breath among her teeth with a hiss, caught her son a hard backhand on the ear, picked up the cup and gave herself some of her own ale.

"It was worth more," Poggio said indignantly, holding his ear. "That mean old tradesman—"

"You used the wrong story on the goldsmith. Once he thought your *mistress* needed the money and had no place at Court, he knew he could name his own price."

Poggio, still rubbing his ear, scowled. Then he demanded, "Who was the Judas? Who put you onto me?"

Sigismondo rose towering above him, sword still in hand. Even Poggio's mother shrank back a little, treading on a hen.

"I am asking the questions, Poggio. Where is the money?"

The sword shone, even in that poor light, and Poggio began a rapid excavation of his clothes, rummaging in his jerkin and untying cords, watched intently by his mother, and unwound a long linen strip full of knots. He deposited this on the ground at Sigismondo's feet with a series of little thuds as the knotted-in coins fell. One of the hens came to peck hopefully at the pile. When he had done and held his shirt up to demonstrate, Sigismondo uttered the one word,

"And?"

Poggio hesitated, Sigismondo whipped the sword to his throat, and he backed, turned and ran to the wall, leapt from one projection to another until he reached his hiding place, and with rear and legs still outside, scuffled till he could drop down with a small leather bag.

"The last. I swear it."

"Save your oaths for the Duke. You return now to Rocca with me."

Poggio flung out his arms again. "I've told you everything. I've given you all the money, everything! Count it!"

Poggio's mother enveloped him again, tearful, and howled, "Don't take him to his death! He's told you everything! You have the money!"

Sigismondo made a small dismissive movement with the sword and hummed a derogatory arpeggio. "If he had—but as it is—" In that hum, at least one of the two listeners heard the well-oiled levers of the rack. Poggio's mother released her son and, seizing the broom from the wall, started to belabour him vigorously. Poggio ducked; the blow caught a hen that flapped up aiming for the rafters. Poggio darted from her, trying to avoid the blows. The pig ran; hens exploded into the air; smoke bellied from the fire; Poggio's mother pursued him wielding the broom, screaming, "Tell him, tell, you fool!"

Sigismondo stood by the door and waited.

Poggio fell over the pig and his mother caught him.

As the outrage of hens and pig subsided and she could be heard, she said, "Will you let him go if he tells you all the truth?"

"First, I will hear it. Then, I have the Duke's authority to do what I think fit."

Poggio, his head clamped in the crook of his mother's arm, was choking. Sigismondo hoisted him from her grip and set him down. The hens in the rafters shifted and peered down, commenting nervously. The sword's tip just touched Poggio's throat, keeping him rigid.

"What did you see when you pushed the door open and looked out into the Duchess' room?"

"I told you: the Duchess' hand."

"Before that."

The sword made a tiny movement and Poggio gasped, his head jerking up. A drop of blood appeared on his neck.

He said hoarsely, "The Lady Violante."

"In the Duchess' room."

"Yes."

"What was she doing?"

"Standing there. Looking at the Duchess."

"How?"

Sigismondo withdrew the sword a few inches and Poggio clasped both hands on his chest. "Like this."

"She was holding something?"

"I thought she was. I couldn't see it. It shone, but it could be her dress. She had gold on her dress."

"How long do you think she had been there?"

"I don't know. I'd heard the man go, but I hadn't heard *her*. She was at the end of the bed; you saw the room? You know the curtains were closed on the bed except this side? She stepped towards the bed and I ducked back. There was a sound—oh, I don't know, I think she sighed. Perhaps she was praying?" Poggio looked up, taken with this idea. "She'd be praying, wouldn't she? Then there were more fireworks going off in the court, and when I dared to look again, she'd gone."

"Were they friends, she and the Duchess?"

"The Duchess wasn't kind to her. She would find fault with her clothes and her manners. Said she was too extravagant and

87

too free—but the Lady Violante, you know, she never quarrelled with her. The lady was brought up by the Duchess Maria, God rest her, like her own child, and this Duchess knew the Duke loved the Lady Violante and of course they wouldn't quarrel. Of course not. I suppose the Duchess wouldn't be much older than she is. The lady's got a good heart. She spoke up for me when the Duke sent me away." He rubbed the itch out of the scratch on his neck and examined the smear of blood on his finger, which he wiped off on his hose. "She's a lovely lady."

Sigismondo had taken off his cloak and jerkin without comment on this and was engaged in wrapping round his body the long rope of linen pockets that had been piled on the ground before him. Poggio and his mother watched yearningly as he put away their golden future, but the sword was at all times near his hand. Jerkin and cloak went on again and he surveyed the pair, not unkindly. Poggio's mother clasped her hands.

"You'll not take him? He's told you everything. You have the money . . ."

"The money is for the goldsmith. Poggio is free to stay."

They screeched, Poggio did a brief fantastic dance and his mother tried to seize Sigismondo's hand to kiss it; but he was too quick for her, turning towards the door with a swirl of the cloak that nearly put the fire out and, filling the room with smoke, made his exit like that of a genie.

Outdoors, it was winter dusk and beginning to snow with more decision. Benno was tired of beating off attempts by children to raid the saddlebags, one of the most successful being a boy who leapt from a roof onto the larger horse, making it rear, however, and slide him off. The saddlebags were firmly fixed and Benno's cudgel effective, and the children had no luck. He was cold, and glad to see his master, whose arrival dispersed the children instantly.

"Thought you was killing someone in there, all that noise," he said cheerfully as they mounted. They rode off through the dusk followed by many disappointed eyes. As Benno followed, a faint hum was borne back to him on the wind, along with a stinging flurry of snow.

Inside Benno's clothes, against his chest, replete with sausage, slumbered the small one-eared dog.

They had not seen the last of Poggio. As their horses picked their way in the twilight and Benno reflected that riding down a steep hillside, whether in snow or not, was an occupation no man could enjoy, a sudden shrill whistle made both Sigismondo and Benno turn. At the crest of the hillside, silhouetted against the darkening sky, skipping and shrieking, was Poggio. When he saw their faces turn towards him, he pointed ahead, where the path wound among the rocks of an old landslide, and drew a hand across his throat. Benno was wondering what this meant, and had almost called to his master to know, when he saw Sigismondo draw his sword.

Poggio saw it, too, and vanished from the skyline. Benno, pulling his cudgel from the strap, took breath, with a mouthful of invasive snow, and tried to feel valiant. Sigismondo had not quickened his pace but rode casually forward.

The attack came with a savage silence. Among the big shapes of the rocks, in the swirls of snow, Benno had to control his scared horse and hit backwards at the man who had landed like an incubus behind him and tried to pluck him out of the saddle. Benno had been made a groom because he had an instinct for horses and he could ride; he pulled his mount in a tight circle and hit at the clawing animal behind. From where Sigismondo was he heard a scream, and the big horse backed into his. Sparks flew from the stones. A curtain of snow blew across; it was thick on his eyelids. His horse slipped and went down on its haunches, then with a trampling slither recovered itself. His attacker was gone. He was soothing his horse, watching all round for danger, trying to see what Sigismondo did and trying to keep hold of his cudgel, which slipped in his cold hand. The little dog trembled against his chest and wet him warmly. Sigismondo, shadowy giant through the snow, appeared and vanished, the sword descending. Benno's horse stumbled on something and an aggrieved voice yelled, "Watch out then!" Benno leant and made out the dwarf, cramming himself away, while on the ground sprawled a human shape. There was blood on the snow.

"Benno!"

He pulled his horse round. Sigismondo was freeing his feet from the stirrups and holding the reins towards Benno, who tucked his cudgel under his arm and automatically took them. He saw Sigismondo stand on the saddle and leap to the summit of a boulder.

"Take care of that one." He saw his master point and made out another figure on the ground. Poggio, in a sheepskin garment that made him resemble a filthy snowball, scuttered towards it, as Sigismondo was gone into the veils of snow.

They had not long to wait. Poggio, standing up by the second man, whose chest now lay open to the bone, called up, "You were lucky with your man—you hit his knife arm first thing." Benno was imagining what it must be like to have a knife go into you when Sigismondo appeared down the track, looming between the rocks. He bent to see Benno's attacker and moved on to the other man. A sound, a wordless, prolonged sound of annoyance, came; then, "I said, *Take care of him*, not *Cut his throat.*"

Poggio said, protesting, "It's the same thing!" and Sigismondo, coming upright and taking the reins once more, replied "*Oh* no. A man with his throat cut can't tell me who sent him."

"Weren't they robbers?" Benno enquired.

Sigismondo swung to the saddle. "Men in good clothes with

well-made boots and at least one purse full of money . . . Had
the others money?"

Poggio slapped his chest, warily.

"So. They had money. They don't need to rob. And they
are not outdoor men; they're city dwellers." He leant down
towards Poggio and said, "We owe you thanks. What brought
you here so fast and so opportunely?"

"I'm not staying up there," Poggio said. "I came the short
way, down the quarry, and I'll guide you the rest of the road.
In this light you could lose yourselves."

"As you will," Sigismondo said. "I told you that you were
free."

"Take me up." He reached an arm, and Sigismondo bent
and seemed to scoop him from the ground.

They rode off down the hillside. Benno called, "What about
them?" and pointed to the bodies, already blanketed in snow.
No one replied. Poggio's voice came on the wind disjointedly:
"If *you* could find me . . . that ring . . ." Once he emerged like
an unexpected birth from Sigismondo's cloak and pointed the
way. They came through trees, the snow whispering, and down
a steep open slope. Benno, alternately rubbing his legs and
putting his hands in to be warmed by the dog, rode almost on
his master's crupper to be sure of him in the fading light.

Past the moving mass ahead, he saw, farther down the hill,
lights clustered about a fire. Dogs' clamour came on the wind
as the firelight disappeared behind a fold of snow. Sigismondo
pulled up well before reaching the encampment, and a trio of
men came forward with a firebrand and quarterstaffs and a pike
to investigate. Before long Benno found himself sitting with a
basin of indeterminate soup, painfully thawing, while someone
rubbed down the horses and Sigismondo talked in a foreign
language to the company.

They made much of Poggio. From their talk to him, Benno

learnt that they counted the meeting lucky. They were camped here waiting for their acrobat and singer, who was missing, probably with some woman in the city. They had not fancied the atmosphere in the city at all, and did not care to stay. . . . A dwarf who could sing, act, dance and, given the right size of instrument, play a lute interested them very much. At this point Sigismondo remarked that Poggio was on his way to an engagement at a nobleman's house; he was a popular and sought-after entertainer. If they wanted him to stay, he was worthy of an important place. There was further talk, and drinking, and Benno and the little dog scratched themselves and shared more soup; finally, hands were struck: Poggio was to stay and travel with them, and if his act—a bravura item of which he displayed—proved all that it seemed, he would be invited to join them as a senior member.

Poggio, who had had a full day, was discovered to be asleep and was helped to one of the carts.

At first light, Sigismondo set off for the city. The snow had ceased during the night, but they rode over ground of luminous pallor. The city gates had not opened yet; the Duke's ring shown at the barred lattice got them admitted with impressive speed through the postern.

As they approached the Palace by the long, open ramp, Sigismondo remarked, "Those men who set on us, Benno— someone is going to know very soon that they failed. Be on your guard."

"Am I as important as that?" Benno asked.

Sigismondo hummed. "They're not to know I don't tell you anything."

"What about the bodies? Up on the mountain?"

"Poggio tells me they'll all be gone as soon as daylight. Someone from the village will find them, all three. There won't be a scrap wasted."

9. "I RELEASE YOU OF YOUR TASK"

Since the Duke was in Council, Sigismondo could not report to him, and chose to seek audience with another member of the family.

The Lady Violante evidently took the Court mourning to affect merely the lower orders. When Sigismondo was announced, she was the centre of a group of giggling ladies. All wore black, but the Duke's daughter's gown was sewn so thick with pearls that the effect was more of moonshine than of sombre night. She scattered her ladies with a brutal thrust of her hands, so that one of them actually stumbled.

"Go. Go! I will speak with this man alone."

As they swept their curtseys and went out, they exchanged glances and looked him over, covertly smiling. The door closed on the feast of gossip she had provided.

"It is kind of you to see me, my lady."

Sigismondo's voice, at its lowest register, was honey or velvet. She responded as a flower to the sun.

She beckoned him to stand before her, running her gaze over his breadth of shoulder and the bizarre shaven head as though she had suddenly found the object of interest she had needed. Her eyes had more than one thing in common with the Duke's: they were a brilliant blue, and they had a dangerous look—in her case that of a child bent on mischief but as yet undecided what form it shall take. Like the Duke, she was tall and slender. Her hair, blonde like his, was worn in a braid twisted with pearls and black ribbons that hung down her back, while casually careful ringlets framed her face. In spite of the necessary formality of dress and hair, there was about her a wildness, a suggestion that she might do anything, at any time, without even knowing she was about to, and that she enjoyed this. In her arms she held an ermine with a fine gold chain dangling from a jewelled collar. As Sigismondo stood before her, the ermine turned its sleek head and looked at him with the same air of unpredictable and happy ferocity.

"Why have you asked to see me in private?" She stroked the animal, held it up to her chin and looked at Sigismondo under her brows as though she expected him to admit an amorous motive.

"I believed your ladyship might be able to help me in the matter of Her Grace's death."

Did the ermine struggle or had her hands tightened? She raised her eyebrows.

"How?"

"Your Ladyship saw Her Grace shortly after she was murdered."

The ermine clawed its way out of the lady's arms and flowed rapidly across the floor, reached the end of its chain and turned back to hide under a velvet stool. Blue eyes stared at Sigismondo, blank eyes. Hands, empty of ermine, slowly fell to her sides. She said nothing.

"You were alone with Her Grace, at least, before the murder was discovered. Did Your Ladyship see anything that might help to prove who killed her? Someone you saw leave the room before you entered it?"

Life returned to the sleepwalker. She swung round and went to the fire as if suddenly cold. She spread her hands, rings shining with the jewels of mourning, pearls and diamonds. Over her shoulder she said, "I wasn't there."

The faintest hum escaped Sigismondo. She faced him again, opened a gold comfit-box that hung at her girdle, popped a sweetmeat into her mouth and continued to stare at him composedly.

"The first time I saw Her Grace after her death, she was lying in the chapel. Who says I saw her earlier?" A fierce energy in her voice and bearing now gave the impression that, could she lay hands on that person, they might at once be short of a tongue.

Sigismondo shook his head, regretful. "I am not permitted to say, Your Ladyship."

"*Who* does not permit? My father is the only one whose permission is valid here."

"As long as your father remains Duke of Rocca."

A scorching blue glare was turned upon him. "How can there be doubt that he will remain Duke of Rocca?" Her hand was on the knife that also hung at her girdle. "You dare say to me—"

"I am the Duke's man. You may be sure of that. But he has enemies, and I did not think you were one."

This brought her right up to him, hissing like a cat, her face distorted and the knife bare in her hand. "You dare, you dare to say I am his enemy!" Her knife, in a remarkably workmanlike grip, went for his midriff. He took her wrist and spoke with sudden force.

"My lady, your father may cease to be Duke if his enemies succeed in blackening his name as they begin to do. They are saying he killed his wife. They say so today in Rocca, and it will be in the Duke Ippolyto's cities tomorrow. Ippolyto will give his help to your father's enemies to drive him out. And kill him."

"*Leandro Bandini* is to be executed for the murder."

"It is likely that he is innocent. Would you allow an innocent young man to die?"

"How can he be innocent? He was found beside her body."

He let go her wrist, and she slowly sheathed the knife, not taking her eyes from him. He said, "His Grace is not satisfied."

A dog, invisible until now in a pile of cushions, grunted in its sleep and stretched all four paws out, quivering. She turned at the sound and walked back to the fire, still rubbing her wrist where he had held it; the fur border of her skirt made a soft noise on the polished wood, not unlike that of the fire.

The deep voice followed her relentlessly.

"Leandro Bandini says that you summoned him to the feast."

She whirled. "That *I*—summoned Leandro Bandini!" The thick rope of her hair flew out and fell across her shoulder. A fine flush of social outrage warmed her face, and her tone was that of a saint accused of summoning lesser devils.

"This is his story: a messenger came from you to bring him secretly to the Palace; you sent a man, when he arrived here, with a cup of wine and a disguise to enable him to reach you unknown."

A flare of the blue lightning. "If he says that, he deserves to die. It is a lie all through. And is *this*, this silly tale, why you think him innocent?"

She stopped and suddenly clapped her hands, bringing a page in past the door-curtain, to be dismissed with a peremptory wave. "No, don't you see? If it isn't Leandro Bandini, if he's innocent, then it's probably true what my stupid women are saying, that Jacopo di Torre sent the message fetching young Bandini here. *They* think him innocent because he's a pretty young man. They say di Torre's daughter is stolen by Ugo Bandini, so di Torre makes sure the son dies for it. It's really very clever."

"You think di Torre would have the Duchess killed to further his revenge?"

"A good revenge would stop at nothing. You know that." She strode across the room, hands clasped against her skirt. "Perhaps he only meant to have young Bandini discovered in Her Grace's room—perhaps by my father. Someone else might have killed her."

"Did you see Leandro there?"

"He must have been hidden. I saw no one."

There was a silence. She turned to face him, her hands flat on the pearly moonlight of her skirt. Then she folded them before her. She closed her mouth very precisely.

The silence lengthened. The folded hands gripped each other. She tightened her lips to a rosebud.

The shadow of a little mocking sound came from Sigismondo. She stamped. Then she flung up her arms and came towards him with the ease of a young woman who knows her position is invulnerable in any case. "I went for my jewel. The cross my—the Duchess Maria promised me. It was always to be mine. I was not here when she died; I wore the mourning for a mother, when I heard. And this one—the Duchess Elena—did not want the cross herself and would not give it to me. I knew where it was and I went to get it."

"Why now, my lady? Why never before?"

"She never dismissed all her maids and guards before, or when she did, there was always Cecilia. So I watched, until I saw, as I thought, the Duchess going away down the stair."

"Why did you think it was she?"

"A cloak with a hood. I thought it was a cloak that she wears. Everyone had put on cloaks to see the fireworks."

"There was no one else?"

"I listened. If I had heard anyone I would have waited longer." She caressed a ringlet, twisting it in her fingers and looking down her nose at him. "If Leandro Bandini did not kill her, was it the one I saw go away?"

"Possibly, my lady."

She looked thoughtful, drawing the ringlet out straight and examining it as if for quality. "She had made sure no one would see this visitor."

"Did Your Ladyship know of any admirers of Her Grace who might have had this privilege?"

"You put that very well," she said critically. "Did I know

who her lovers were?" She let the ringlet spring back, laughing and looking him in the eyes. "No. There were lovers. Cecilia knew. Some of her women will have known, I suppose, but nothing would make them tell, even you."

Sigismondo certainly knew that anyone can be made to speak, but he asked only, "Did His Grace know?"

"He never spoke of it. If he suspected, he never accused her. Not even in their quarrels." She smiled wickedly at the memory. "They were at each other's throats a few days ago when she found that my father had given one of his villas to Caterina Albruzzo. So stupid, being jealous. The Duchess Maria never was. She wasn't jealous of my mother, or at least she was never fool enough to show it. When my mother died, she had me brought to the Palace and treated me as her own daughter. My father loved her for it."

A scratch at the door. It opened, the curtain was drawn back and a page bowed to her. "My lady, His Grace's Council is over and he wishes to see you."

The Lady Violante extended a hand to Sigismondo. "Come with me."

As the page withdrew, Sigismondo took her hand on his and bowed over it. She stood still. "Do you intend to tell my father that I was . . . there?"

"If he does not ask me, I have no reason to tell him."

The fingers of her other hand pressed his lips. She leant a little towards him. "Silence, then."

Her hand resting on his, she allowed him to escort her to the Duke's presence.

Way was cleared for them by the Duke's page and the lady's, walking side by side. The Palace seemed filled now with grave elderly men talking excitedly or arguing in voices that stopped abruptly when they saw who was near; backs bent all along the way. The debate continued when they had passed. The general effect, now that mourning was universal, was of a scattering of crows cawing among themselves. Corvine glances examined the man who surely ought to be following behind the lady, not pacing at her side.

The doors were opened for the approaching pair and closed behind them, shutting them in with silence. The Duke sat absorbed in thought, his great carved chair askew from the head of the long table, his arm along its Turkey carpet of deep blues and reds. His secretary shuffled scrolls and papers together and fussed at attaching his inkhorn to his girdle. A wine-cup stood untouched before the Duke.

Against the wall by the window, watching his brother with a concerned look, was the Lord Paolo. Beside him on the cushioned window-seat, his son Tebaldo sat awkwardly, shifting himself to ease his body from one pain to another. In this proximity, family likeness and difference were very clear; Tebaldo had inherited the melancholy fold of the upper lid, and his face had the particular sadness of one who is often ill.

The Duke's reverie lasted no longer than it took for him to realise that his daughter had come into the room. He surged to his feet and advanced to embrace her. Tebaldo stared openly at Sigismondo, unannounced and, to him, unexplained.

The Lady Violante looked back at her escort from her father's arms and said, "This man tells that Leandro Bandini claims that *I* invited him, *and* in secret, to the Palace."

The Duke exclaimed. His brother strode forward, saying "What insolence!" and in his anger the resemblance to the Duke was suddenly strong. "I hope no one knows of this. People will say such dangerously foolish things. Has anyone else heard this tale?"

"No one but the lady, my lord, and I."

"You spoke with young Bandini?"

Sigismondo bowed, and Paolo, after a long, considering look, turned to his niece. "It may be di Torre used your name to lure the boy. We must never forget that the terrible quarrel of their houses may be the root of all this."

The Duke's voice broke in furiously. "*God's bones*, I'll make them pay for their wreckage of our peace. If this can be proved on di Torre, it is his own death. Yet I cannot believe that, even to destroy Bandini, di Torre would murder his Duchess. Can it be possible?"

He seemed to ask himself, not his audience, but Paolo replied with a shake of the head, reluctantly, "Men will stop at nothing when they seek revenge. They see nothing but their own aim. The past gives us too many examples of it—it's like a spell blinding them to their actions. Di Torre must have done this if the Bandini boy is innocent."

The Duke had listened to his brother, but now he turned the falcon stare on Sigismondo, who, even standing without movement or words, made his presence felt.

"Did you find the dwarf?"

"I found him, Your Grace, and have the money to restore to the jeweller."

"Your Grace, was the dwarf then found who stole the ring? I thought the jeweller could not tell which it was. Which was it? Might he have killed her for it?" Paolo had come to his brother's side and both, so like and so unlike, looked at Sigismondo.

"Poggio, my lord, the one you banished, took the ring. But no, I do not believe from all he said that he could have killed Her Grace. He found her dead."

Paolo leant forward, intent. "Then, did he see no one? Can he bear witness to one who might be the murderer?"

"He saw no one. And he cannot bear witness."

"He cannot? Did you not bring him back?"

"I was bringing him, Your Grace, when we were set upon

by robbers. We drove them off, but Poggio died in the fight."

"Poor little wretch," Violante said. "He always made me laugh." She looked up at her father, leaning against him, and he stroked her hair.

"Let that be his epitaph, that he made you laugh. I would have punished him for the theft, but I would not have had him dead. God rest his soul."

With the others, Sigismondo gravely signed himself. Violante took her father's hand as it descended from touching his shoulder and plaited her fingers with his, saying coaxingly, "Your Grace does not mean to execute Leandro Bandini? If he has indeed been tricked, you would kill an innocent man."

The Duke sighed, raising their interlocked fingers to look at them. "When cities are to be ruled, the innocent do not always escape. I must take measures that will guard Rocca against my enemies, far as well as near. Duke Francesco is a bird of prey that doesn't sleep—"

His brother made some involuntary movement and the Duke glanced at him. "That tireless advocate of mercy, your uncle, has persuaded me only now, in Council, that I must not be ruled by these fears, that Rocca cannot be taken if its citizens remain loyal. But how do I ignore things that have happened? When I—"

"The blood on the gates?" Only his daughter dared interrupt. The Duke slightly nodded.

"That, and other things."

"What things?" She clasped her fingers with his into a double fist. "What have they dared to do?"

Her uncle put out a soothing hand. "Some jailbird, some agent perhaps of Duke Francesco—some one man may be responsible for it: daubing His Grace's statue with blood, putting rhymes on the walls. If His Grace stands firm and ignores such provocation, all Rocca will be behind him. Rumour is not—"

Violante stamped her foot, an action making up in force for its lack of effective sound. "They *cannot* think for one moment that Your Grace—they can*not* think such a thing of you."

"They will say I found her with a man."

"But if you had, who could say it was wrong to kill her? Others—yes, princes—have done so."

"You forget Duke Ippolyto. Is he to accept that his sister had a lover? It attacks his honour; he will demand proof."

She was silent, swinging the Duke's hand for a moment, thinking, and then she released it.

"How will you keep the peace with him, then?"

The Duke went to the window, putting a hand on the shoulder of Tebaldo, who had made an effort to raise his wasted body as the Duke approached. He pointed.

"There, in a week's time, someone must die. It may have to be Leandro Bandini. I lose support of the Bandini faction to keep my alliance with Ippolyto."

"Can someone not be found, some story made that would convince Duke Ippolyto—that would earn time while you find who is guilty and save the Bandinis' loyalty?"

Paolo put out his hand to draw Violante to him. "Niece, you become a statesman, but think, Leandro Bandini may not be innocent. Remember how he made open love to the Duchess at the feast in his guise of Wild Man. He spilt wine on her dress so that she was forced to withdraw. He follows her, forces her and would have escaped if Her Grace had not, so bravely, struck him down. Who can swear that he is innocent?"

The Duke spoke from the window. "Sigismondo says that he was given drugged wine, brother."

Paolo gave Sigismondo another thoughtful stare.

"Who gave it to him?"

"My lord, he does not know."

Paolo made an incredulous sound and smiled. "You take his word for it? If he took anything in his wine, and I don't doubt that to act as he did he must have drunk freely, then he took some aphrodisiac. Forgive me, niece, but young men do such things."

The Duke watched Sigismondo as if waiting for a response. "Might it be so? Are you so sure of the drug?"

Sigismondo's bow and turn of the hand could have implied anything. The Duke took it to be assent. He strode to the table and, as if reminded, drank off his wine and spoke with fresh energy.

"Justice will be done. The people shall see it done, and we can put this behind us. Look no further, Sigismondo. I release you of your task."

"With Your Grace's leave: there may be more yet to uncover." The deep voice was respectful, yet it objected, and the Duke was hesitating when Paolo spoke again.

"There is always more to discover, as there are secrets and things unknown in every family. What His Grace wishes is for peace to return. Render up your authority as His Grace desires."

Sigismondo took off the ducal ring and brought it to its owner. The Duke slid it onto his finger and extended it to Sigismondo to be kissed.

"You will be rewarded. We'll talk later." It was dismissal in more ways than one. Sigismondo backed from the presence. The Lady Violante's gaze followed him with speculation.

Benno was vacantly chewing something when Sigismondo found him propped against a pillar outside the Council chamber. Two guards were eyeing him askance, unused to any but official lack-wits in the Palace. He was pleased to see his master and looked him over with a proprietary air. As they set off through the corridors and passages, he said, "Ring's gone, then, is it? Duke take it back? That means now we can go and look for the Lady Cosima, doesn't it?"

10. "THE OMENS ARE EXCELLENT"

The smell in the tiny out-of-the-way room chosen by Sigismondo when he bore the Duke's authority could be traced, past Benno, to the dead pigeon hanging up. Benno showed it off proudly, parting the feathers to check on the state of the flesh beneath.

"Coming on nicely, but it'll need a while longer. We'll take it with us, come in handy. Where're we going?" He stuffed the pigeon into a bag and was about to follow it with his master's rolled-up cloak when Sigismondo's hand intervened and took it from him. "Oh, yes, you'll need it, a-course. Wish I had something as thick." On the bed, an unexpectedly white, furry object emerged from under a horse blanket Benno had come by and shook itself, cocked its ear at Sigismondo and wagged a plumy tail.

"You've washed him. It was time."

"Well, I wouldn't have, but it was the fleas." Benno stopped and put a hand to his mouth. "Oh, there was something I had to tell you, but I expect you'll want to be off."

Sigismondo surveyed the room, stripped of their few belongings, and fastened his cloak over one shoulder. He made sure that the purse of gold given by the Duke's steward was securely stowed, and turned to Benno.

"First, you'll tell me what it was, or we go nowhere."

Benno shouldered his bag and looked resigned.

"One of Ugo Bandini's men came. I told him you was with the Duke and he could tell me. He knows me because we always used to fight when we met, me being a di Torre man. I've given him more black eyes than would fit out a Turkish brothel."

Benno rubbed a corner of his jaw as though remembering what he had got in return. "Ugo Bandini wants to see you."

"Is he still with the Cardinal Pontano?"

"Not him. Back at the Palazzo Bandini tearing his hair out over his son. I'm told the Cardinal got tired of his moaning and lamentation, so it was a case of *We will meet at the execution, I'll be praying for you, my son.*"

Benno was already hurrying to keep up with Sigismondo, whose passage through the Palace was attended with as many glances and whispers as before—but with a subtle difference, as though the absence of the Duke's ring could be sensed somehow.

"Bandini swore his innocence on the ltar of Saint Agnes?"

"He'd have sworn his son's into the bargain, if they'd have let him. The Duke was furious he went to the Cardinal for safety. Said he wasn't a tyrant and Bandini could trust his justice. Strikes me"—Benno skipped to keep up—"that's what he's afraid of. Anyhow, he's back in the family hovel and wants to see you. I suppose we're going? We'll look for the Lady Cosima after, won't we?"

The reply was a ruffle of his hair that made Benno stumble forward, ahead of his master for once. They left the Palace not by the Castello gates and the long ramp, but by the modern door onto the square, and the dog began to cast in circles after the new smells.

"Thought I'd call him Biondello," Benno said, "like the other one. He's not as pretty, I mean he's not a lady's dog, but he's little and he's white."

"He is now," said Sigismondo.

They threaded their way through the city by the lanes, alleys and courts known to Benno as the most direct route. Biondello scorned direct routes. The city was the place of miraculous smells, and he ran at least double the distance without ever straying far from his masters' heels. One extremely fine heap of garbage, though, was in the possession of a family of pigs, who drove him off in short order. He was also kicked out of a shop and hit accurately by a blind beggar he investigated. He was frisking down a narrow street between high houses, in front of the two men, when the second attack on them took place.

Benno, when the muffled figure rushed on him from the mouth of an alley, simply dropped like a scythed flower. His assailant's blow fell with deadly force on the man beyond, who was attacking Sigismondo, who thrust this sagging form aside and was about to deal with Benno's attacker when a third skirmisher came from above. He had been crouched on a wall, and most likely intended to bear Sigismondo to the ground, but the slight noise made by his falling body was enough to assure him a welcome. He was seized in irresistible hands and slammed against the wall. While this operation was being repeated, the first assailant crouched over Benno and and swung his right arm back for a neck punch. At this moment Biondello's young, sharp teeth closed on the back of his thigh and he rose, Biondello attached, with a supernatural cry.

Sigismondo dropped the man he was holding and brought his fist down on the angle of the howling man's neck.

Benno was the only man to rise to his feet. The lane had recently been traversed by the pigs. Biondello shook himself and released his feelings in a fury of barking. He had, in defending his masters, outraged the conditioning of all his short lifetime, and he was utterly confused. Sigismondo saw the assassin's knife in one attacker and looked where Biondello's victim lay with eyes open to the cold sky and blood at his mouth's corner and in his ear. Biondello, calming as nothing further happened, lifted his leg over the nearest body.

Sigismondo picked up the man from the sky, taking his head between his broad hands.

"*Speak* to me! Ah . . ." And a hum of disapprobation followed.

"*Still* no one to tell us anything." He let the man drop. "Do you know any of these, Benno?"

Benno, who had been searching them, stopped to examine their faces. "No. They look like tavern roughs to me."

"So who hired them? Benno, we're just getting too good at this."

At the use of the word "we," a slow smile dawned in Benno's lamentable beard.

The Palazzo Bandini was a far more modern building than the Casa di Torre. This latter may have represented established wealth, but Bandini's house was constructed to let the world know the family could afford the most fashionable architects. A classical portico framed the entrance from the street, with columns flanking muscular marble statues showing rather more strain in supporting the Bandini arms than was perhaps tactful. Inside, everything that could be gilded had been, and every ceiling had a pagan sky brimming with nymphs.

Benno was denied these revelations. He judged it politic to remain in the street outside, fearing to excite Bandini henchmen because of his previous affiliation or to get thrown out on account of his filthy state. He prepared comfortably to spend the time watching any interesting female who passed.

His master was ushered past a complicated marble representation of Apollo and Daphne, past a very large relief panel of a goddess rewarding either Piety or Learning, through an over-pillared lobby into Ugo Bandini's superb new library filled with books for which he had paid a fortune and which were unlikely to be read, especially if his son died.

Since Sigismondo last saw him, before the Duke, Bandini had aged—even more than his enemy di Torre over his Cosima's loss. Every lugubrious fold of his face had deepened as though tugged down by grief, and the eyes examining Sigismondo peered from swollen lids.

"Did you tell the Duke I had asked you to come?"

"I no longer work for His Grace, sir. There was no further need."

A gleam came into the eyes bloodshot with weeping. "You're at liberty to work for another? For me?"

The hum was neutral, enquiring. "What work would that be, sir?"

Ugo Bandini beckoned Sigismondo closer with an oddly furtive little movement of the hand, until he stood within a foot of him, when he uttered in a hoarse whisper:

"Find di Torre's daughter and I will pay you more than the Duke could ever give you."

If Sigismondo found this request ironic he gave no sign, but continued with his head politely inclined so that Bandini was unpleasantly reminded of a priest hearing confession, and of the final one his son might be making in so short a time. About to take hold of the man's sleeve to emphasise the urgency of his task, he found a reluctance to touch him. The attentive silence, however, forced more explanation than he had intended.

"His Grace has sent to me. He believes now"—and by *now* Bandini meant *now that he believes my son murdered the Duchess*—"that it was not di Torre but I who spirited away that wretched girl. He has enjoined upon me to produce her before the week be out." Again, both men knew what lay at the end of that week.

"Where do you believe she is, sir?"

"In that old fox's country villa! That's where you should look." Ugo Bandini brought his fist down on the polished crimson marble of his new library table, making some account scrolls skip. "He is trying to kill me and mine. I can in no way imagine how he has contrived it, but I am sure in my soul that he is the cause of my son's doom. If he murdered Her Grace to effect it, that is well within his nature. He would stop at nothing to cause me suffering." There were tears in the folds of the cheeks that would certainly have rejoiced di Torre.

"Have I liberty to conduct the search as I wish?"

Bandini's reluctance gave way to the pure urgency of his feelings: he clutched the man's arm. "Yes, yes. And you shall have gold, anything you want, my best horse, my household at your command, only find the girl. Find her, and the Duke may have mercy. *My son must not die.*" The tears ran among the furrows of his cheeks, and one fell on Sigismondo's hand.

A tap at the door interrupted them as a man in an indigo gown looked in.

"A messenger, sir. Says it's very important."

Bandini frowned in irritated surprise, seemed inclined for a moment to wave the interruption away, then, releasing Sigismondo's arm, he went to the door, where the man whispered in his ear, the sound like a trapped fly. Bandini's frown darkened, he patted the air towards Sigismondo, indicating that he was to wait, and hurried after the secretary from the room.

Sigismondo, thus left alone, strolled along the shelves, pausing from time to time to take out a book, examine the gilded binding with appreciation and, opening it, read a little. He was doing this almost half an hour later when Bandini returned and stared at him in suspicious surprise. Sigismondo, with a hum of amusement, turned with the book in his hands.

"I was consulting the *sortes Virgilianae*, sir." He read: "*Nusquam abero, et tutum patris te limine sistam*, which may construe, Nowhere will I leave you, and I will set you down safely on your paternal threshold."

Bandini's mouth, whose lips had peeled apart when he saw a man, hardly more than a hired bravo, reading Latin, closed again without his having found anything satisfactory to come out of it.

His manner had curiously changed; he seemed as anxious

as before for Sigismondo to leave and stood there making unconscious twitching movements of the hands towards the door. All the personal urgency, however, had left him.

"Anyone will tell you where to find the di Torre villa; perhaps you'd do well to say you came from the Duke."

Sigismondo shook his head with decision. "His Grace would not care for that. If he were by chance to hear—"

"Oh, quite, quite. You must do as you think best." Bandini picked up a silver bell made to resemble a pear and shook it. The man in the indigo gown had been at the door, for he popped immediately into the room and held the door wide for Sigismondo to leave; he, however, paused as he came to Bandini and genially murmured, "Expenses, sir?"

Bandini looked fretful. His hands took on their own life, brushing the air towards the door. "It is arranged. My secretary will . . ."

"And the horses?"

Bandini's expression would have been a good response to a request for camels, but he waved his hands more spaciously still, and said, "He will see to it. Go with him."

Sigismondo inclined his head and left the room, hearing Bandini release a gusty sigh before the door closed.

Benno looked the horse over with a professional eye, not impressed.

"Nothing like the Duke's lot."

Sigismondo slapped the rump of the big bay he had chosen. "We were lucky to get these. If Bandini had come to the stables himself we'd have been awarded a pair of jades with the bots." He felt in the breast of his jerkin. "If you don't like the horses, try the money."

Benno grabbed the purse from the air and weighed it. Then he undid it and looked in. He raised wondering eyes.

"Buy Biondello a bone, Benno. It won't run to much more."

The newly christened dog, which had come to circle Sigismondo in delighted wriggles, barked at his name as though he had learnt it already and perfectly grasped the reference to dinner. Benno, at a nod from his master, lost the purse somewhere in the unsavoury recesses of his woollen tunic and went on to tighten the girth on the bay, which was blowing itself out in a practised fashion. Benno was too inquisitive to observe the rule of no questions, and divined Sigismondo's indulgent mood.

"What's the money for, then? Milking a gnat?"

"Advance payment for finding the Lady Cosima."

Benno let go the girth, and stared.

"Hasn't he got her, then? Or is it a blind? If it wasn't bandits, who else would've taken her? The old villain—fancy asking you to look for her."

The horse had inadvertently breathed out, and Benno got the girth tight.

"He must think you won't be able to find her. Wrong again, isn't he? Why's he want her found, anyway? Does he think my old master will rush up and slobber over him and say all is forgiven now my daughter is found, and I'd just like to say it was me set up your son, pity about the Duchess, so sorry, Your Grace." Benno scratched his beard, out of breath but triumphant in his conclusion.

Sigismondo acknowledged the speech with a wag of the head, and Benno, finished with the horses, picked up Biondello and cuddled him, crooning, "Going to see your lady, we are. You wait." He watched Sigismondo mount and the horse toss its head and sidle in trial of the controlling hand; then, stuffing the dog once more into the bosom of his jerkin, he mounted too. "Where we off to, then? That money won't take us far. Nor that horse, neither. It may be the only one up to your weight but it's been ridden too far too lately."

Sigismondo, moving forward, said, "The money speaks, Benno. Bandini doesn't care if we find the lady or not."

"But didn't you say that's why he sent for you?"

"And, to start with, it's what he wanted above everything. Then he saw someone who changed his mind. Who came to the house while you waited?"

Benno considered, scratching his beard again and then Biondello's protruding head, with much the same sound and very likely with the same effect on the active inhabitants of both.

"Hardly a soul, bar a couple of nuns. All bundled up like they'd come a long way in nasty weather. Mounts in a bad way, muddy and tired. I got talking to the groom before someone called him in. Funny accent he had, and sure enough he comes from Castelnuova. Seemed to think we're all murderers here, kept eyeing me like I'd get out a knife and stick it in his ribs just for kicks. Wouldn't have been worth it for what he was wearing, I can tell you."

"Nuns. What convent did they belong to?"

"I didn't get around to asking."

"Always ask questions—of other people."

Benno grinned. "They were Benedictines, I know that much. There's a big Benedictine house over in Castelnuova. Why?"

Sigismondo for answer took his horse forward, and Benno followed, showering a beggar with dirt from a frozen puddle and ducking as a stone was thrown after him with a curse on his journey. He stuck out his fingers against the evil eye without slackening pace, and he prayed that wherever they were going he would see the Lady Cosima soon.

The villa of the Widow Costa was on a hill, like the hovel where Poggio was born, but all resemblance ended there. The sharp wind was here tempered by tall ilex hedges, shuttered windows and well-tiled roofs. A small avenue of poplars led from the road to the wrought-iron gates, which stood hospitably open and, as the travellers rode up, a man raking the gravel before the villa looked up and took off his cap. Guests were certainly no novelty here. Benno, who had no idea where they were, or why, was glad to get down, stretch his legs and rub a bit of feeling into them, let Biondello water the gravel, and be led by a fat girl to the servants' hall for a meal. The man with the rake took both horses round the house to the stables, while a cheerful serving maid of about fourteen in an apron too big for her asked Sigismondo whom she was to announce. Sigismondo put his finger to his lips, so she dimpled and led him to the widow's door, where she left him to his surprise.

"Hubert!"

The woman in black who sat reading, a candle prodigally already alight in the winter dusk, rose with a delighted cry. The book skimmed along the inlaid table; she hurried forward, arms wide, skirts of heavy silk rustling like autumn leaves before the wind. Her face, like her body, was all curves, the almond-shaped dark eyes, the full mouth smiling as she came to Sigismondo's embrace.

"How long is it? Two winters, and here you are looking the same as ever. Would that time treated us women so." She turned to the other woman, who had also risen but was holding her rosary as though it might be in requisition to repel demons at any moment. Time had treated her less kindly than he had touched the widow; though they were much of an age, in her the curves had sagged and her features were distinguished, though not markedly improved, by a moustache.

"Allow me to present Hubert, my dear. Your brother's comrade-in-arms and my own true friend." She hung on Sigismondo's arm, looking fondly up at him. "I hope you've come to stay for a long time."

Benno had an abundant meal in the kitchen and impressed

the fat girl and even the cook with his appetite and an account, enhanced by mime, of the wedding feast at the Palace. He hoped his master was having as good a time. He was assured that the widow was a good mistress, and kind, and liked to see company; he hoped in the most disinterested way that his master would not be distracted from their quest by this kind and welcoming lady.

Biondello, making uncouth noises over a bone at his feet, was not troubled by any such fears. He was a dog who lived for the moment. Since leaving his native village he had passed his days in Paradise, and his fleas—such of them as had survived his bath—could hardly believe their luck.

The night was spent pleasantly by all, perhaps not least by the widow. Even her sister-in-law had been charmed at supper by Sigismondo and was moved to add, to the already long list of petitions she recited before bed, a special prayer for brave soldiers. Equally concerned for their welfare, the widow did not spend time at her prie-Dieu.

Benno, even though he slept before the kitchen fire with Biondello rather than the fat girl as he had hoped, was perfectly satisfied. He had seen more interesting things in the past few days than ever before in his life, and he slept secure in his trust that Sigismondo could restore the Lady Cosima, whatever hazards might stand in their way.

Benno's fear that they might make a lengthy stay here were banished some time towards dawn when he was roused from sleep and given orders. He stumbled to his feet, muffled Biondello's enthusiasm for action and set about procuring food to pack. By the time he was in the stables, he could hear laughter upstairs in the house. The gardener-groom, sleepwalking, helped him lead out two of the Costa horses; Benno collected his bag with the pigeon in it, increasingly easy to find, was given some dried apricots to stuff into his mouth and his pockets and, clicking fingers for Biondello, crunched out across the gravel to lead the horses to the front. Before mounting he kissed his medal of Saint Christopher and pressed Biondello's willing muzzle to it.

Over the hills a lemon sunrise cast a pale light on the walls of the villa, and on an opening shutter. As Sigismondo, heavily cloaked and hooded, settled himself in the grey gelding's saddle, a hand waved from the open window. He raised an acknowledging hand in salute.

The wrought-iron gates were still open as they rode out, and Benno, turning to look back, saw that his master was smiling. He also appeared, under the deep hood of his cloak, to be wearing a wimple.

11. "CALL ME MADAM"

Benno asked no questions because he thought himself still asleep, imagining things, but as they passed out of sight of the villa, descending the steep path between poplars, Sigismondo let his hood fall back.

Benno stared.

The strong jawline was disguised by the lines of the wimple, drawn over the cheeks to a point below the mouth, making a triangle with the low band to the eyebrows, a deliberately feminine triangle that showed only the dark eyes, the nose and the mouth. Benno noticed for the first time the thick sweep of eyelashes, and that one could see the sensual mouth as womanly too. He had seen matrons on the Rocca streets with faces just as commanding. Sigismondo smiled and lifted his hood forward again over the black lawn veil. Biondello thrust his head out of Benno's cloak to have a look.

"You serve a widow now, Benno: Donna Maria-Dolores, Spanish relict of a di Torre cousin. Ride beside me, and tell me all that you know about the childhood and relations of the Lady Cosima."

Benno, at first of the opinion that he knew nothing of the subject, found that in pleasant converse with this weirdly female figure he could tell a good deal. As time went by, the person beside him seemed to become more and more feminine in bearing and behaviour. The voice modulated to a deep contralto, and, gradually, Benno began to see just such a woman as he had often met: big, somewhat masculine, but with a score of differences that Benno could not place but which made him all but lose sight of his master, and made him able to accept the transformation. He talked about family celebrations of the di Torre household, about gossip among the servants of the guests, and long arguments on winter evenings about such matters as the relationship of old Matteo di Torre to one of the Christmas guests, of Jacopo himself to the godparents of the little sons who had not lived; repetition, and Benno's pride in the family he served, had printed a good deal on his memory. By the time that they drew off the road onto a sheltered spot under a contorted cliff and ate and drank, the widow could say decisively: "Yes, I am Maria-Dolores de Cornuto, and I was married to that Venetian cousin. But you'll offer no explanations to anyone. You'll call me Madam. And from now until I tell you otherwise, in any company you'll leave your mouth open and let nothing come out of it."

"So where are we off to, Madam?" They were not in any company, and the Widow Cornuto was in a relaxed mood. Benno remembered the laughter upstairs in the villa at dawn.

"Do you know none of the roads round Rocca? Can you not tell our direction?"

"I never was anywhere but Rocca and the villa. I'd like to see the world, like Kiev and Compostella and that."

"For now we're going to the Benedictine house you spoke of. If nuns from that house came to see Ugo Bandini and, after he had seen them, he no longer wished me to search for the Lady Cosima, it must be because he then knew where she is. And where better to hide a young, unmarried girl than in a convent?"

"Who took her there, if it wasn't the Bandini?"

The face so strangely feminised turned to him with raised brows that touched the linen browband.

"When I find the answer to that, Benno, I may even tell you."

They rode on in silence, Benno mentally digesting. He had let Biondello stay on the ground for a run. The little dog kept close to the horses, uncertain of, but interested in, the roadside. He avoided a woodcutter who, muffled to the eyes in sacking and with rags bound round his feet and legs up to the knees, met them, leading a donkey and not sparing the woman and her groom a second glance. Biondello had learnt that most human beings kick or throw things, and he kept to the far side, safe behind his gods, who did neither. They met an ox cart creaking behind the two blond creatures who looked as if they walked in their sleep, their dewlaps aswing. Farther back one of them had dunged the road, and a flock of birds was pecking without much hope. Biondello saw them off.

"Leandro Bandini, then." Benno, getting some answers, hoped to air a few more of his questions. "You really think he didn't do it? Why'd he act like that at the feast, then, giving his heart to the Duchess and not the bride? Dancing about like that on the table?"

"You thought he did it well?"

"In and out the plates and cups, a tumbler couldn't have beaten him at it. Until he knocked the wine over the Duchess. But then he must have meant to do that."

The grey, going ahead on the path as it narrowed, picked its way carefully among the stones on the slope, and Sigismondo's voice came back to Benno, "Quite the professional, as you say. Have you ever tried dancing on a table like that? There were two Wild Man costumes; Leandro could wear only one."

Benno hurried forward to ride alongside as the road opened out again, and he leant to scoop Biondello off the bank. He tucked the dog under his cloak against his body to warm the paws icy on his palm. "You think it was a tumbler killed the Duchess?"

The bewildering face was turned towards him again in amusement. "M'm-h'm-h'm. You could be right. It's a thought,

Benno. Some tumbler could have a grudge against the Duchess, sent the spare suit to Leandro with a false message, knowing he'd need a disguise, as a Bandini, to get into the Palace. It would be interesting to know where the tumbler is now. He could tell us something."

"Or he could've been paid to kill her. What about Poggio, though? *He* had a grudge; she'd got him kicked out of his job *and* the Palace. Why couldn't he have killed her?"

They both crossed themselves as they passed a wayside shrine. The statue of the Madonna, her blue robe chipped at the edges, looked serenely down at a spray of ivy somconc had put in a pottery jar at her feet.

"It's not impossible that Poggio did."

"But you let him go!"

"I know where to find him," said Sigismondo, "and he'll think he's safe now. He'll stay with that troupe unless he quarrels with them."

Benno brooded for a while, his cloak twitching as Biondello got in a good scratch under one ear. "Did Poggio see anyone there, then, if he didn't do it himself?"

"He saw nothing to begin with, and then his mother persuaded him that to keep quiet would hang him quicker than the truth would. And my sword may have helped."

"Then he did see—"

Biondello, with a particularly ecstatic flurry of his hind legs, ejected himself from the cloak and landed in a surprised condition on the path. Sigismondo swerved the grey aside, and by the time Benno had dismounted and collected the dog, his master was ahead again.

"*Did* he see someone?" Benno was afraid that the indulgent mood might be over and the answers dried up, but the answer he did get earned him a mouthful of cold air. "The Lady Violante? What was *she* doing there?"

"Come to take something she thought belonged to her, at a

time when she was sure the apartment would be empty. A jewel promised her by the former Duchess. So she tells me. Equally she might have gone there to kill the Duchess, or to have taken the opportunity of finding her asleep; the lady saw somebody going away, cloaked, whom she took to be the Duchess, so she says; it could have been anyone, male or female. Perhaps she came into the room, took the jewel and then saw the Duchess and believed her theft had been seen and killed her. She's an impetuous young creature."

"If it was her," Benno pursued the idea with awe, "and you said so, you'd be for it, wouldn't you? —Well in fact, Your Grace, it was the Lady Violante who did it— Ah, thank you so much; guards! Take this man out and hang him."

Another wagon groaned and creaked its way towards them, the four oxen plodding, scattering stones and crushing the ice of puddles, not altering their pace for the whip that flickered and cracked around them or the shouts of the man trudging alongside. His exertions had made him warm and he offered them a cheerful greeting, demurely acknowledged by the widow. It was a little time before Benno spoke again.

"Why'd His Grace send you away? Does *he* think it was the Lady Violante?"

"I doubt if he's thought of that. What's on his mind is what I put there: I told him there were no signs of forcing on Her Grace, no bruised wrists, no bruises anywhere. She had lain with a man, and she had been willing. Poggio heard no cries of protest and he was in a closet off her chamber, only a matter of yards away. The Duke does not want to hear about her lovers. As his brother said, there are secrets in every family."

Benno rode in silence for a little, accommodating himself to Biondello's efforts at settling in comfort. Then he ventured, "If the Duke'd found her with a lover—"

"Young Leandro wouldn't be waiting to die now."

"No one would've blamed the Duke for it, would they?"

"Even Duke Ippolyto might have had to accept his sister's death."

"Know what I heard in the Palace afterwards? They were saying, only, like, behind their hands, that the Duke's killed her in one of his rages, same as he killed the Duchess Maria."

"And what's the version you've heard of *that* story?"

"He set his dogs on her, and they tore her throat out." Benno said it with a gossip's relish. "Everyone's heard that. A-course, at the time it was given out it was an accident and the dogs had gone mad, they'd jumped on a monkey she was holding. The Duke killed them himself. I was that sorry when I heard. I was just a boy in the stables. Poor dogs, how could they know?" Benno fondled the dozing Biondello. "I should have been sorry for the Duchess Maria; everyone said she was good and kind. D'you think the Duke killed this Duchess too?"

The widow gave a little forward shrug of the shoulders. "Whoever did it arranged for Leandro Bandini to take the blame. It may indeed have been the Lady Violante who sent him the message. The Duke himself is set on healing this feud that damages his state—is it likely he would provoke it further? There have been riots in the town since the death, Bandini against di Torre, street fights from which one man is near death. Is this the Duke's peace?"

They had reached the top of a hill and paused, the valley spread out before them touched now by sunlight, the walls and buildings of a distant town white and red against the far-off hills, blue like the bloom on a plum. It was warm now, and the widow let her hood fall back, arranging her veil with one hand.

Benno had been visited by an uncomfortable thought and gazed at the view without seeing it.

"Could have been my old master, you know. Lord Jacopo could've sent the disguise and that to Bandini's son, hired the dancer to get the Duchess to withdraw to change her dress, and dumped Leandro—believe me, he could have done it. You don't make a fortune like he has if you're afraid of dirty tricks. And he did pretend my lady had been snatched."

"How would he get the Duchess to dismiss her ladies? Do you propose him as her secret lover?"

Benno snorted. Side by side, they surveyed the landscape. The grey whinnied and rubbed its nose on its foreleg. A bird, from its size a raven, flew heavily into the distance towards the town; another group of black birds, dots in a field, moved busily, foraging. Benno undid his cloak at the neck, whereas half an hour ago he had been envying the widow's enveloping skirts.

"It's a lover, isn't it? Her lover did it. Has to be, if she was expecting someone. Might be Leandro after all, eh?"

The strong profile under the veil was thoughtful. "He may be lying, just as Poggio may; but if a man lies with a woman, there are traces that cannot be concealed. I helped him strip off that Wild Man suit in prison soon after, and there was nothing; and I smelt herbs on his breath that made me believe his tale of a drugged drink."

"Why'n't the Duke kill him when he found him?"

"He didn't find him. Leandro was meant to be found, as I see it, at the Duchess' side, and found by the Duke, perhaps, who would be likely to kill him, or by the guards. But, half-conscious, he tried to move and fell between the bed and the curtains; by the time I found him, he was not conscious and the Duke would not kill him."

"I know he's a Bandini, but I'm really sorry for him. I'd be really sad to watch him executed. But if it isn't him, how can you find who the lover was? Not likely to come running to the Duke, is he, saying, *Sorry*. And the Duke doesn't want you to go asking either. That's what's called a dead end, I'd say."

Sigismondo gathered the reins and touched the grey's flanks. "That's to be seen, my Benno. And now take your vow of silence. You've talked enough to last you for the next four days."

The widow, her groom and his dog rode on towards Castelnuova.

12. NO TIME TO WASTE

The travellers did not at first glance impress the portress at the Benedictine house in Castelnuova, but the tale of woe that came at her through the grille prompted a speedy unbolting of the postern and necessitated a helping hand for the bulky woman bundled in cloak and veils who could hardly step over the high threshold. Her lack-wit groom, trying to help, only precipitated her forward. The woman was ill, exhausted, a pilgrim who had been set on by robbers, deserted by her attendants, left with this poor fool who understood nothing but horses. The man's mouth hung open; his eyes clearly conveyed nothing to his mind. He was sent round to the stables, accompanied by a lay-sister in case he lost his way, and to vouch for him.

The widow herself, now revealed as truly imposing once she had cast back her hood, was in need of care. Her plethoric build was not suited to the trials she had endured. She sank into the portress' chair as soon as she saw it and lay back, with eyes turned upward, lips parted, near to fainting, a hand pressed to her heart. It was a case for the infirmary rather than the guest house.

"Mother Luca, the infirmarian, is at Nones this half hour, but she will, I don't doubt, be with you before Vespers. This sister will take you to the infirmary and there you will be looked after until Mother Luca comes from chapel. She will be told of your arrival as soon as Nones is done."

The widow, very grateful, made an effort at a smile and thanked her in a husky whisper. The portress watched her set off across the great court, leaning on Sister Rosa, whose robust arms, strengthened by years in the vegetable garden and in the laundry with its heavy woollen robes, she trusted would be able to support their guest. With a jangle of keys, the portress sat down in her chair, breathing the musky scent the widow moved within and suppressing worldly speculation as to the Venetian gentleman, not surprisingly dead, who had dared take her to wife.

The infirmary was of a size befitting such a famous and well-endowed foundation; there was first the chapel, from which the sound of chanting came. Sister Rosa remarked that Sister Benedicta was very ill and constant prayers were being said. She supported their labouring guest across the long dormitory. The chanting came very clearly here through the window that opened onto the chapel. "The sick have the benefit of the Blessed Presence," Sister Rosa said. Incense smoke also drifted in.

"What a comfort!" whispered the widow. She glanced at the tall stone walls, the beds enclosed in wooden boards giving them considerable resemblance to coffins, a helpful *memento mori* for the sick. "I shall not have to stir far to make my prayers for my dear husband's soul . . ."

The infirmarian's assistant nun came towards them just as the murmur continued: ". . . and make offerings for thanksgiving at having been brought to a harbour of kindness after such travail . . ."

The sister took the widow in charge with respectful care. Here was a woman of substance in more ways than one. The widow paused to gaze at the huge crucifix on the wall and her lips moved silently.

She was escorted to a small private room suitable to her status. There again was a lack of show, no more than a narrow cot curtained; a small scrubbed table beside it for candlestick, book of hours and medicines; a stool for a visitor; and another crucifix, on a more economical scale, opposite the bed, to concentrate the sufferer's last gaze. The widow sank upon the bed as though her legs would take her no farther, gave a great sigh and, fixing her eyes upon the crucifix, wiped away what must have been a tear.

"I thank God I have been permitted to reach this haven." She joined her hands and said an Ave in which the sister took part. Then, with a curiously sweet smile on a face which was not prepossessing, she murmured, "I have escaped so many dangers. A great number of travellers must be grateful for this protection. I cannot be alone in finding it at this time."

"You are the only one to arrive today, Madam, but we have another—ah, here is Mother Luca herself."

The sudden nervousness of the infirmary assistant did not appear to be justified by the mild sweetness of Mother Luca's greeting, but it did not escape the attention of the widow. A thin hand pressed her down as she attempted to rise; she fell back, gasping with exhaustion.

"I can see you are overtaxed, madam. You must rest." The hand was laid lightly on the brow under the linen band and skimmed to what part of the cheek was not covered. "No fever, I see, so I shall prescribe a draught to strengthen the blood. Sister Ancilla, bring our guest a cup of the wine that is mulling for Sister Benedicta. Be sure that it is not too hot."

Once the nun had gone, gliding with as much haste as the Rule would permit, Mother Luca, slipping her hands inside her sleeves, turned all her attention to the widow. Even the plainest face can gain distinction from the simplicity of a nun's head-dress, but the infirmarian's face, though no longer young, would have turned heads anywhere. The olive skin had still a glow, though the dark eyes under the melancholy fold of lids looked as if they had seen a good deal of sorrow, whether in the world or here. Her smile, however, when it came as now it did, was charming enough to put heart into her patients.

Her assistant reappeared with eager speed.

"When you have drunk this wine," Mother Luca said, offering the cup with quiet authority, "you must eat. I will have a *minestra* prepared for you. With lettuce, which will be sedative. Later perhaps a draught of valerian."

"You are so kind, Mother. I think I am almost too weary to eat." The long sleeve concealed most of the hand the widow placed on her midriff; the husky murmur faded under the reproof of Mother Luca's raised eyebrows.

"That is precisely the time when one must force oneself, my daughter. Discipline is needed for many things in this life, and the recovery of health is foremost for you. Now you must sleep." She extended a hand for the cup, from which the widow had drunk in genteel sips, making little appreciative sounds at the healing warmth.

"May I go to chapel, mother? I cannot sleep till I have prayed."

"Tonight you shall pray here, Madam. I shall come to see you after Compline and by then I trust you will have recovered from the worst effects of your journey."

Smiling, Mother Luca wafted her assistant before her and shut the cell door softly but with decision.

Left alone, the widow straightened from her drooping docility and sat for a moment or two listening intently. Not far away, chanting came more loudly for a moment, then was cut off by the sound of a door shutting. The widow rose, gathering her skirts, and prepared to disobey the infirmarian.

The arched corridor was deserted. To one side, the door just closed by Mother Luca or her assistant led to the big dormitory and the chapel. To the left were three other doors beyond the widow's, and opposite them, two long, thin windows like arrow-slits but filled with fine grey glass. Most of the illumination came from a candle inside a small lantern in front of a Madonna between the windows.

When, on her arrival, the widow had been led through the dormitory, only two patients had been lying there; both had lain on their backs, hands crossed on their breasts in the fashion proper to a sleeping nun, and on both, divested of their veils as of their outer garments, the white cap made their faces more sickly yellow by contrast. Neither had been young. If Cosima di Torre were in this convent, she was not in the main dormitory. She might be in the guest quarters, but the widow believed in looking under one's hand. She softly lifted the latch of the door next to hers.

The room replicated her own. The narrow cot held only a bare straw mattress.

The next room held an occupant, evidently the Sister Benedicta for whom the prayers were being said. Privacy was hers, probably because she was about the business of dying. She too lay flat, hands crossed and eyes closed, but she was even more pale than her sisters, with grey shadows in the hollow face. Candles stood by her head as though to anticipate that final state in the chapel, where Sister Benedicta would be surrounded by candles saved by her on each Feast of the Purification against her lying there in death. At the foot of the bed, her back to the door, a nun knelt, rosary moving silently. The table by the bed held flasks and a cup; a scent of herbs lay heavy among the scent of wax. The widow crossed herself and withdrew.

The last room also had an occupant. Lying with eyes closed but with hands at her sides was what at first sight seemed to be a boy, because of the cropped hair. The face, smooth and ivory-pale, was that of a girl of perhaps seventeen. The widow smiled, moved forward and shut the door as softly as if it were a shadow.

The girl did not stir when the widow bent over her, close to her face. She did not even wake when the cup on her table was picked up for the widow to sniff that also. The flask beside the cup was examined, a drop tipped from it onto the widow's finger and licked. As the flask was set down again the girl's eyelids flickered and the widow sank onto the stool and took the limp hand. In spite of the brazier burning in the room, the hand was cold, not responsive to the encouraging pressure of the broad hand.

"Cosima?"

The eyes were hazel, more green than brown, all the larger in the pale face for the dark shadows beneath. Her gaze held only mild surprise.

"Is it time for supper, Mother?" She frowned a little, as though trying to bring her thoughts together. "I'm sorry . . . It's not Mother Luca . . . Are you a new sister?" A nun's dress, being adapted from that of a widow, was easily mistaken. Her voice was slow and confused, unable to adjust to the waking world. The widow patted her hand and spoke low, with cautious urgency, alert for any noise outside.

"Cosima. What do you recall about coming here?"

The girl was puzzled. "I can't . . . I was brought in by travellers . . . Mother says they rescued me from robbers. I was very ill. A fever. They cut all my hair," she added plaintively.

"Are you ill now?"

The girl's eyelids drooped. She was beginning to tire. "But sister, didn't Mother tell you?"

The widow's ear had caught the sound of a distant door. With agility astonishing for one of her bulk and so voluminously beskirted, she was at the door, putting a finger to her smiling lips as she turned for a moment towards Cosima. She had just time to shut her own door behind her before Sister Ancilla went past to see how far Sister Benedicta had loosed her soul from its earthly moorings. The widow, anticipating a check on her own condition, sank to her knees by the pallet and set up a flow of prayer in a husky murmur.

She had to pray long enough for the sub-infirmarian to visit both the other occupied cells, then a tap on the door preceded her entrance, followed by a lay-sister carrying a board with a covered dish, the soup ordered by Mother Luca. The widow, rising, confessed herself to be a little better but suffering from great agitation of the heart. She was not altogether surprised to hear that Mother Luca had already prepared her a calming draught with her own hands and would, as she had promised, be coming to judge of its effect after Compline.

There was no time to waste.

Left alone, the widow drank her soup, considered the calming draught, disposed of it in the necessary under the bed and, holding the pot under her robes, added to the contents by way of disguise. All this took but a short time, and she was then ready to slip along to Cosima's room. It was all but dark now on this winter afternoon; the narrow windows showed blackly by contrast with the lantern's red reflection on the walls. The bell over the chapel rang for Vespers, and the nuns would be in chapel, except for the one by Sister Benedicta and those, like the sub-infirmarian, with permission to stay at their work, and Sister Ancilla had just visited her patients and was not likely to be back for a while.

In Cosima's cell, the brazier's coals had been replenished and, unfortunately, so had her cup. It was empty now and Cosima lay motionless and dumb. The widow, even by shaking her, could win no response. She did not linger but returned briskly to her own room, where she sat for a time on the bed, deep in thought. Then she removed, and folded on the stool, her outer garments and veil and got into bed, pulling the coverlet up to her capstrings, snuffing out the light and closing her eyes to wait for Mother Luca's visit in a few hours. Only those without resources waste time in repining and, before minutes were out, the widow's sleep was genuine. When at length Mother Luca and her night lantern went round, she left the widow in satisfaction with the efficacy of her draught.

The widow was accustomed to sleeping lightly and to waking when she chose. She heard the chapel bell for Matins at two in the morning, for Lauds at five. As the bell began ringing again for Prime, she calculated the hour at not long after seven, by the faint grey round her window shutter strengthening to daybreak, and she had established that before each Office, Mother Luca or Sister Ancilla, sometimes both, made the rounds of their patients. They passed along outside the cells almost without a sound, and only sharp hearing would have detected the raising and dropping of latches on each door. A nun's training to be noiseless in performance of her duties was demonstrated finely in the care of the sick.

The widow had also discovered, by the most acute listening, that the nuns who prayed by the dying sister would be relieved before an Office was due.

Mother Luca was pleased to hear that the widow had slept well but concerned that she found herself still weak, indeed hardly able to stand.

"It seems—I fear—that I must trespass upon your patience. Indeed, I intend to remember this house of succour in my will as well as in my prayers. And I can pay for such things as you may think necessary, any drugs and food. The robbers, I thank God"—she directed pious eyes briefly towards the ceiling—"were driven off enough for us to escape before they could take what I carried." She produced a small, clinking bag from her robes.

"You may do whatever God puts it into your heart to do, daughter, but this foundation is, thanks to Him, well able to carry out the duty to relieve and serve. We do not ask payment. God be praised that your life was spared, let alone your possessions."

Sister Ancilla began to say that indeed robbers were a danger to all, to other—and perhaps she would have spoken of the other traveller so close by, but Mother Luca's calm tone, without emphasis, rode her down.

"I shall send you a carminative to strengthen the vital energies. You will like to wash, and hot water will soon be provided before you break your fast."

She left, Sister Ancilla a flustered second after. Mother Luca had saved her from useless talk.

It was important for the widow to have time to use the hot water before any sister arrived with food. What she did in the interval required haste, skill, the temporary removal of her headgear and a razor-sharp knife. By the time the lay-sister came with bread and half a cold fowl and wine, and took down the shutter to let in daylight, the widow reclined fully clothed, the wimple in place over cleanly shaven cheeks. She lay back exhausted and feebly expressed anxiety over her groom's care of her horse. She felt a responsibility for the lack-wit and would be glad if she might see for herself how he did. The lay-sister doubtfully suggested that permission might be given for the lady's groom to come to the porch of the infirmary, if the lady were only strong enough to walk there. The widow professed complete confidence in her recovery with the help of Mother Luca and suggested that her groom might be summoned when the noon meal was in progress and he might be less likely to disturb devout eyes.

The lay-sister had been admiring two pilgrim seals the widow had placed beside her bed, of Saint Godelieve from Ghent and Saint Hubert from Brussels; she undertook to mention the groom to Sister Ancilla at least. Sister Benedicta was failing fast, and the drugs that soothed her pain required Mother Luca's particular skill in the delicate adjustment that would allow her to give her soul into God's hands in consciousness.

Sister Giuseppe and the widow crossed themselves at that thought. The sister left, aware that she had stayed longer than was necessary with their new guest, who, in spite of the pathos of her condition, was somehow a little disturbing.

It was after Mother Luca's round, at the time for Tierce, when the widow took her chance. She left her room.

The corridor had been washed down and was still damp. She paused in thought before placing her footprints, so betrayingly large, but it was to be hoped the stone would dry before they could be seen, or that they would be brushed over by her skirts. She went first to the Madonna and paused again there, listening. Risks had to be taken.

Cosima was alone, and less drowsy than yesterday. She smiled and, though her voice was faint and anxious, she spoke. "Have you come to pray for me, sister? Am I getting worse?"

"You are well, Cosima. All that is wrong with you is the drink Mother Luca gives you. It's that which makes you sleepy and confused."

Cosima's eyes widened. "Mother Luca says I need sleep to recover from what happened and my illness—the fever."

"I think you never had fever. Did you wonder why your father sent no letter, no messenger?"

Cosima's fingers struggled in the warm grasp. "Mother said news has been sent. He knows I am safe."

"In his villa in the country? No. He believes you have been snatched away by his enemies. He does not know where you are."

Cosima brushed her eyes with her fingers as if to dispel cobwebs. "I don't understand. I was rescued from robbers."

"A trick. The sisters may believe it, but it was all arranged, to hide you from your father so that he may suffer."

Her eyes were thoroughly alive, and frightened. She made an effort to sit up. "I must tell Mother Luca. She'll help me."

"Mother Luca is not your friend."

"Who are you? How do you know all this? How can it possibly

be true?" She fell back on the pillows, breathing hard, bewildered. The widow turned her head, listening to a distant door, and then spoke in haste, still keeping her voice from its natural depth. "I'm your father's cousin Caterina. I saw you at your christening. That cross you wear was my gift. Your groom Benno is here, and together we will take you back to your father. But, if you wish to see him, you must do what I tell you, and *say nothing* of me, of all I have said—"

"Benno? How did he get here? Did father send him?"

"Tell no one what I have said. *No one.*"

The widow rose and pressed a forefinger to the girl's lips. There was barely time to whisk into the corridor. Mother Luca and Sister Ancilla, coming from the dormitory, found the widow on her knees before the Madonna.

"You are recovered, daughter, I see." Mother Luca's eyes, so sad under the folds of their lids, were perfectly observant as she stood, hands clasped in her sleeves, looking down at her patient.

"Oh Mother, thank Our Lady you have come. I was wondering how I could reach my bed without help. I thought I could pray here, ask Our Lady's help to make me better; I was foolish. I can't get to my feet." She extended her arms to be helped, and both sisters responded, but she got up more with the aid of strong leg muscles than they could realise; they thought she leant all her weight on them. The husky babble continued in a voice that weakened as she shuffled between them to her room. "My dear husband had so special a love for the Virgin . . . He had her name on his lips as he died . . . I am so afraid . . ."

"Of what are you so afraid?" Mother Luca, trying for the widow's pulse, was prevented by her sudden clasping of her hands, half-hidden by the long sleeves, to her mouth.

"That I shall die. I'm so weak."

"Of course you will not die, daughter. It is true that you are weak, but this is often seen after undergoing danger." She reached for the pulse again, and the widow stumbled; at this moment a nun appeared in the doorway.

"Mother Luca. Sister Benedicta."

Mother Luca did not hesitate. "Daughter, rest. Do not stir from this cell. I shall send you a draught." It was a voice not raised but accustomed to command obedience, and it held a trace of irritation. The widow must be prevented from rambling about so freely. The great silly was something of a nuisance.

During the next hour, her dying sister claimed all Mother Luca's attention. Other problems receded. She sent Sister Giuseppe to pour the girl's medicine and return swiftly; Sister Benedicta must be supported in the only position that for the moment eased her pain. Mother Luca must go to the dispensary. Sister Ancilla must inform Reverend Mother. Sister Benedicta must be persuaded to take the stronger draught prepared. To Mother Luca's practised eye, tonight would see Sister Benedicta's joyful departure from this agonised body. Tonight, the Lord in His mercy might, as so often He did, grant a complete recession of pain so that the nun could go from this life as she ought. Father Vincenzio would be here then.

The widow had to pass the door of Sister Benedicta's cell to reach Cosima. The afternoon light shone clear and the door of the sick nun's cell stood ajar. Nevertheless the bulky figure went soundlessly along, pausing as before at the shrine to check whether anyone had noticed her. She went into the girl's cell with a finger to her lips.

The eyes were open. Cosima once more struggled to sit up. Indeed, she succeeded, although the arm on which she propped herself trembled.

"Is Benno really here?" she whispered. "I don't understand. And I did have fever; I saw father here, and thought I was at home, and Biondello—and the robbers killed him."

The widow pointed to the cup. "That made you see visions."

"I didn't drink it this time. I said I would, and Sister Ancilla was in such a hurry she didn't wait. I wanted to think. Why is Benno here? Why didn't my father send all his men?"

"These people have hidden you. Your father does not know where you are. They would have denied you were here."

"I have been thinking. It's the Bandini, isn't it? They carried me off. Who else? They don't want the marriage with their Leandro any more than we do." She fell back on the pillows and clenched her fists. "Ugh! The very thought."

"More urgent is the need to get you away from here. Can you walk? I doubt it; let's see."

With no need for modesty before the widow, Cosima pushed back the covers and managed to get her feet to the floor. The widow's left arm supported her, and she clung to the right hand through its sleeve.

"I don't seem to have any legs," Cosima reported, breathless. She was lowered to the bed again.

"A little practice. But at the sound of anyone approaching, to bed. You must appear confused and half-asleep. You must practise. I can support you, but to carry you"—the widow smiled demurely—"would look suspicious, wouldn't it, if we were seen? There's a journey ahead of us. You will need all your courage."

"Can't we get Mother Luca to help? I'm sure that she would. She's understanding, and kind."

The widow looked intently at Cosima.

"What would you say if I told you she was a Bandini?"

13. COUSIN CATERINA

A strengthening draught and mutton broth so thick with vegetables as to be almost pottage were duly supplied to the widow and found their way to Cosima during Nones. It was also during Nones that a cheerful whistle sounded all along the courtyard side of the infirmary, and the widow, in her own room, stood on the wooden stool and slit the oiled paper of her window. After a moment during which she allowed the knife-blade to show beyond the outer embrasure, the whistler came to a halt outside and Benno coughed.

The widow peeled back a corner of the paper and in a vigorous mutter informed him that Cosima was found but was in no state to travel as anything but a parcel. The widow made enquiries about the stables, and Benno, leaning idly against the wall, replied. The widow gave directions, and he listened.

"There's a couple of the servants," he said at the end, "that don't have no duties. They're not visitors like me. They get fed here and they go in and out, to the city. One of them came in soon after daybreak and was over here right off like he had news. Reporting to this Mother Luca, eh? Because a tall nun came over and put a new bandage on his wrist and talked to him all the time without looking up, and he kept nodding, and then he left. By all accounts the servants give, she runs the whole place and Reverend Mother just nods."

Biondello, who had been ranging the purlieus, returning always to his idol and source of all earthly delights, now noticed that Benno was talking and stood still, cocking his ear and giving an enquiring whimper.

"?"

"*That* one's going to be noticeable no matter how the rest of us disguise," remarked the widow.

"We could dye him brown."

"And cut off the other ear? Keep an eye open for those doubtful characters, Benno. Do you all sleep in one room over there?"

"I thought if we was to move off on the quiet, the servants' loft is the last place I should be. I sleep with the horses."

"Good," said the widow, and, tucking back the oiled paper as neatly as was possible, she descended from her perch as Benno went off, circled rapidly by Biondello.

The day wore on. More nuns were now with Sister Benedicta. The low murmur of prayers, now said aloud, pervaded the annexe. When the widow, pausing as before at the shrine, took her supper to Cosima, she found her lying just as she had first seen her, but at her approach the eyelids fluttered and Cosima sat up.

"I knew your scent," she whispered. "Oh, Cousin Caterina, I've been listening, and thinking—and look!" Once more she pushed back the covers, swung her feet to the floor and stood up. "I've been walking. There's no room, and it was dreadful at first. I kept falling—I longed for you to come and help me—but see." She walked to and fro, then lay down again far too thankfully for her boast to be true. The widow gave her the supper and watched as she ate it. "I'm so hungry! I'm not allowed much, because of the fever, but I didn't mind until today. What are *you* eating, Cousin?"

"Oh, they gave me plenty," said Cousin Caterina, with a benign smile. She was used to fasting.

Cosima ate. She had been on a low diet and this was a stew with roborant herbs and spices.

The widow took plate and spoon and stowed them about her person. As Cosima finished the wine, she asked her, "What would you do, Cousin, if sister came in while you were walking?"

Cosima unfocussed her eyes. She bore, of a sudden, quite a resemblance to Benno at his most vacant. "Like that. I shall pretend I don't know where I am." She handed over the cup and lay back.

The widow gave a soundless chuckle. "Cousin Jacopo didn't get his riches by being a fool," she said. "You're his daughter."

Cosima's small face under the cropped hair became fierce. "That Bandini woman shall *not* get the better of me."

Cousin Caterina nodded and turned to go. The door opened, no warning tap being necessary for a drugged girl, and Mother Luca stood there. Her hand still on the latch, she stared at them. Cosima lay as one dead, her eyes closed, her face washed of meaning, and the widow stumbled forward, catching herself from a fall by grabbing the inner side of the latch, jarring Mother Luca's grasp of it. Her eyes showed the whites hideously.

"Oh Mother, at last. I went to the shrine . . . I felt so strange . . . How did this girl come to be in my cell? Is she dead?"

Mother Luca's face expressed quite plainly that she would have been indifferent had the widow herself been *in extremis*. She summoned up a smile that gave new meaning to the words *lip service* and stuffed her hands in her sleeves as if to spare the widow a box on the ear.

"Go to your cell, daughter. This is not it. Go to your cell and remain there. I will send you medicine to calm you. This child is gravely ill, but, if she is not disturbed, she will not die."

The widow, almost whispering her apologies, her thanks, made her way out, helping herself along by the wall as Mother Luca stood aside to let her go. The door was shut. She could only speculate as to what Mother Luca was making of Cosima's state. The medicine she should have taken was in the chamber-pot and suitably diluted.

Once in her cell, she listened acutely, but the drone from next door overcame all other sounds. It would be unwise to visit Cosima again until the final time.

The day drew early to its ending. Dark clouds slowly obscured what remained of the daylight, which in these cells was never strong. Doors opened and shut. A distant chanting made itself heard, drawing nearer, and there was an impression, rather than an actual noise, of a lot of people in the corridor outside. Someone pressed against the door. A small bell rang, and the widow opened her door and knelt, and remained so. The sisters were escorting the priest who brought the Sacrament to Sister Benedicta.

Nothing could be better.

Sister Ancilla appeared, her veil a little awry as if she had come through a press of people, and looking more distracted than was compatible with the Rule. She carried in both hands a horn cup, rather full. She gave hurried instructions that this medicine was to be drunk immediately and that the widow must lie down and rest. She did not stay to see it drunk but turned to collect a candle from a sister waiting at the door, who carried two. The door closed.

The widow, sniffing the cup, raised her eyebrows and slowly nodded, pursing her lips: a draught for meddlers indeed. Father Vincenzio might have had to look in here when he had finished in Sister Benedicta's room.

A shuffling next door initiated a general exodus. The procession reversed. The widow, opening her door a minute crack, watched Sister Benedicta, her bed carried by her sisters, on her way to the chapel in a dazzle of candlelight. As they processed into the dormitory, the widow was out of her own door and along to Cosima's.

The girl lay still, eyes shut.

"Cosima."

The eyes opened and Cosima sat up; the eyes were brilliant even in the gloom.

"She tried to wake me, but I pretended to be far gone. She took my pulse and I'm sure it was wrong. I hardly dared to breathe. I don't think she was very satisfied. Do you think she would suspect?"

"I don't doubt it. As a doctor of medicine she knows what she is about. She sent me water-hemlock in a dose of valerian. Waste no time talking. Benno's waiting and he has horses ready."

Cosima, standing up without having to grasp at her cousin for support, held out a fold of her shift in dismay. "I can't go like this—"

Cousin Caterina turned aside and was busy with her own clothes. Cosima relaxed. Of course that would have been thought of. Then the door opened.

Mother Luca stood there. She saw Cosima standing, and she advanced. Then the door shut and Mother Luca seemed to disappear among Cousin Caterina's flying wide sleeves and then to throw herself forward as though fainting, held up by the widow's grip.

"What happened?" Cosima shrank from the woman whom the widow now laid down on her side, eyes closed, on the bed. "Is she ill?"

"Quickly!" Her cousin had whipped out from somewhere a strip of material very like a stocking and, amazingly, was gagging Mother Luca with it. Next, as Cosima still stared, off came the nun's veil, wimple and cap, revealing a head as dark and cropped as her own and alarmingly vulnerable. The neck and chin showed that she was not a young woman; the planes of her face, that she had been a very beautiful one. She seemed unconscious; the face jolted as Cousin Caterina turned her over in the process of taking off more clothes.

"Put these on."

Cosima took the garments thrust at her and, half in a daze, began to put on stockings still warm, then to assemble the habit round her, drowning temporarily in the darkness as the tunic dropped over her head, tying strings at her waist, putting on the scapular, still shocked at Mother Luca's immobility and vaguely conscious that parts of the habit she was assuming had been blessed and it was surely a sin to wear them. Mother Luca looked nothing like a nun by now, and the more secular she looked, the more it became credible that she was a Bandini.

"Turn round."

She turned, a puppet, and had the cap put on and the strings thrust into her hands to tie. Her cousin was now tearing her petticoat to make strips to bind Mother Luca—the Bandini woman—and fasten her to the bedstead. The covers were then pulled up to her nose, hiding even the gag.

Her cousin turned to her, took the strings of the cap she was fumbling with, gave them a professional twist and tucked them in; wound the linen of the wimple into place and pinned it, flung the veil over all and pinned that—holding the pins in her lips like any lady's maid—and then led her to the door. Cosima glanced back for a second. Another Cosima lay there, just the closed eyes and the dark cropped head showing.

"I had clothes for you, but those are better."

Cosima was not strong yet. It was in a daze that she walked beside Cousin Caterina through some big room and out into the open air. Here, she was supported. Cousin Caterina leant over her. Anyone might think she, a nun, was holding up an ailing guest! They reached, at last, after crossing about a quarter mile of the great court, stables. There was Benno, ducking over her hand, hustled by Cousin Caterina. There was a dog who was for a moment Biondello. There were horses.

They were in the open, riding across heath and into trees. She was held in a steely arm against Cousin Caterina. It was not possible to make things steady or clear in her mind, but she kept seeing Benno's delighted face turned towards her. Summer at the villa, freedom, riding with dear, scruffy Benno . . .

They were on a road. She saw countryside. Leaning against Cousin Caterina, she glanced down at the hand that held the reins. It was broad, muscular, with hair along the back, quite unmistakably male.

Cosima sat upright, the horse sidled and her head swam. She looked at Cousin Caterina, who smiled. She looked at the face closely.

"Who are you?" she demanded. Elderly women might be downy-faced or outright hairy, but never smooth as if shaven. Thick eyelashes and a sculptured mouth, yes; but so strong a nose? The dark eyes glanced towards Benno and an eyebrow rose.

"It's all right, my lady. It's a friend. We're taking you back to a safe place and then to Rocca. You'll see your father soon."

"But he's a *man!*"

An astonishingly deep voice replied, "But if you're asked, my lady, you must swear you were always properly chaperoned," and he gave her a wide, benign smile.

14. "You've Lost Your Hair!"

The kitchenmaid was supposedly slicing cabbage, the cook in theory preparing pork to go in the soup, but neither of them had been able to resist the pedlar's tray; the cook had been drawn towards it but still carried her knife as a token that she was at work. With that, she pointed to a length of cherry ribbon that would do well to lace her bodice on Sunday; the kitchenmaid's eyes lingered more on the face of the assistant carrying the tray. Not only did he look like one of the angels straight from a painted church wall, but his hair was the strangest colour she had ever seen, gold with a warmer tinge to it. She touched and examined the buckles the pedlar pointed out to her, but when she held them to the light it was only to steal glances past them at the young man. The pedlar himself, enormous with red beard and black leather hat, bulked huge even in the space of the kitchen, and with his patter in a foreign accent engaged the attentions of the cook. It seemed that dinner for the Widow Costa and her companion would be late today.

Visitors were not uncommon at the villa; the widow had a quite wide acquaintance and kin, who came to stay, but that was usually in the summer. The pedlar, who had his own budget of news about what was going on in Rocca after the Duchess' death, made idle enquiries about such guests, and the kitchenmaid wondered if he hoped to sell her mistress the length of black silk he said he had in one of his packs. Suppose Angelface were to display it; who could resist? They were an odd pair, the tall, broad man like a wrestler, and the slight young man who needed only wings to fly away over their heads. She tried to catch his eye and smile at him, but he kept his eyes warily on the tray.

"Can it really be your mistress has seen no one since Christmas? No chance to show your skills?"

The cook bridled, a considerable displacement of flesh. She had allowed the cherry ribbon to be held against her bosom but now threatened the pedlar's hand playfully with the knife and took the ribbon from him to try it there for herself; he, nothing daunted, held a mirror from the tray for her to see the result.

"It doesn't take a feast to show skill. My lady can appreciate my work whether she has company or no. And there has been company. Why, last Wednesday there was the soldier that fought alongside my lady's husband, God rest his soul, in France, a great big man like yourself with a shaven head like a priest."

"More shaven than that," said the kitchenmaid, delighted to see the young angel raise his eyes. They were grey as glass, but he looked at the cook and then at the pedlar, not at her.

"A soldier with a shaven head? Maybe he'd turned priest to atone for his sins. What retinue did such a man travel with? Some old cut-throats that had been in the wars with him?"

The cook put out a fat hand to adjust the mirror he held. She would have replied, but the maid broke in with a giggle, still trying to attract the eyes that would not look her way.

"Cut-throat? More like a natural. Never shut his mouth though he put away half our stores in it. Couldn't even answer a question—he'd just gape. Kept a bag that stank and he wouldn't let me see what he had in it. Something dead, you could tell that much. And he had a little white dog fuller of fleas than an egg is of meat and that had one ear bit off."

She ended her breathless description suddenly. As though conjured by her words, into the kitchen from the yard there trotted that very minute a small dog with one ear, its tail wagging expectantly.

The tail wagged more slowly, then drooped. Looking from

one face to another, it sensed something awry. The kitchenmaid and the cook, with human perception more dull than his, took longer to see that the situation was all at once out of their control. The men, after a moment staring at the dog, acted at speed. A glance went between them, then the angel-faced lad ducked out of the leather neck-strap of his tray and, displacing a half-sliced cabbage and slivers of pork onto the floor, slid it on the table. The kitchenmaid, following this with puzzled gaze, felt first the unexpected bliss of the young man's arm tightly round her waist from behind, and then the very different thrill of his knife-point under her ear. Over her shoulder the glass-grey eyes challenged the cook, who was, by the heave of her bosom, getting air into her lungs.

"Scream, and kill her." He sounded interested in the possibility.

The pedlar had vanished with the same turn of speed, even more dismaying in a man of his size. He had the cook's knife out of her nerveless hand and was gone by the door into the house. The dog, with that same strong instinct that had preserved it from becoming soup in its native village, left just as fast by the yard door it had come in by. Unfortunately for its present owner, it had from earliest puppyhood found barking indiscreet in moments of acute danger.

Benno was therefore more pleased than disturbed to be joined in the stables' straw-smelling warmth by an affectionate Biondello, whom he had to urge away from his feet several times as he rubbed down the horses. He whistled as he worked, unaware that, to sharp ears in the kitchen, he was signalling both his preoccupation and his whereabouts.

The maid in one of the rooms at the front of the villa, passing a soft broom over the marble floor, dreamt of a handsome stranger. She would have been surprised to know that one was waiting for her in the kitchen.

Happening to glance idly from a window as she moved forwards, she recognised the man walking across the flagged terrace before the house, throwing the hood off his shaven head. There was also a nun, presumably a visitor for the mistress' companion, arriving simultaneously, for she did not seem a likely companion for Master Hubert.

She lost no time, propped the broom against the wall, shook out her apron and, as she ran out into the hall, pulled a curl or two from under her cap. Certainly she did not see, as she opened the great oak door, the other man, the one who stood behind the tapestry of Venus and Paris in the shadows at the back of the entrance hall, or she would not have smiled and bobbed her curtsey with a free heart, as she did.

This time, she was determined not to lose the privilege of announcing the main guest, and as he had been expected back from day to day and there was no point in surprise, he allowed her to precede him up the green marble stairs. He did not mention the nun, although he had handed her in at the door. The maid did not suppose that the Widow Costa would mind much about this extra guest, and she would be a boon to her sister-in-law, who delighted in nuns. Her slippers, and the man's boots, and the nun's soft step, padded on the worn green marble whose treads were white-flecked so that it seemed like walking on water.

The pedlar was unamused by this miracle. He would have preferred the maid to join the little party hosted by his assistant in the kitchen. He waited, close by the kitchen door, and they passed out of sight. A door opened. There were distant exclamations. He waited, knife ready, as the maid ran lightly down the stairs smiling to herself, looking forward to returning to the company on the *piano nobile* with the wine the widow had commanded. She put aside the tapestry, whose edge was blackened and buckled by a thousand such handlings; she did not see anyone behind its folds; she skipped into the silent tableau in the kitchen.

Her try at an apposite sound-effect was stillborn; the pedlar's knife was at her throat. She stood, eyes wide, in grotesque imitation of the kitchenmaid facing her, a mirror image of terror. The cook clasped both fat hands over her mouth as if to cram back screams that would vomit forth. Her face was the exact colour of the turnips on the table, cream with a greenish tinge.

Angel-face, presented with another charge, repeated his assertion that a scream would precipitate the death of the kitchenmaid. To reinforce the notion, he permitted a drop of blood to flower, as if by magic, on her neck and observed the silent jump all three performed for him.

The pedlar, having left the maid in hands so far from safe, once again vanished.

Upstairs, the Widow Costa had very cordially embraced both her guests, and Sigismondo had kissed the hand of the companion, who preened herself like a little elderly bird and hoped, though not aloud, that there would be exciting stories at dinner as before; and that such stories would not be muted by the presence of a religious. She was ignorant that she was about to become part of an exciting story herself.

Sigismondo did not immediately explain the nun, and the Widow Costa, seating the girl safely by her sister-in-law, drew him to a low-backed chair facing the window so that she might watch his expression, while she sat herself with her back to it, being of that age where a woman prefers to be seen by candlelight rather than by winter sun. She leant to take the broad hands in hers and, patting them, began—not to question him about his journey or the nun, for she had been his friend long enough to wait for what he chose to tell her—but to amuse him with trivialities about life during his short absence. She was telling, with well-acted indignation, how her companion had discovered that two of her pilgrim badges, those of Saint Godelieve of Ghent and of her guest's name-saint, Hubert of Brussels, were missing, when the door opened. She did not look up, expecting the maid with the wine.

If the companion and the nun had not looked and uttered a simultaneous shriek, the knife might have found its mark in Sigismondo's back. As it was, Sigismondo had dropped to a turning crouch and the knife stood juddering with the force of the throw in the wooden jamb of the window.

It was no loss to the pedlar, to whom the cook's knife was merely fortuitous. His own was in his hand, longer and fully as sharp, and he leapt. Sigismondo's chair met him halfway, jarring his arm so that the knife jumped from his hand. He wrested the chair aside and the men grappled. The Widow Costa and her companion clung together, holding breath in acute anxiety and terror, as the men trampled and then rolled about the room, the face of one muffled in the other's sleeve, as they struggled, Sigismondo to drive his knife home, the other to prevent him. The leather hat soared across the room like an ungainly fowl, the men grunted and the floor resounded. By a twist, Sigismondo emerged on top, forcing the knife down in a swoop that veered abruptly and embedded the blade in the floor. Both men, quite still, stared.

"Barley. You scoundrel. You've grown a beard!"

"Martin! You've lost your hair!"

The three women disbelieved what was happening as devoutly as they had disbelieved what went before. After a moment, each reacted: the companion remained rigid, pressed against a tapestry of Philemon and Baucis, gabbling a litany of prayer; the widow seized the chair Sigismondo had used against Barley and stood ready to wield it; the nun wrested the knife from the window jamb and waited her chance to plunge it into the man who could only be a Bandini.

The two opponents were busy helping each other off the floor, laughing, embracing, a bears' reunion. Sigismondo retrieved his knife and sheathed it. They regarded one another with relish. Their lethal fight had plainly been a fillip to their taste for life, had raised their spirits.

"Who paid you to kill me, eh?"

"Who's a traitor to Duke Ludovico?"

Sigismondo put a hand to his shaven head and smoothed it down to the nape, humming thoughtfully. "Ah. That's the way the wind blows now?" He jabbed Barley in the chest, a chest that could take any jab not delivered by steel. "You'll remember Federico Costa?"

"I don't forget a man I fought beside, God save his soul."

"Meet his widow."

Sigismondo led forward Barley, now a bashful bear, to kiss the widow's hand. She had lowered the chair, albeit watchfully, and looked at the men with growing anger, charged by her recent fear.

"What's the mystery here? You come to kill my guest under my roof, and you say you are my husband's comrade? Is this the common usage among men of the sword?"

"He is an Englishman." Sigismondo's statement was an exoneration for all eccentricities, even with knives. Who could need more explanation? But Barley was aroused.

"A *Scot*, man! I am a *Scot*. Take that word *English* off your tongue. You're such a mongrel yourself, you understand nothing of these things, or so you pretend." A playful blow hit the chest as impervious as his own. It looked as if they had more wrestling to do before they could work off the pleasure of this meeting.

"You are not a Bandini? Nor hired by one?"

Barley took in for the first time the young, frail-looking nun with fierce eyes and a knife to match, with which she was suddenly threatening his ribs.

"I'm no Bandini, sister, nor have I taken money of one. I've come from Rocca, true, but on the Duke's business."

"You lie! He told me *he* works for the Duke."

"No longer, no longer." Sigismondo deftly retrieved the knife from the nun's hand. "Let us sit in peace and, with your permission, my lady"—bowing to the Widow Costa with a warm smile—"drink some of your excellent wine." As he spoke, some dark thought flashed on him and he swung abruptly to Barley. "Are you alone?"

Both men thought of Benno. Barley also thought of Angelface, who by now might have had a visitor in the kitchen looking, as Biondello had done, for welcome and food. Both men plunged from the room.

Nun and widow sank onto chairs as if their knees had abdicated responsibility. The companion, in a catatonic trance quite unbroken by anything yet said, remained pressed against the tapestry beginning another decade of Hail Marys, perhaps in a certainty that, if she stopped, the sky, or at least the ceiling, would fall.

Benno, when he finished with the horses, whistled to Biondello, slung his bag on his shoulder and strolled towards the kitchen, enjoying the spring sun. It glowed more warmly than of late, and he raised his face to it, anticipating, as Biondello had done, good food from the hands of the cook and, with luck, more than a kindly pat from the kitchenmaid. He did not notice that Biondello had prudently failed to come along.

He stood in the kitchen doorway, living up to the kitchenmaid's unkind description of him, though to call his appearance half-witted at this juncture would have been generous. The urgent, frozen scene did not change, though eyes moved towards him. Even the soft invitation from the angelic one to despatch the kitchenmaid from this world by an untoward move was the same. He had issued it effectively twice before and it should have been adequate for even the most clouded mind. Benno, however, had his priorities. He spared a sad thought for the kitchenmaid but he scrambled into a headlong rush along the gravel, to run round the house to the front. He understood danger, and his master was the man for that. He hoped that the great oak door had not been bolted. He even hoped that the lovely young viper with the knife would take time over cutting the kitchenmaid's throat, but he doubted it. Something about the creature connoted speed. The house was much larger than he had thought. He fled along the front terrace, hearing the quick spurting of gravel behind him. Arriving with a thud against the oak door and struggling with the handle, he found it not bolted and shoved it open and flung himself inside yelling. At this moment Angel-face caught up with him and a vast red-headed man came running full tilt down the green staircase ahead of him, followed closely by Sigismondo. Luckily for Benno, he then tripped.

Angel-face hurdled him without faltering, the knife leaving his hand to skim past Sigismondo's ear, strike the wall and clatter down the stairs underfoot. The big redheaded man bellowed like a baited bull while from the kitchen regions long-pent-up screams bore witness that not everybody's throat had been cut.

Another knife seemed to grow in Angel-face's hand. A fierce grappling hold from Barley prevented him from attacking Sigismondo yet again. He was finally placated with an oath from Barley that the apparent pursuer, their intended victim, was a friend.

Sigismondo stood, thumbs in belt, enjoying the noise and confusion with a broad smile. A dwindling hysteria in the kitchen prevented any humming from being heard. Benno raised only his head from where he lay prone on the marble, to judge when rising would be safe, and justified once again his absolute belief in his master's mastery. Upstairs, a door had opened and the Widow Costa and the Lady Cosima peered down the stairs.

Persuaded at last to put up his knife, the beautiful viper, introduced by Barley not surprisingly as Angelo, bowed to the ladies, acknowledged one man he had tried to murder with a salute and helped the other to his feet. Sigismondo had picked up the knife thrown at him and held it out hilt-foremost, still smiling.

"It's my day to stand for target. I must try it at a circus one day and get paid for it. It's thirsty work."

"Spoilt this blade on the wall," Angelo remarked.

"He's too fast. I missed him too," Barley assured him. "But this is Martin: you name it, he's knifed it."

Benno had not the nerve to enquire about the kitchenmaid, though he had eyed the knife his master so genially restored. Now quieter voices in the entrance hall reassured the kitchen. The tapestry veiling the door shook and the cook's face peered cautiously out. The sight of Angelo nearly drove her back, but she perceived that he was in converse with the lady of the house as well as the appalling pedlar, and curiosity and the absence of any corpse drew her farther into the hall. On this day of knives she, too, had armed herself afresh. With her came a strong reek of burnt feathers, explained by the sight through the open door of the housemaid lying on the stone floor, not yet responding to the kitchenmaid's efforts. Angelo also had his priorities, and the disposal of Benno rated above that of the kitchenmaid. It was flattering, and Benno was glad to be alive to feel it.

The widow, a woman of serene temperament besides good sense, led the way upstairs again. Benno was sent to the kitchen with the cook to convey the good news that no one had been, or was about to be, murdered, and with strict orders to carry up the wine which, but a short time ago, the maid had failed to bring.

The cook had the more difficult task of getting dinner for five extra guests while her chief assistant was ministering to a hysterical maidservant in a muddle of cabbage slices and raw pork. However, as her advance into the hall with a knife showed, the cook was a woman of courage and resource. Vinegar proved better than burnt feathers in resuscitation, and the process was completed by a brisk clapping on the cheeks with hands capable of shifting huge pans on the stove. The cook had her assistant back, though excited and reluctant to wash the cabbage and pork, and liable to talk ceaselessly about the fair devil who had nearly killed her.

Benno still smelt of stables, with a whiff of the bag he had dropped when he ran and, of course, of himself, as he brought the wine upstairs, where Angelo, with a grace as natural to him as knife throwing, took the tray, poured the wine and offered the glasses round to the company. Benno regretfully, at a nod from his master, took himself back to the kitchen, where he saw that Biondello was not only present but was covered in pigeon feathers and a vibrant smell of his own. He had rifled Benno's bag in the yard.

Upstairs, the party so strangely convened was beginning to liven. There was relief in the air, the relief that comes after battle with the realisation that Death has passed you by. The companion had been coaxed out of her prayerful trance and sat making little gasps from time to time, taking comfort in holding the hand of the girl she believed to be a nun and gazing at the face of the angel who had fallen from Heaven to sit opposite. There was stirring, somewhere in her mind, the idea that she might soon, perhaps later in the spring, go on pilgrimage again. Certainly on such a journey she would, this time, not sit dumb in her corner when each pilgrim contributed a story. She now had her own tale to tell!

The widow, although she felt more and more entitled to an explanation of all that had exploded round her in the last half hour, managed to keep quiet and to drink a good deal of her own wine. It might be that she would not get the truth until it was told in privacy that night. The thought of this put her into an excellent mood, and she was glad to note that Benno had brought several bottles. At a request from her, Angelo rose and filled glasses yet again, his hair shining in the gathering dusk, dreamily followed by the gaze of the companion. The widow smiled and set herself to attend with greater concentration to the story Barley was telling, with embroidery by Hubert—had he really been known as *Martin?*—which involved some astonishing ambush which they, and her husband, had survived. Men were the same the world over, and you had to be grateful that some of them came home.

The cook contrived her dinner, not a little hampered by her assistant's repeated and irrepressible descriptions of her ordeal and demonstration of the tiny mark on her neck, to Benno and some of the farmworkers who had come in with firewood. These were vociferously confident of their powers to deal with any intruders had they been there, and they inclined to shrug off the women's vivid descriptions of the size of the pedlar and the demonic attributes of his henchman as feminine exaggeration. Benno's confirmation was dismissed indulgently. What nobody could understand was why the mistress and her formidable guest were drinking wine with this murderous pair.

The servant, who doubled as groom and by virtue of this did meet foreign, city folk occasionally, was sure it was politics; the cook thought it might be a curious joke such as the gentlefolk often liked; the maid believed they would all have their throats cut in the end, and was continually having to be fetched back from the hall, where she had crept out to listen as if she expected to hear horrid groans from above and see a river of blood flowing down the marble stairs towards her.

Benno said little but took all that came his way. Whatever happened, his master would prove victorious; had he not retrieved the Lady Cosima? Biondello, with quite equal trust, laid his head between Benno's knees and accepted willingly his half of all Benno received.

Not groans but laughter came from upstairs, and what flowed freely was the widow's good wine. Sigismondo and Barley, capping each other's stories, strayed into fantasy and bawdry as time went on. The widow laughed; the companion laughed, though not because she understood the humour, but out of general euphoria. Cosima di Torre, an unmarried girl in a rich household, had had less opportunity than anyone for meeting people, so that even more of the talk was as strange to her as was the whole situation. She kept up her pretence because, like Benno, she had grown to trust Sigismondo, and he had not told her to declare her disguise. She therefore drank little, kept her eyes down and did not laugh.

Angelo also said nothing. His contribution was to fill the glasses and look beautiful, tasks he performed to perfection. It crossed Cosima's mind, she did not know why, that the pale gold of his hair might not be its natural colour.

Candles were lit. Barley put another log on the fire, the substantial branch in his hand appearing as a twig. The long oaken table was set with silver dishes which the maid fully expected would leave in the pedlar's pack when the food was eaten. The food was as good as the wine, more of which was brought up by one of the men from the kitchen, inquisitive to see the strangers. He, on his return, admitted that the maids and cook were innocent of exaggeration as regards the red-haired giant, but that the blond boy looked no better than a girl. Even a kitchenmaid could have twisted a knife out of *his* hand.

Angelo's skills were under discussion at the table also. Barley described some of his own activities since he last saw his friend Martin; how, recovering from wounds that for a time made him unable to hire his sword out, he had led a vagabond life, even joining a troupe of performers who journeyed from city to city, dancing, singing, selling ballads, doing a bit of juggling, fortune telling and wrestling. It was in this troupe, whose members came and went like summer clouds, that he had met Angelo. Over the pork and cabbage soup, he described with large explanatory gestures an act they had great success with. For Barley it had involved wearing a bearskin—and from the expressions of his audience they appreciated how convincing this must have been—and wrestling with Angelo, who each time eventually vanquished him and led him, in triumph, round the crowd collecting money. Angelo could sing like a bird, like a cathedral chorister . . . and dance! Barley leant across the table to seize his friend's sleeve.

"I tell you he is the best dancer in the world. He can trip it like a whoreson fairy. Up, Angelo!" Barley swept a vast hand above the dishes—"Up, and show them!" He wagged his red beard at them all, looking round, and then assured his hostess, "Don't fear! He'll not touch a dish nor break a glass."

Angelo, whose eyes had remained as modestly downcast as any nun's while he was praised, submitted to the general encouragement. One foot on his bench, one on the table, and he was up, and began, to Barley's handclap and deep singing of an *estampie*, to dance among the dishes and flasks and glasses, the spoons and pieces of bread, on the table. The companion, who was now very flushed, beat her hands in rhythm as loudly as anyone, and was reminded in a muddled way of having heard how angels dance upon the point of a pin. Even the nun clapped her hands. Sigismondo waited until Angelo had leapt down and had accepted another glass of wine from the admiring widow. Then, as Barley had done to him, he leant across the table and seized not the sleeve but the breast of the young man's tunic, bunching it in his grasp.

"You have a tale to tell me, *Wild Man*."

15. "LIKE GRASPING A CLOUD"

For a moment grey eyes stared into brown, and then the table witnessed the resurrection of the viper; a knife glinted in Angelo's hand from nowhere. Sigismondo released Angelo's jerkin and clamped on his wrist, Barley uttered a roar and jumped up knocking over the bench, the companion shrieked shrill as a whistle and the maid, carrying in a dish of baked onions stuffed with ham and cheese, dropped it and hared for the door. Sigismondo repelled Barley with a punch to the chest that sent him over the upturned bench into the onions, and gave such a twist to Angelo's arm that the knife fell spinning onto the table, chipping a glass his dance had not touched.

"Peace. I'm your friend. All I want is your story, man!"

Angelo, snarling and gasping, Lucifer after the Fall, glared unconvinced at Sigismondo, from where he was held down on the table. The companion had closed her eyes the better to concentrate on screaming.

"My oath on it, I mean you no harm," Sigismondo repeated above the noise.

"You've not come to kill me?"

Sigismondo released Angelo's wrist and began to laugh. Barley, asprawl among the débris on the floor, joined with a bass bellow of enjoyment.

"Kill you? Didn't you come here to kill *me*?"

Angelo, rubbing the wrist still white from Sigismondo's grasp, began reluctantly to smile. He stood looking at Sigismondo, who made no effort to impound the knife or to rise. The deep voice, however, was now serious.

"If you think your life is in danger, it is for the same reason that Barley was sent to kill me. There's a mystery here, and we need your help too to unravel it."

Angelo took up his knife and sheathed it, docile again. Barley, sampling an onion close to his hand, was still chewing and brushing cheese off his jerkin as he righted the bench so that they might sit. The Widow Costa put down the napkin she had been holding tightly to her lips; the nun shifted her hold on her ivory-handled knife to a less aggressive one, and Sigismondo, by clapping the companion on both cheeks and then taking both hands in his and warmly kissing them, made her open her eyes and stop shrieking.

"Dear lady, all is well again." Taking the nearest wine-jug, he topped up her glass and folded her fingers round its base. "It is time for another story."

"First things first," the widow said, rising. "I must see what is to replace the onions."

"We owe you apologies," Sigismondo said, also rising.

"Nothing very wrong with the onions," Barley protested. He, and the other men, had certainly eaten food far worse than that to be retrieved from a well-kept floor. He was at that moment removing an onion, very much the worse for his weight, from the rear of his jerkin. He spread his napkin over the tapestry of the bench to protect it from what remained.

Their hostess, however, was picking her way towards the door when it opened boldly to admit Benno with a meat axe, followed, not readily, by two farm men with more of the cook's armoury.

Benno lowered the axe on seeing his master genially at ease and the reported assassins seated, not threatening—one of them chuckling still.

The widow gave orders about the onions and about further dishes, and came back to the table. She said, "Truly, Hubert, no apologies are due. I've not had so interesting a time since Federico, rest his soul, left this earth." She sat down and, settling herself in the big chair, said, "And now, this story."

"We are going to hear the tale of how a Wild Man danced for a Duchess and who set him to do it."

"That, I can't tell you." Angelo's voice was soft but definite. "I saw his face but I don't know who he was."

"Or for whom he worked? Was he a man of rank, perhaps?"

"No; a servant, but not in livery."

"Tell from the beginning what happened."

Angelo accepted Sigismondo's own glass, full, and drank consideringly. The widow leant forward to hear; this was news even the citizens of Rocca had not heard.

"Barley and I were in Rocca for the wedding, along with a crew of others."

"Everyone knew there'd be pickings," Barley interrupted, stretching a long arm to take the wine-jug from Sigismondo and pouring for his hostess and the pretty nun, whose eye he had been quite unable to catch. "We went to the Palace to see if the festaiuolo would take us on."

"So everyone knew you were together?"

Angelo and Barley exchanged a glance. Barley shook his head. "There was a whoreson great crowd, dwarves and all, waiting to show their acts, and Angelo got called out alone because they wanted a special dancer. I was hired too." He threw out his chest and looked around. "I was to have been a giant. The festaiuolo thought I would look well with the dwarves at the end. Then *you* wrecked it all." He gave Angelo a friendly shove that nearly sent his golden head into the companion's bosom.

"I was supposed to do as I did! Those were my instructions: to dance along with the dwarves, to mime, to offer the heart to the Duchess, to spill wine onto her dress. It's not easy, sending wine to spill where you want it to go."

"It was beautifully done," Sigismondo's voice soothed. "I was there. When were you told to do that?"

"Just before the feast started. This man—he had come to me before when we were rehearsing and offered me money, if I would execute a jest, he said; an admirer of the Duchess would pay me well for it. It was a lot of money, because he said it might well get me into trouble."

"Did you get the money?"

Angelo smiled. "And kept it, though that I wasn't meant to do."

Silence supervened while one of the servants brought in another dish and served it. Another swept up the onions into a pan and wiped the floor. They departed together to tell the company below stairs that it was like supper in a monastery.

"What was to happen when you'd kicked the wine over?"

"Clear out quick, and I didn't need telling." Angelo rubbed his ribs. "I wasn't popular."

Sigismondo hummed. "Her Grace gave orders you were not to be beaten."

"They didn't wait for orders. Everyone got in a swipe at me on the way out. I earned that money."

"What became of the Wild Man suit?"

"I was to get out of it, quick, and hand it over to this man who'd told me—he was waiting for me in one of the antechambers. Helped me get the skin and mask off and bundled them up, inside out. He gave me my money and said I'd done well and I was to clear out." Angelo paused and drank, the companion watching him devotedly. "I wasn't intending to hang about and get everyone's opinion taken out on me. I don't like messing up a good act in the first place, but money's money. So I went out the way he took me, back ways through the Palace—"

"He knew the Palace well?"

"Like a mole. He didn't need his eyes. He shut me out of this little door that opened on the courtyard where they had the bonfire. People were coming out to see the fireworks and I was sorry to miss them." The beautiful face became wistful. "On my way, I looked back to see if they were going to set any off, and then I saw him. Lucky I did."

"Saw the man who'd paid you extra?"

Angelo showed his teeth—crooked, more like a devil's than an angel's—and nodded. "Him. He was chucking the skin right in the middle of the bonfire."

"Why'd you call that lucky?" Barley thumped the table. "Cost money, skins. That bearskin, now"—he drank—"and it stank."

Angelo wrinkled his nose. "Who had to wrestle with you? Who got hugged to it? No, it was lucky I looked back because I got suspicious. Why was he so close behind me? Why was he burning the skin? I thought, Some people don't like parting with money, and it's a good sum; and burning the skin looks like the Wild Man was set to disappear. When I got out on the street I kept my eyes open."

"*Especially* the ones in the back of his head." Barley clapped Angelo with a fond, crippling hand on his shoulder; "*they* can see in the dark too."

"For God's sake, sir," said the widow, "let him tell his tale. Did he follow you?"

Angelo nodded. "For a little way. I made sure that's what he was doing. Then he jumped me with a knife."

There was a pause while everyone pondered the foolhardiness of this move. The companion made a noise like a trodden-on cat.

"What did you *do?*"

Surprised at the question, Angelo said, "I killed him." He frowned. "I thought at first that he'd simply wanted his money back. He wouldn't be the first. When I got back to the inn, I found word was going round the Duchess had been murdered, and I knew I was in the shit. When he"—the golden head jerked sideways at Barley—"got back to our lodgings he told me Leandro Bandini was in prison at the Palace for killing the

Duchess. I started to breathe again. I thought that let me out. Then he said Bandini was found dressed in a Wild Man skin."

"So it was *Bandini's* man who hired you!"

They all turned to look at the nun, who had spoken for the first time. There was no question of her keeping custody of the eyes as she leant forward to stare at Angelo, her pale, pretty face intent. "Bandini planned that you should take the blame. The action of a murderer and a *coward*." It was clear, as she spat out the words, which category she thought was the worse. "He had to have someone to do the dancing, which he couldn't do." She was scornful. "To kick the wine over the Duchess so that she would have to retire—I see it all—and then he could kill her!"

Suddenly she was aware of their attention upon her, and she flushed vivid pink. The Widow Costa, patting her hand, thought it a shame so lively a spirit should take the veil; judging by the men's faces, this girl would never have lacked for offers.

"But, sister, why should he want to kill her?" she asked.

The nun gave a small shrug, as if to imply that no one need ask why a Bandini should murder. Sigismondo was silent, watching.

"One can see," Barley spoke through a mouthful of braised turnip and leek, "that the Duke tries to mend the di Torre–Bandini feud by marrying the di Torre girl to the Bandini boy and of course"—he flung his arms wide—"they don't like it. Saving your presence, sister, it's hate the world runs on, not love. They hate the Duke for it. And they'll ruin Rocca between them."

"But why kill the poor Duchess?" the widow persisted.

"It's easy." Barley sprayed some turnip and wiped his mouth with the back of his hand. "Revenge, isn't it. You don't have to get at a man direct to hurt him. And now what they're saying in Rocca about the Duke . . ."

"That he is the murderer." Sigismondo roused to pour wine. Barley pointed a spoon at him triumphantly.

"You've heard. It's all whispers in corners, but it's being said."

The widow put in impatiently, "She can't have been murdered by Leandro Bandini *and* by the Duke."

"Lady"—Barley was a patient bear—"if you're Duke you can't kill your wife just *so*, pouff!—she has kinsfolk, she's highborn. Dukes need scapegoats."

"That's not sense. One minute you say the Bandini boy did it out of hatred at the idea of marrying the di Torre girl—am I right?—and next minute you say it was the Duke himself. Was the man who hired your friend Angelo, then, working for the Duke?"

"What I would like to know," Sigismondo's deep voice cut in after the widow's contralto, "is why you called me a traitor to the Duke. Someone hired you to kill me for that?" He folded his arms on the table and regarded Barley under his brows. The companion, pleasurably dazed though she was with wine because Angelo had kept her glass filled, put her hands to her heart and hoped that no fight would start anew between these redoubtable men.

"He told me, this one that hired me, more than I needed to know. The name and the money was all I needed; or a passable description if there was no name. But these people—they want to be at ease with their souls about what they do, so they tell you their reasons." Barley laughed indulgently and drank. "So this shaven Sigismondo has become privy to the Duke's secrets and has then gone and hired himself to the Bandini—"

"*The Bandini!*" cried the nun, on her feet.

"Be at ease." Sigismondo's hand sat her irresistibly down. He shook his head at her and smiled. "Barley is telling us this man's excuses. One who wants me dead is not on oath."

She subsided, doubtfully.

Barley scraped his plate with bread. "But I dare say the rest is true, knowing you: that you've found your way into Palace secrets."

"The Duke trusted me, but he trusts his brother more. It was the Lord Paolo who feared I had seen too much."

"There's a good man!" cried the widow. "I'd a Mass said in Saint Agnes' for Federico on his anniversary last year"—her hand moved in a cross—"and Lord Paolo spoke to me in the great doorway as I left. There he was, a man with a great place at Court, stopping in the middle of the crowd of folk to talk to a crying widow; good, sensible, comforting words, too, nothing mawkish. I remember on that day when I was walking back to my town house, we were held up by a great fight in the square, di Torre and Bandini men, all among the market stalls—poor folk packing up their goods as best they could to save them, fine potters' ware shattered and trampled, good cloth thrown down, and I took up a little child to save him, half-dead with a broken arm. I can see I have a di Torre partisan at my side"—and again she patted the nun's hand—"but Rocca will never prosper while those two fight."

"The Duke should banish the Bandini, then!"

The nun seemed surprised that the others laughed at her fierce reply. Barley said, "One story is that Jacopo di Torre had the Duchess murdered and the Bandini boy left at her side."

The nun looked, for a moment, horrified, and Sigismondo said, "Rumours, rumours. Truth lies at the bottom of a well, and I dare say was drowned long ago."

The door opened to servants with more dishes: apple fritters, pumpkin fritters, a compôte of mulberries, and little biscuits. The maid, taking away dishes of the former courses, avoided Angelo and watched him with wary, fascinated eyes. As the door shut, Sigismondo continued, to Angelo, "One thing we may be sure of, that the man who hired you was not alive to hire Barley. But is the same person behind them both?"

He smiled, widely benign. "It's someone who hires men who are strangers. But let's consider that in the morning. Tonight, there's good company and good wine and food."

"And I drink to our hostess. May she enjoy peace all her days." Barley raised his replenished glass and bowed to her. She, murmuring that peace was not always concomitant with enjoyment, acknowledged also the others at the table who raised their glasses to her and echoed variations of Barley's toast. The companion hiccuped loudly in the quiet while they drank.

"Oh! Your pardon . . . unaccustomed strong wine . . ."

Barley looked round about him on the floor. "What was it? Did a mouse fart? It is excellent wine, lady. Blame nothing on the wine."

Perhaps not unconnected with this, the widow now decided that the men had best be left to their drinking while she saw the women to their beds. Sigismondo said that Benno could wait on the drinkers, and she did not demur but sent her servants to their beds as well.

Benno brought, as she had bidden, another great flagon. More wood was put on the fire, one candle snuffed; the men moved to the fire, Barley bringing the silver basket of nuts and each man his glass. Sigismondo sat in the big carved chair; Barley sprawled along a Venetian daybed. Angelo folded himself down on the wolfskin rug; Benno hunkered with his back to the stone pilasters by the hearth at Sigismondo's side. He cracked walnuts with the fire irons, but Barley used his fist alone. The house sank to quiet about them as they munched and drank, and they heard the hunting call of an owl as it ghosted outside in the night. Barley heaved himself round to throw nutshells in the fire and said to Sigismondo, "There's altogether too much you haven't said. You listened to Angelo's tale. You know why *I'm* here. The Duke wants you dead. So what have *you* done?"

"Did the Duke himself tell you he wanted my death?"

"I heard his wishes from the lips of the Lord Paolo."

"M'm-h'm. And why choose you?"

"Who else looks like me?" Barley sat up, throwing out his chest, and smiled in his beard. "He saw me trying out an act for the festaiuolo. I'm not to be missed in a crowd."

"A crowd of dwarves," said Angelo, and rolled away from Barley's kick. "The Lord Paolo oversaw the entertainments on the Duchess' behalf. He watched us all try out and came to see us rehearsing too, making suggestions—and not bad ones either, for an amateur."

"He loves his brother like his own life," said Barley. "Like that crippled son he dotes on. He'd kill for that one. Every time that boy puts his foot to the ground he steps on his father's heart."

"You're a poet, Barley. Of course they say the English are a race of poets—"

Benno ducked and dropped a nut into the ashes as his master seized Barley's wrist as the hand grabbed for his throat. He relaxed as Sigismondo broke into laughter. "A Scot, a Scot! The English are nothing but rhymesters, and only the Scots are poets." He threw the hand from him, and Barley sat back. "So Lord Paolo and the Duke think me a traitor. Do they think I am an agent of Duke Francesco?"

"Are you? By God, Duke Ludovico's days are numbered, then." Barley shouted with laughter and, tilting his beard at the ceiling and its painted beams, threw a handful of nuts into his mouth. "Why were you in Rocca in the first place?"

"I came looking for work, as you did, my sweet Scot. I'd done the Duke a service in the past, and he trusted me enough to employ me in the matter of the late Duchess."

"What could you do there? The Bandini boy is a lamb to the slaughter if the Duke himself killed her. Were you hired to make it look otherwise?" Barley's small eyes surveyed Sigismondo acutely, and Angelo too rolled over to look at him.

Holding out his glass to Benno, Sigismondo hummed.

"That's more than I can tell, as yet. Much in this whole business"—he extended a broad hand and closed it on the air—"is like grasping a cloud." He leant forward and put the hand on Barley's massive thigh. "One thing for sure: it's a cloud will rain blood soon."

He paused and looked round, at Angelo, at Benno, again at Barley. "We must leave for Rocca at dawn."

16. "WHAT SORT OF MONEY?"

"You're anxious to get us all killed?" Barley, staring, crushed a handful of nuts and held them in his fist, thumping it on his knee to mark his points: "Rocca? Here's Angelo: he's dyed his hair and killed the fellow who wanted his money back, but we all know that wasn't the man who hired him and who could recognise him as the one who played the Wild Man." He paused while Angelo turned up his eyes and drew the edge of his hand not across his throat but, to Benno's surprise, across his belly. "He'll end up spilling his guts on the scaffold with the Bandini boy."

He stopped to sort out kernels from shards and to bat them into his beard. "Then, there's me," he went on. "I was supposed to kill you, remember? If I turn up without your head in a bag, someone is going to require mine instead. And people notice me. My death too is waiting for me in Rocca."

"Death waits for us all, even the most overgrown Scot amongst us; but with some, he is forced to have greater patience than with others." Sigismondo held his glass towards Benno to be filled and went on, "And I am officially a traitor and so in Rocca any man's hand can be my ending. We must all seize the moment when our watchful Death yawns, and we tiptoe by."

The vision of Sigismondo and Barley tiptoeing past anything, whether or no it were equipped with a scythe, gave Angelo a silent spasm of amusement. Benno, however, was anxious about someone else.

"What about the Lady Cosima? They'll be looking for her, won't they? Now you tied up the nun and all."

Barley and Angelo both turned to look at Sigismondo, who sat fondling his chin, smiling.

"*Tied up the nun?* That's my Martin! What now? Was it the pretty nun at supper? I'd tie her up myself if she hadn't the look of one who'd bite. Who is the Lady Cosima?"

"She. That is the Lady Cosima. The nun who was tied up was Mother Luca, infirmarian at the Castelnuova convent. She objected to losing her patient by other than natural means. It's her clothes you saw at supper."

"Tied her up *and stripped her?* Infirmarian at the big Benedictine house on the hill near the border? In Duke Francesco's country? Martin, you have a *genius* for trouble." Barley thumped a paw down on the shoulder beside him and leant to gaze admiringly into Sigismondo's face. "Not content with stirring it up in Rocca, you have to thumb the nose at yet another Duke. Had you all the lives of a cat, you couldn't satisfy them all."

Angelo shifted on the wolfskin and, firelight gilding his face, looked up too. "Why, if you're Duke Francesco's agent, are you raping his nuns?"

Barley broke in, shocked. "He said no word of rape—"

"Who is this nun who is Lady Cosima? The Lady Cosima who was snatched by bandits?"

"By *Bandini*. That's what they say in Rocca."

"They say in Rocca!" Sigismondo's cynical hum rose up the scale. "They say anything in Rocca. They say what they're told in Rocca! But listen to a Bandini, you will hear how di Torre stole his own daughter to put the blame on them, then stabbed the Duchess and, stuffing Leandro Bandini into Wild Man rig, knocked him unconscious and threw him on her bed."

Angelo was sitting upright, grey eyes narrowed. "Did he? Was it di Torre who hired me?" A quality in the light voice suggested he was ready to go back to Rocca knife in hand once he knew who had hired both his assassin and himself. An unexpected answer came. Benno spoke.

"The Lord di Torre? He wouldn't do that, not my old master he wouldn't. Not stab the Duchess. Not ever so much to spite a Bandini." He looked round the faces turned to him. "What I reckon is, whoever killed Her Grace really hated the Duke, *really* did, wanted to fix things so it'd stir a hornet's nest, what with the Duke being called a murderer and the di Torre and Bandini tearing Rocca apart. Say there is an agent of Duke Francesco in Rocca, I reckon that's what he'd be pleased to fix up."

He nodded his head with finality, unaware that in the eyes of two of his audience he had graduated from being a half-wit to being one of the party. Sigismondo's hum was deep, like that of a bee in a flower.

"Come on, Martin. What's your story after the Duke gave you the push?"

"Ugo Bandini hired me to find Cosima di Torre; the Duke had ordered him to produce her, no matter how he swore he hadn't an idea where she was. So I was to find her, to prove to the Duke that di Torre had hidden her in the first place."

"Did the man truly think the Duke would believe him if you turned up with the girl, swearing you'd found her in a field with no Bandini in sight?"

"A man whose son and heir is scheduled for a public garotting is not at his most logical. For the boy's sake he was ready to do a deal with the Devil."

"And along you came." Barley's punch was affectionate, easily fielded. "Poor bastard. I understand all right. But what gave you any thought of Duke Francesco?"

"Because Bandini changed his mind. At the start, he was sweating blood, ready to shower gold on me to find the lady, so he could bargain for his son's life. Then his steward came whispering in his ear, and he bustled off and left me for the best part of an hour. When he came back, he was singing another song, and not even in the same key: he grudged any money save what would guarantee my leaving the house fast. I thought then that it was because he'd been told where the lady actually was. Now I've changed *my* mind." Sigismondo picked over the palmful of nuts Barley held out to him.

"How had he heard? How did you find her?"

"By following the wrong clue, perhaps. The only messengers to arrive were nuns from Castelnuova, and so we went there. While I was busy preparing to abduct the Lady Cosima from the convent, Benno, who as you know is little better than an idiot, was in the stables, and he was interested in two men who had little to do there. They seemed to wait for word from Mother Luca, infirmarian of the convent. You note that he much resembles a bundle of old rubbish, and it was as such that he listened to her instructions; these were from Duke Francesco; Bandini was to be told that the wolf would be at the door on the feast of Saint Benedict. There was an instruction in the same words to someone else whose name they did not speak, and to Jacopo di Torre."

Barley clapped his hands together, and Benno jumped.

"I see it. You're right, the old fox Francesco has everyone by the colpouns. Di Torre and Bandini do his will to protect their children; Duke Ludovico is branded *murderer* and his own people believe it—but the wolf at the door?"

"My old master doesn't have to do what he's told now," Benno said. "We've got the Lady Cosima."

"Di Torre doesn't know that." Sigismondo picked up his glass from the floor. "That is one of our reasons for going to Rocca."

"Give us another," Barley invited, hunting round his feet for a dropped kernel. "I like to know why I'm going to die."

"We have the Lady Cosima, but Leandro Bandini is still in the Palace dungeons. As long as he's there, Ugo Bandini's life, and what may be more important, his cash, is at Francesco's disposal."

"What kind of money does Bandini have?"

Sigismondo's hum was respectful. "The sort you lend Popes."

Barley whistled. "And you are proposing, my crazed Martin, to disguise yourself as a rat, slip into the dungeons and gnaw the Bandini boy free?" His gaze sharpened. "There'd be quite a reward, eh? Bandini'd cough up a few ducats to have his son and heir in his arms again."

"I knew you'd want to come," said Sigismondo, draining the last of the wine.

17. A FRIEND TO TRUE LOVE

The small cavalcade left the Villa Costa a little later than dawn because of the preparations involved. A white spring mist lay in the valley below the villa and clothed them as they rode in ghostly silence. Benno cuddled a warm, drowsy and replete Biondello under his cloak and reflected with happy trust on what lay ahead. He knew from the talk last night that it was a future full of danger to all of them, himself no less, but his confidence in Sigismondo's powers had not been dented in any way. Here was the Lady Cosima, whom he had found when she could not be found and had rescued from an impossible situation, who now rode with them. Benno had seen in church a fresco of an angel, finger to lips, leading Saint Paul out of prison, and although Sigismondo would make a bulky and demonic angel, Benno foresaw a similar miracle for Leandro Bandini.

The Villa Costa was empty, save for servants and the sister-in-law, now paying for the enjoyment of so much wine the evening before. She would not have cared if the Last Trump had sounded, provided it put an end to her misery. She was past registering that the Widow Costa, visiting her briefly at dawn, was out of mourning for the first time since Federico's death; nor would she have known the nun of last night, dressed in clothes long cast off by the widow's daughter. Had she searched for Angelo's beautiful face among the party ready to leave, she would have been flabbergasted to find it framed in yellow silk ringlets twisted with lilac ribbons before the ears. A dress long preserved for sentimental reasons in the widow's wardrobe, which had once fitted her younger, slenderer form, was, though not up-to-date, ravishing on Angelo, who had gathered folds of veiling modestly over his flat chest.

The widow, as dignified in mulberry velvet as she had been in black, rode in the character of her own sister, accompanied by daughter and maid, on a visit to her town house in Rocca. There members of the family stayed now and then, and, owing to the timely death of her steward two months ago, the staff had changed and no one was there who had ever seen the widow's sister. Two servants attended her: a half-witted fellow carrying her little dog, and a burly great brute in a hood, whose bare chin looked sore; at her side where the road permitted it rode her chaplain, cowl over his shaven head, grave in his robes, reading his breviary with devout attention.

The Widow Costa's new steward, put out by the arrival of guests without notice, was struck by the strong likeness of the sister to the widow herself. The letter she gave him, with her seal attached, was hardly needed to prove her identity and, with respectful obeisances, he made her welcome and despatched his family about airing mattresses, hanging bed-curtains, lighting fires and dressing meat for dinner. The Lady Donati's daughter kept her face veiled before the steward, as any highborn maiden should, but if her looks could be judged by her not fearing competition with those of her maid, Angela, they must, he thought, be exquisite indeed.

The chaplain wielded formidable authority. It was evident to the steward that everyone in the party looked to him for earthly as well as spiritual guidance, though he spoke so little. The steward was quite unaware that while he was in the kitchen examining the provisions, deciding what could be served and what must be procured, this same chaplain was slipping about the house with a sinister turn of speed, exploring staircases and passageways, checking on the exits to alleys and streets bordering all sides. Three separate doors were found, the bolts tested for ease of drawing, the bars shifted in their sockets in case they jammed. Each door, from the judas at eye-level, looked out on a different alley, one within all-but-touching distance of the house opposite, and dark as a rat-run. A maid coming up from the cellar with a bundle of faggots tucked under her arm, for the fire in the great drawing room, was confused to come on a priest peering out of the door at the street, but collected her wits enough to bob as he turned and blessed her.

One thing which did surprise the steward was that the witless servant was sent to exercise Madam's rather horrible little dog not in the street but in the gallery, where he feared one of his family would have to be sent to clear up after both of them. The steward could not know that the lovely Angela had offered to remedy the dog's identifying characteristic herself by removing the other ear, but he had heard the indignant yell of the lack-wit as he snatched the dog to his unsavoury bosom.

Another surprise was Madam's summoning the vast brute of a groom to her bedchamber, when the fire had been lit there. Certainly her daughter and the maid were there; it was not improper. Luckily for the steward's sanity he never saw this same brute seated in Madam's chair in a strong light, trying not to blink while his sandy eyelashes were re-darkened, with oil and candlesoot, by Angela's professional hand.

Angela left, her golden hair covered in a linen kerchief, herself shrouded in a dark wool cloak, a basket on her arm. She respectfully reported to him before she went, so *someone* of the party, he reflected, knew the proper conduct of a household. He could have made no sense of the fact that her errand was to an elderly dwarf at the Palace, and that the word employed to gain the confidence of that dwarf and fetch him to the servants' entry of the Palace to sponsor the beautiful creature in, was "Altosta," home village of the late, lamented Poggio.

By the time that Angela returned, the steward was satisfied that he had the house in a fit state for his mistress' guests, and that the dinner now being prepared for them by his exhausted wife and niece would be worthy of the Lady Donati's praise. It had been hard to manage, for the city was in such a ferment— people in shops more ready to talk politics than to serve, and supplies short because the Palace was buying in for the Duke Ippolyto's visit, expected at any minute for the execution of his sister's murderer. Such vegetables as there were at this season, coming in out of the country every morning, went at high prices to the Palace, and even the pigs in the street were at risk of being abducted. Madam Donati was surprisingly affronted by his assumption that she was in Rocca to see the execution. After that, he did not see how to object when she asked for his keys in order to look out something that her sister had asked her to bring back, from the rooms kept locked since Federico Costa's death.

"Well, yes, Madam. I have them on a separate small ring; here. I would point out that on Madam Costa's express instructions I have not entered the rooms myself, save to ensure that damp or rodents—"

"It's no matter at all. I shan't look at the dust."

He was more relieved than he could say, as he could not have induced his wife or daughter to enter the rooms to dust them. They were possessed of the idea that they were haunted, and it would not be tactful on his part to imply that Madam Donati's brother-in-law was an unwelcome guest, in however translated a form.

For a party newly arrived in the city, the visitors showed themselves highly restless. Their journey here did not seem to have taxed their energies. Shortly after the beautiful maidservant returned, she and Madam Donati's daughter, heavily veiled, set out on an unexplained expedition, accompanied by the huge groom. He looked, in his close-fitting black hood, unnervingly like the man who would shortly appear behind Leandro Bandini on the scaffold being erected in the grand square.

Cosima's first reaction to the part proposed for her had been a violent refusal.

"Never, never, never! How could I, a di Torre, do such a thing? How could you ask it? Never. I will not."

In the silence that had followed, she was aware of their eyes upon her, considering, while her cheeks flamed with her— surely righteous?—indignation. She had expected at least Benno to speak up in support, but the only sound from him was the scratching of his beard in uncouth concentration. What she did hear was Sigismondo's deprecatory hum, so much deeper than the voice she had first heard him use.

"I didn't think you would do it," he said. "I told them you couldn't bring yourself to it. We must think again."

No one spoke for a bit and her breathing quietened. Then Angelo, sitting up straight in his green wool dress as though he had studied feminine deportment all his life, remarked in that light, incisive voice, "We are all risking our lives here, and you are unwilling to risk your pride. *You* have been rescued; Leandro Bandini has not."

Barley broke out, "Do you know what death he faces, lady? What they do to a traitor? First—"

"No." Sigismondo raised a hand; she noticed that Barley at once fell silent. "You can't know what this lady feels. A di Torre could not give a cup of water to a Bandini were he in Hell flames. This young man is innocent of what he is to die for. He has done the Lady Cosima no harm. He is to die a terrible death but, as a di Torre, she must rejoice in it."

"That's not true." She knew she had flushed again; she was so angry she could have wept. "I'll do what you want. *No one* shall say a di Torre is without Christian charity."

She had not known what it would be like.

All her life, she had only rarely been permitted out of doors, for instance to Mass at the church nearest her father's house, rather than hearing it in the family chapel. She was now out in the streets far from home. She was grateful that the young man in skirts who walked a step behind her, just as Barley loomed a step in front, was in charge. Since she left her father's house less than a week ago, she had crammed more astonishing experiences into her life than she had dreamt possible. Now here she was walking among crowds of people in an ordinary street, in the cross-talk and hubbub of a city square, seeing beggars holding out stumps or revealing hideous sores, seeing ragged children fighting over a filthy piece of bread, hearing hammering and shouts and looking up to see a curious platform being erected in front of an ornate balcony; behind her, Angelo said flatly, "That's the scaffold."

She supposed they must be near the Palace, then. She already felt tired. She had walked farther than ever in her life. Angelo, stepping forward, offered her an arm. Cosima thought vividly of Sascha, whose arm she had leant on in walks through the country park. She was here to avenge Sascha, too, against those who had killed her. For the moment it slipped her consciousness that she was leaning on the arm of a young man, and when she thought of it, she faltered. Angelo misunderstood.

"You don't have to speak when we reach the door. I've got the money; the guard will let us in. Leave everything to me."

At the door, while Angelo in his new light tone talked and demurely repelled flirtation, Cosima repeated to herself what she was to say.

Angelo now led the way and followed the guard. Barley, stopped at the door, lounged there so unconcernedly that Cosima took heart. Smooth, cool stone under her feet was a blessing after the rough streets. The guard kept looking back and slowing sometimes as if he hoped the lovely creature at his heels would collide with him. Cosima, who had seen the lovely creature with a knife in its hand, was aware of a glow of excitement, of adventure, as though she were being swept towards something dangerous that she wanted to meet.

They were being taken deeper and deeper by dark passages down into—not the heart, rather the guts of—the Castle. She noticed that they met no one. The guard was bringing them by unfrequented ways, giving them full value for the small leather bag that Angelo had pressed into his hand. Of course, though, he was probably as anxious to avoid notice as they were.

They met one person now. They had descended a final flight of worn stone, lit by a torch in a bracket on one of the sweating stone walls, and here was a man who could only be a jailer. He stood there at the foot of the steps, large, suspicious, blocking their way, the lantern he carried sending an additional upward and infernal glow onto his gross features, while the torchlight was reflected oddly in his eyes, red like a rat's.

"What's this?" His voice grated; she had the fancy that this was because he seldom used it and it had rusted up. "Who are these? No one is to come down here without my leave."

"Visitors for the Bandini. That's all I know." The door guard, with a last look at Angelo, who returned it, took himself and his own torch away, having come to the end of what their coins had bought. The jailer stood where he was, eyeing them with increasing disbelief.

"Bandini? No one sees Bandini till he dies." A grin split his face like a wound. "Then you'll see more of him than anyone's seen before—more than he'll enjoy." The grin seamed itself shut again. "What you want with him?" He raised the lantern to shine on Angelo's face. "Pretty bird to fly into my cage." The wound once more gaped, showing teeth at its edges black as gangrene.

"My lady must see her affianced before he dies." Angelo approached the jailer—Cosima instinctively holding her own breath in sympathy—and whispered in his ear, at the same time transferring another small leather bag into his free hand, which closed readily upon it. Angela's golden, ribbon-trimmed plaits mingled for a second with greasy grey curls and, as the rat eyes swivelled to look Cosima over, she was glad of her veils.

"Ah. *That's* the case, is it? Piero's a friend to true love, he is." He weighed the bag and pushed it into the front of the stained leather tunic. "Just a few minutes, then, because Piero loves a lover." His chuckle sent a miasma of garlic and rotting teeth through Cosima's veils and she felt her stomach heave. *Of all things, I mustn't vomit now.* She was too innocent to know that her involuntary spasm and swallowing were convincing evidence to Piero of the condition Angelo had hinted.

"My lady." Angelo's hand, thin and hard, was under her arm, supporting her, leading her in the wake of the jailer, who had turned and was stumping down the passage. "All is well; but a moment and you will see your beloved."

My beloved! My mortal enemy! What would my father say? This beat in her head as she heard the key turn in the lock of a huge, low door. The jailer held up the lantern to peer through the judas first, and now as the door groaned open he cried with dreadful joviality, "A little bird to see you, Master Bandini! A little lovebird!"

Angelo supported her across the threshold. The moment had come. A shape had got up from the straw, was standing there. She could sense bewilderment. Boldly, she did as Sigismondo had rehearsed her: she stepped forward, flinging back her veil and holding out her arms. They closed round a young man's shoulders, the first she had ever touched, and she pressed her cheek to a rough one, whispering urgently in his ear, "Pretend to know me. If you want to live, join with what we say."

She felt his sudden tension, his deep breath. Then hands held her shoulders. He said aloud, "My love?"

Cosima put her forehead down on his shoulder. She heard Angelo speak. Leandro Bandini crushed her to him and said again, "My love! You came—you came at last!"

And, unaware that it was Cosima di Torre he held in his arms, he kissed her with heartfelt enthusiasm.

Cosima di Torre, who was well aware she was being kissed by a Bandini, almost at once lost appreciation of that fact. Her lips seemed to be connected to the whole of her body in a completely new way. If this was what being kissed by a young man was like, then it was perfectly obvious why unmarried girls should be protected from the experience. Rapturously she returned the kiss. His arms tightened, wrapped round her farther, so that suddenly she remembered the situation and who she was. Flushing, horrified, she made an effort to release herself and they sank together on the straw. The jailer had set his lantern down in the doorway and was engaged in a muttered exchange with Angelo; a bar of light fell across the faces of the two where they sat in the straw, gilding the faces of each to the benefit of the other. Cosima was amazed that a Bandini could be so handsome; her imagination had foretold a face marked by generations of evil. Leandro thought it only fitting that someone who had come to rescue him should resemble a being from Paradise.

"My lady." Angelo bent over them, plaits swinging, blocking the light, to their mutual disappointment. "We must go, but we'll return with a priest. Piero has agreed to allow the marriage."

"Marriage!" Leandro's start and cry brought an oily chuckle from the jailer.

"They get you in the end, lad, even with the gallows waiting."

"Sweet Leandro—" How strange the name sounded in her mouth. She bent her head modestly and managed to utter the words she had rehearsed, wishing she could sink through the ground. "It is for the child's sake."

Leandro snatched up her hands and bent his head to kiss them, most likely to hide the astonishment she had momentarily seen. Cosima felt it appropriate to her role to lean forward and kiss his rumpled hair, and managed to breathe "Trust us," as she drew back.

Angelo helped her to her feet before the jailer could, and with professional swiftness arranged her veils over her face against his leering glance as he raised the lantern.

"No more kisses, little bird, until the priest says so. Been too many already, eh? Oh, how lucky you are to find Piero here. He's got such a soft heart for lovebirds in distress. Such a soft heart."

Wagging his head in approval of his nature, Piero ushered them out, clanged the door to and clashed the key in the lock while Leandro peered through the judas until it was shut on him. Cosima thought she saw such a look of hope on his face that her heart melted. Poor young man, to have been brought up a Bandini.

18. "ESCAPE, WOULD YOU?"

It was getting dark, the sky an intense green behind the distant hills, the pale violet of spring twilight overhead, when Cosima, weary, set off on her second journey through the city streets to the castle prison. Again, she was accompanied by Angelo, wrapped as she was herself in a cloak now that the bitter little wind of evening keened round the alley corners. There were as many people in the street as before, but an unease struck her; there were groups who talked in low voices. The man who went ahead now was not Barley but Sigismondo, cowled and furled in his black robes. She observed something strange: although he parted the crowds with easy confidence, as they approached the Palace his gait altered, grew less sure; his shoulders hunched, as though he shrank from what was to come. For the first time Cosima thought truly what peril they were all in: that even Sigismondo, on whom she had come to rely as implicitly as Benno did, had good reason to fear.

The guard at the door had changed. Cosima's heart missed a beat at the unfamiliar face, but evidently they were expected. The new guard seemed just as entranced by Angela's face and just as ready to accept a bribe to let them in as the other had been. His colleague, who had not been at this door either, was inclined to take his bribe from Angela in the form of a kiss, to which the maid acceded very readily. The priest, clicking his tongue, called them to order, and they continued on their way, Cosima increasingly disturbed at Sigismondo's stumbling walk.

"Can you manage the steps, Father? Not easy at your age, I know." The guard seemed a kindly man, if amorous; but as he put out a hand to help Sigismondo, Cosima sent up a piercing prayer that he would not feel, through the woollen folds, the steel muscles of this ageing priest. She understood now why Sigismondo's height seemed to have lessened and his step become shaky. He must seem pitiful and not threatening. She remembered his saying that he had already visited Leandro in prison. The jailer might well recognise him. The guard was now pinching Angelo's behind, and got a back-handed little feminine punch on the arm for his pains. He left them at the top of the last crooked flight of steps. Cosima picked her way down the worn treads, skirts bunched in her hands—telling herself that her heart beat so fast because of the danger they were in, and not because of the coming meeting with Leandro Bandini.

Piero had heard them and waited, lantern in hand aloft, in an expansive mood suitable to a wedding. From the extra layer of smell on the air, he had been drinking their former bribe in anticipation. He greeted Sigismondo with a respect that from him was gruesome, bending his knees and head together.

"Your blessing, Father. Makes a change from hearing confessions down here, having a marriage. May be the first the place has seen, who knows? The Romans built this," and he slapped the wall. "A wedding, and then straight to the last rites, eh?" His laugh, Cosima thought, sounded as a rat might if it choked on a gobbet of flesh, and she pinched her nostrils shut as they followed him down the dank passage to Leandro's cell. He was still expatiating about the Romans as Sigismondo tottered at his heels making little yaps of assent.

"Here is your bride, Bandini!" Piero flung wide the cell door with a flourish, jangling his keys like wedding bells. Leandro was ready for them, Cosima saw, anxiously smiling. She was touched to see he had brushed the straw from his clothes and combed through that thick hair with his fingers. How he must have suffered in this place! What had he thought, all these days, as he waited for death?

Sigismondo was bent over his breviary, tilting it towards the lantern, his shaking hands making it tremble as he muttered words that Cosima was surprised to recognise as good Latin. What kind of man was this who had first emerged into her life dressed as a widow? But here was Angelo, putting back her veil for her, handing a ring to Leandro, standing beside her with meek bowed head while Sigismondo maundered on, turning the page. The jailer held the lantern near, the light sending shadows swimming across their faces, Sigismondo's all but invisible beneath his cowl. She was aware of Piero's eyes on her, his head cocked to see into her face. Leandro, directed by the "priest", took her hand and put the ring to each finger and at last onto the ring finger itself. He had said the words; *she* had said the words . . . If Sigismondo had really been a priest—and she was visited by the chill idea that perhaps he *was*—she would now be married to Leandro Bandini and her father would die to hear of it. If he saw her now he would certainly succumb to apoplexy.

"Is it all over, Father?" Piero put the lantern down on the threshold and, horribly, advanced on her. "First kiss from the bride! Piero's reward for a soft heart."

She had no time to shrink from the foul breath that preceded him, hardly felt the grip of Leandro's hand draw her back, only saw a violent movement behind the advancing Piero like a whirling darkness against darkness itself. Piero's face lurched towards her, large as nightmare, eyes suddenly starting like a hare's, tongue thrust out as though it would reach her first. A curious loud retching sound filled her ears and the next second she found herself pulled round against Leandro's chest, held against his thudding heart.

"The keys. Right . . ."

Despite Leandro's hand, which tried to keep her head against his chest, Cosima twisted round to see. The lantern's light flickered, protected though it was, as if the wind of struggle had nearly doused it. But its uncertain light showed Sigismondo and Angelo busy over something on the floor in the corner. As they stepped back, she saw a huddled figure on the pallet and Angelo twitching the ragged blanket up over the grey, greasy curls. Sigismondo was unwrapping his rosary from his wrist and knotting it again at his belt. She felt once more a heave of nausea as she knew what she had seen: Piero being strangled . . . *He deserved it*, she told herself with dismissive anger. This was not a time to be squeamish. Sigismondo was pulling a dark robe of fine wool from under his habit, and he and Angelo flung it over Leandro's head like a couple of bizarre tirewomen. Sigismondo was thus restored to his usual figure. Angelo took up the lantern, Leandro seized her hand and they left the cell, Sigismondo bringing up the rear. She heard him lock the door.

She needed both hands to manage her skirts up the narrow flight of worn stairs, and Leandro, letting go, whispered, "I'll never forget this! Never! You shall have anything in the world—"

He was cut short by the sudden appearance of a figure, carrying a lantern of its own, at the head of the stairs. Leandro halted a moment, Cosima gasped. It was another figure out of nightmare, too small for a man, too thickset for a child, and with an iron-grey beard. So, far from challenging them or raising an alarm, he put a finger to his lips and then, turning, beckoned them on and led at a rapid pace down a passage branching off the one they had used before. Cosima, as they all followed, fancied for a moment that they had slipped into one of the tales told by her nurse or by Sascha, and that they might see a witch or a monster barring their way before they could come to the world outside again.

This did not happen until they had traversed quite a few passages, some so narrow they had to edge in single file, one so low that only the dwarf could walk upright. Cosima understood that he led them by ways known only, perhaps, to his own kind. She had heard of the Palace dwarves, and she imagined, as she parcelled her skirts close to her chest and felt her veiling catch on rough stone, that the whole ancient castle was honeycombed with such ways where the small people might go about their lives unseen. The present passage seemed to be a tunnel cut in the rock. She thought they might almost have made it themselves.

Here she stumbled on some débris, and Sigismondo's hand was instantly under her elbow. If *he* was bringing up the rear, any danger must be expected from behind, pursuit rather than confrontation. He said, "I hope Durgan takes us nowhere straiter than this."

They began to hear the sound of people not far off, talking; the clash of what might be halberds; the barking of a hound farther off. It sounded as if it were barking to the sky; there was no echo from a confined space. They might be near an outer door, with its guardroom. They must, she thought, and could feel her heart drumming, they must be very near freedom. Here the walls were of dressed stones.

It was here that they met the man with the torch.

He came suddenly from a small door and wheeled to look at them, holding the torch high. The dwarf slid his dark-lantern shut. So, at the rear, did Sigismondo. If Piero had looked like a large rat, this man was like a weasel, with small, glittering eyes and a long nose that twitched.

"Who are you? What do you here?"

The voice was sharp, but educated. He was no jailer, no guard, in his long gown. Durgan said, "They are friends of mine. I vouch for them, sir—"

"*Master Leandro!*"

Cosima heard herself let out a short cry like a yelp. Leandro stepped back against her, shielding his face with one arm from the torch's flare. The weasel-man had thrust aside the protesting Durgan and dashed the torch at Angelo as he forced his way past, hand out to grasp Leandro.

"You'd escape, would you? We'll see—"

What he, in that confident plural, had been going to see dwindled suddenly into realms of conjecture. Cosima, pressed back against Sigismondo, knew she hampered him from acting; the weasel had only to cry out, it might fetch those guards and lead to all their deaths. Angelo had snatched the man's torch, even as he continued to come forward, hand outstretched, mouth open; but instead of words, blood poured out.

Leandro staggered under the man's sudden weight, sending Cosima back to be steadied by Sigismondo as he crammed himself against the wall past her and supported the man's body. She, with a fearful glance into the dark they had come from, flattened herself all she could, and he got by. She saw Angelo now pulling his knife back, wiping it on the man's gown, slipping it out of sight to where he had produced it from. The beautiful face between the gold silk plaits had neither anger nor satisfaction, but, though serene, he breathed fast and had moved even faster.

There was now silence. Sigismondo was listening. No change came in the sounds they had heard beyond the walls. He murmured to the dwarf, "Where can we put him?"

"But it's my father's secretary," Leandro whispered, "What—"

"Ask later. Durgan?"

The dwarf had pursed up his mouth. Now he nodded and pointed the way they were going. Angelo put out the torch on the floor and pushed Leandro and Cosima ahead after Sigismondo, who carried the body. The light of Sigismondo's—Piero's—lantern presently brought up the rear in Angelo's steady hand.

Leandro said, "But he was going to—"

Cosima, surprised that he should speak, was not surprised when Angelo, in the language of the stables, told him to shut up.

Durgan stopped and closed his lantern. Angelo at once closed his. They were in the dark once more until a door opened ahead.

A veil hung there, it seemed, hiding lights. Then she saw it was tapestry. Durgan's shape appeared against it, peering into the lit place beyond. He beckoned, lifting the cloth. They hurried across a wide hall bright with flambeaux. Cosima could feel her pulse in her throat, and every inch of her body seemed aware of its awful visibility. She expected a guard's shout.

They hurried down a long, straight stair on the other side; then, on a landing where two pillars rose either side of a statue, Durgan seemed to vanish. Sigismondo, sidling, got with his burden between the statue's plinth and the pillar. Cosima saw that Leandro would have offered to let her go first, but Angelo stuffed him into the gap. He was the one whose presence could still betray what they were up to. A small door yawned behind the plinth, and he ducked into it. Cosima followed, Angelo joined them and Durgan opened his lantern. They were at the top of a flight of precipitous broken steps and had to go down.

The steps started as dressed stone and ended as rock. Angelo's lantern could give little help; there were shifting shadows. Once, Sigismondo stumbled, and a rattling stone went down ahead of them into the dark. They were feeling their way foot after foot and into an increasing foulness of air. Once more it was cold. When she slipped, Leandro took her hand to help her. His hand was strong and smooth; a Bandini ought not to have pleasant-feeling hands.

She wished she had thicker shoes. The raw edges of stone hurt her feet.

They had reached a level floor. The dwarf went forward, and the smell told Cosima that once more they must be near dungeons. He stopped and, raising the lantern, showed a round grating in the floor.

Sigismondo put down the body in its stained blue gown and set to work. He had to wrap his hands in his sleeves to grip the rusty grating, and it took him a long few minutes to heave the metal from its bed, but no time at all to roll the body into the dark void. They heard, after a long pause, a thud far below.

Cosima feared—she would have sat down had the floor been dry, while Sigismondo put back the grid—that they would now have to go back the way they had come. Durgan, however, led the way on. A long ramp that curved as if it were inside a circling wall went upward. The stone was smooth as if it had once been used often, but their feet raised dust. The air freshened. Amazed, Cosima smelt incense. They came out onto the level and Durgan opened a door that gave onto the vast marble floor and echoing space of Saint Agnes'.

19. "YOU WANT MY FATHER TO COMMIT TREASON?"

They were next to a side altar. Cosima hurriedly veiled herself. She saw Sigismondo bending to have a word with Durgan, then the door, shutting, became invisible.

People were leaving after Compline, in groups and singly, crossing the great floor. Sigismondo gathered his group about him. Here they kept to the shadows, for here he and Leandro could not cover their heads. He put Leandro's arm round Cosima and told him to lean his face over her as they walked, following him. He walked slowly, his cowl pulled high round his neck. She said, "Can't we hurry?" and Angelo, at her heels, muttered, "Yes, if you want people to stare."

Outside the door—had she ever been so grateful for the dark?—the men put up their hoods. The dreadful shape of the scaffold loomed to one side. Then it was behind them. Sigismondo hurried his steps now. They entered the confinement of streets after the open square; Angelo allowed a crack of light to shine at their feet. Cosima felt the cold and shivered. No one spoke. They stopped before a door whose threshold lacked a step—it was at knee height above the ground. Sigismondo rapped softly to a pattern. The door gaped into darkness. He turned, took her by the hips without ceremony, and put her up into the doorway. She was steadied by someone unknown, then she smelt Benno. He drew her away from the door, for the others were entering.

Then there were lights. They crowded up a small stair. She had to stop and put her veil back to see her footing. A landing full of crumbling plaster led into a big room lit by fat candles where a large man was getting up from a chair by a brazier; she saw the incredulity on his face as he took a hesitant step forward. Leandro ran to him.

The pair embraced, exclaimed, held each other at arms' length to look, embraced and kissed once more. At last they brought themselves to remember that they were not alone.

"Ah, father, here's my fair saviour!" Leandro came and seized her hand, very freely it seemed of a sudden in this domestic and social atmosphere, although on their adventures they had touched hands without question. He led her towards his father. "A courageous lady! She played her part perfectly. Whatever you paid her can't be enough."

Cosima stopped dead, making him turn, and dragged her fingers from his clasp; and with the word *paid* singing in her head she brought her hand across his face as violently as she knew how. He reeled, his eyes amazed, his cheek reddening. Bandini and Angelo began to speak, but she forestalled them.

"I am a di Torre!"

If they had been startled before, it was nothing. Ugo Bandini drew breath raspingly, his son became for a moment a caricature of a handsome young man surprised, straight from her father's book of physiognomy.

"I am Cosima di Torre." She reinforced their surprise. "I did what I did because I had been rescued and you had not. If you suppose for one instant that I, or any of my family, could be *paid* to do any service of *any* kind—"

"Lady Cosima"—Ugo Bandini's voice, being male and powerful, unfairly made itself heard above hers—"be assured my son spoke in ignorance—"

"I could not know." He touched his cheek tenderly and then flung his hands wide. "Lady, most admired, most worthy lady, I have been rescued by your means and with your valiant help. I beg your forgiveness. I understand nothing. The Duke's agent"—he turned towards Sigismondo, but Sigismondo was not there; only Angelo stood douce and vigilant behind Cosima—"the Duke's agent rescued me, and my father's trusted secretary tried to prevent my escape."

"Giulio? To *prevent* it?"

"Yes, sir, there was no mistake. He would have laid hands on me to prevent it." He put the back of one bloodstained hand to his forehead, and his father took hold of him at once, looked at his hands in horror, began to pull at his bloodstained gown to get at suspected wounds he had but just envisioned. "I'm not hurt, sir. That's Giulio's blood. He tried to stop me; he would have called the guard. *She* killed him." He nodded at Angelo, who, as Ugo Bandini wheeled to see him, curtseyed politely. Cosima, sinking onto the bench and wondering what had happened to her knees, thought that the Bandini, father and son, had had all the surprises that they could manage for the moment.

Apparently Fate disagreed, for the door opened and Cosima had her own surprise, ushered in by Sigismondo. Her father, his furred hood falling back as he came in, entered and stood, mouth open, staring from her to Bandini, who gaped back at him.

Cosima had risen to her feet at sight of her father, ready to sink into her filial curtsey, with an automatic smile of welcome as she waited for the joyous recognition, the embrace for a daughter restored, like the one Ugo Bandini had given his son. Her father stared, and her smile faded. He strode forward to shake his fist at the Bandini.

"Traitor! Murderer! Is this your revenge, devils? To bring me here to show me my disgraced daughter?" He swung on Sigismondo, who stood behind him by the door, gravely attentive to all that passed. "You called yourself the Duke's man, but now I see the stories are true; you work for Duke Francesco. Spare me your excuses!"—though Sigismondo showed no sign of making any—"the *evidence*"—and he flung a pointing hand out towards Leandro—"is here! None but a traitor would free a murderer." He struck his brow with both fists, almost dislodging his fur cap. "But you have failed! I disown her!" And a sweep of the arm at Cosima brushed her out of his life. "She is no daughter of mine. You have dishonoured her, and she is no di Torre! Do what you will, give death for her shame, she is no longer mine!" He was weeping as he shouted, and Cosima, astonished and angry, thought: *Perhaps he cares about me after all*, and simultaneously, *I hadn't realised he was so old*.

"Your daughter, my lord, since her abduction by Duke Francesco's men, was at first in the charge of the nuns of a convent in Castelnuova. She was then in the care of the Lady Donati, in whose sister's house we are now. Everywhere, she has been suitably accompanied, and her honour is unstained."

"Nuns?" Sigismondo's firm tone had carried conviction, and Cosima saw hope begin to dawn in her father's face. The Bandini, father and son, had also made no protest against the accusations, but watched as though at a piece of theatre whose plot escaped them.

"Nuns." Her father turned his head from Sigismondo to her again. "Nuns brought me her hair."

"They cut it off," she heard herself saying, putting her hands up and feeling the still unaccustomed shape of her shorn head under the folds of lawn. "I was a prisoner there." *How pathetic I sound!* Leandro was regarding her with sympathy.

Her father's face had changed. "Duke Francesco . . . ?" And he turned again, to Ugo Bandini. "Then you had no part in this?"

"I swear it. On my son's life."

This, which seemed to convince di Torre, raised other questions. "Your son—" Di Torre pointed.

Sigismondo came forward, raising his hand magisterially.

"My lord, that's another story. Let it suffice that your daughter has behaved with all the courage and breeding of a di Torre." Jacopo turned once more towards her, she saw Sigismondo beckon and she at last sank into her curtsey. Her father came hurrying to her, and as she rose she was clasped to his fusty furs. He kissed her, rubbed tears from his beard and then started and whispered urgently, "Your veil, girl! Good God, have you forgotten there are *strange men* present?"

Cosima reached over her shoulders and brought her veil down. Sigismondo for a moment smiled, and she, remembering how boldly she had thrown back her veil in the prison, began to blush, the confining lawn making her face feel hotter still.

He was speaking, however.

"Sirs: your children are, for this moment and in this place, safe; but you and they are in danger and so is all Rocca and the Duke himself. I think you know this. You know that Francesco of Castelnuova is about to attack—that his mercenaries have crossed the border and are encamped tonight on Roccan soil."

Neither man showed shock. It was true. They had known. Ugo glanced down at his son as if to conceal any expression. Her own father, who had released her almost at once from his embrace, had a conscious air. It was Angelo who, smoothing his dress, remarked, "Artful bastard," and drew all eyes.

"Well, he's chosen his time, hasn't he?" Angelo spoke still in his upper register, as a girl. "The city's steaming like a midden. They don't like their Duchess getting murdered, and they don't like Ippolyto's men either, swaggering about sneering. They don't like the street fighting that ruins their goods." He nodded at Leandro and showed a hint of the crooked teeth in the lovely face. "They'll be pissed off properly at not seeing the colour of your guts tomorrow. Some of them's connoisseurs."

Bandini indignantly enveloped his son once more in a protective embrace, but Sigismondo addressed Jacopo di Torre.

"You were given instructions, my lord: the price of your daughter's life and safety."

Di Torre tweaked at the veil on his daughter's shoulder, as if arranging it were of importance.

"What were those instructions?"

Cosima found her wrist taken by her father, who displayed her and spoke in a quick loud tone. "What was I to do? Could I let my child die? My only heir? A di Torre?"

An object, a possession, a pawn . . . Cosima found these thoughts, which she had entertained all her life, rising to the surface. Her father never looked at her as Bandini looked at his son. Leandro was an heir, and he would keep his father's name, perpetuate his line. She struggled a little to free her wrist, and her father at once let go without looking at her. She was deadly tired, and her feet burned, but her young lifetime's practice kept her upright, with the face of complaisance expected in a young girl.

"Indeed, my lord. You could not let her die. Nature and your love for her demanded that you obey those orders. What were they? How were you to come to the aid of Duke Francesco tomorrow?"

Di Torre pointed once more at Ugo Bandini. "Understand, sir, that I believed these instructions came from you."

"We are quits there, sir. I believed that the mind behind all these machinations was yours."

Sigismondo hummed genially. "So that both of you were prepared to sacrifice your Duke to save your children."

"I am no Brutus, sir, to send my son to death for my country's sake." Ugo Bandini put out a preventing hand to Leandro, who would have interrupted. "I too had no choice in the matter." He and di Torre were regarding each other now as if reassessing their enemy as a possible human being.

"You must understand, my lords." Sigismondo's voice gathered force, had an urgency that brought Cosima a sense of the danger still surrounding them, of an enemy not conquered. "You have been tricked, both of you, and by the same person. Both of you have had spies in your house, the slave Sascha and the secretary Giulio."

"Sascha!"

"You left the city unconscious in a litter. She left wearing your dress and riding with one of the bravos; she let your dress be seen, as he let the false Bandini colours he wore be seen. She was bitterly paid for her treachery."

Cosima could only think, Why did Sascha do that? Did I treat her badly? Did she hate me and I never knew?

"They will not have been the only spies. There's no time now to explain all that needs to be made clear, and you must trust me and, for once, each other. Your children are both safe for this moment, but their lives, and yours, depend on the events of this coming day."

He had moved to the windows and peered through a crack in the shutters as if to estimate how close that day might be to its dawn. Now he turned and spoke almost casually to di Torre. "And your instructions, my lord, were?"

"To open the gates. That is"—Cosima heard a constriction of the throat, an effort at dignity in this admission of being a traitor—"as a Chief Councillor of the Duke, to send messages with my seal that no alarm was to be raised, nor any effort made to prevent, when armed troops arrived and entered; that they were the Duke Ippolyto's men, come to help our Duke to put down riots."

"Riots?" Bandini asked.

"Riots would be provided," Sigismondo answered drily. Cosima, once more seated on the tapestry bench along the bedfoot, saw her father's face and was sorry for him for the first time. After all, it was for her sake he had been ready to do this, even if she were not a person but merely his daughter.

He now raised his head and said to Bandini, "What did you have to do?"

Bandini made a giving gesture with both hands, his tone almost conciliatory. "Money. Troops, mercenaries, must be paid. If you were to let in the men Francesco has hired, I was to be their paymaster"—and he put a hand on Leandro's shoulder—"if the boy were not to die."

"Instead of which"—Sigismondo's voice held a note of ironic cheerfulness—"Duke Ludovico was to die. Now, if we are to prevent that, you must do as I say."

"First, first"—Jacopo clicked his fingers towards Angelo— "look after your mistress. Put her to bed. What an hour for her to be up."

Angelo curtseyed and came to give Cosima attendance. At this point Leandro sprang from his chair and hurried forward. Sigismondo, humming in strong deprecation, drew him sharply away.

"Angela, the Lady Donati will certainly be waiting. See your mistress to her room."

Di Torre and Ugo Bandini were left on either side of the great hearth where the brazier stood. Sigismondo fed it with wood, and it gave out a grateful warmth in this hour before dawn.

Bandini took his son's face between his hands and kissed him on the brow. "You should rest, child. You are exhausted . . . and your hands are still bloodied."

"All is ready." Sigismondo opened the door, and Benno came in at once, laden with a vast swathed jug of steaming water. He set it down on the hearthstone and fetched a big earthenware basin glazed with a pattern of dolphins. He filled it with a splash that made the brazier hiss like a cross cat and stood back. The light caught his face, and di Torre started.

"What the devil is that rogue doing here?"

Sigismondo had observed that the sight of Benno seemed to

arouse in people the desire to kick him, or at least shout at him,
Di Torre, affronted at the vision now gaping amiably at him,
reached out and shook him hard. "Answer me!"

Sigismondo said, "He is one who risked his life to bring your
daughter back to you."

"He?" Di Torre stepped back. "He?" One might have thought
that he would on the whole rather not have had her back on
such unsanitary terms.

Sigismondo picked up the great cloak that lay on the bed
and brought it to Ugo Bandini, whose son was already peeling
off his shirt and preparing to wash, kneeling on the hearth.

"Sir, before light discovers you, you must be home. Whatever
you do, show no joy for what you have seen here. Continue to
mourn, and do exactly what you will be told to do. My man,
who brought you here, will come with word."

Bandini bent once more to kiss his son's face, wet though
it was, and then folded himself in the cloak.

"You too, my lord di Torre. You must return home."

"But my daughter? Am I not to remain to escort my
daughter?"

"You mistake, my lord." Sigismondo was benign. "You came
to see that she is safe. She can't return with you yet. There is
still at least one in your house who might betray that she is
there. Our enemy will not have relied only on the slave-girl.
They will be watching you. That was why you were brought
here in such secrecy and by a long route. I'm told that you
complained of it, but you do not know how much you have to
fear. Ever since we took the lady from Duke Francesco's power,
they will have looked for her to be brought back to you. Your
part in this is to do just as you engaged to do by him."

"By Duke Francesco?" Di Torre's face was that of acute
alarm, and he resisted Sigismondo's guidance towards the door.

"Do just as he bade you. Trust me."

"My daughter . . ."

"Is in her bed, in the room of the good lady who has taken such excellent care of her since her rescue." Sigismondo was as convincing with a disingenuous statement as with the truth.

They reached the outer door. There was some grunting as Bandini, even assisted by Sigismondo's arm, made work of getting from the high sill down to the street. A gruff young man in a hooded cloak, quite unrecognisable as the maidservant, was there to guide them both home, but he lunged at the wall and did not help. Bandini might have laughed as di Torre was helped down—his old enemy clinging to the door-jamb like a frantic old badger in his furs. Sigismondo closed the door softly, barred and bolted it, and returned upstairs.

Leandro lay on the bed. He had pushed back the covers but not pulled them over him. Sigismondo tucked them round him while Benno dealt with the basin and water-jug. Leandro roused a little. He had a thousand questions to ask, not least about Cosima, but the only one that was in the forefront of his mind and that he could, so to speak, lay hands on was, "What *is* my father to do tomorrow?"

"Tomorrow? It is today." Sigismondo drew the bed-curtain. "He too must do just what the Duke Francesco ordered."

"You *want* my father to commit treason?"

Sigismondo smiled. Leandro's tired mind attempted to wonder whose side Sigismondo was really on, but he slept.

20. "THERE IS HER MURDERER!"

Leandro woke, with the brisk resilience of youth, because of shouting in the street in the still early morning. He had a moment of disoriented wonder at the size of the place, the painted ceiling, the tester and his own ease. As a crescendo of shouting ended in a metallic clash, he rolled from bed, taking the padded quilt and swathing himself as he went, and peered through the shutters. Disappointingly, he saw only people running away, but in his mind was Sigismondo's *Riots will be provided.*

It was not unlike prison in two respects: it was cold, and he was hungry. He hurried to dress, found that the brazier was extinct but that there was a covered dish by the bed holding the chicken and bread he had been unable to eat the night before.

A third thing, he thought as he ate. I am still a prisoner. Whose?

He stopped eating of a sudden. Comfortable in his nest of quilt and pillows, he began to think about the day. His father and di Torre had to carry out the tasks Duke Francesco had laid on them. Whose agent *was* Sigismondo, after all?

It was inconceivable—surely—that he himself was destined to carry out what had been laid down for him this day? That his rescue was a cruel farce to ensure his father's obedience? And that incredible girl, could she really be Cosima di Torre? The old villain had not shown much affection for her. Was he acting a part?

Leandro lost his appetite again. He wrapped himself closer and brooded.

Jacopo di Torre refused his early sop and wine too. He stayed in his bed. The household had come to know that he had received the young mistress' hair; indeed they could scarcely have helped knowing from the outcry and wailing, the execrations of the Bandini, the broken crockery of that day. Now the steward reported that he was sitting holding the ribbon-threaded plaits with their little gold clasps. He had written letters with his own hand and his Councillor's seal and sent them.

Ugo Bandini had already left the city. He had the Duke's permission to do so, for the Duke's own implacable fury against the man had been softened by his brother's pleading. Paolo had prevailed on him to believe in Ugo's innocence of conspiracy with his son and not to force him to remain in the city during his son's execution. He was to take refuge in the country villa of a friend, and his pass allowed him out before dawn, riding with a laden pack-horse and a giant bodyguard.

The Lady Donati was waited on immediately after her morning devotions by the anxious steward, his wife and niece. The women were white as their caps. They apologised profusely. The niece wept. They could not—could not stay. It was the old master's chamber. They had been sweeping out the big dining room below for the lady . . . but they had heard it . . . footsteps! They came at once to see if the guests were all present or if it could be one of them in the master's chamber—and here they all were! Yet there had been—they had both heard it, and called the steward—he had heard it—they could not stay in the house—footsteps, soft, to and fro, in the room of the dead.

"Piero's sleeping it off late this morning," his mate said. "He'd better rouse up by the time the priest comes to young Bandini."

"Is it true Bandini had a whore in there last night?"

"There's a lad!"

"Horny young devil."

"Never. Piero wouldn't stand for that."

"With the Bandini's deep purse?"

"Did someone ought to take the lad's food along?"

"Piero don't like it. Let the young murderer go to his death fasting, anyway. Would you believe he was sleeping when I looked through the door? And what's the odds what he puts in his guts when they're going to be on view anyway?"

No one could speak to the Duke Ludovico that morning. He was in a savage temper. Even his brother steered clear of him. Only the Lady Violante, who was carrying her baby half-brother for an airing on the loggia, received a civil word when the Duke paused to look at his motherless heir. The attendant ladies drew well back. They knew that pallor and that falcon stare.

On the wide sills of a palazzo's barred windows, a woman had set up her wares, woven rush pokes and wicker baskets. Two of Duke Ippolyto's men paused, watched by those standing about.

"God in Heaven. What are these messy objects?"

"The people round here use them for hats, hadn't you noticed?"

As they went off laughing, one of the Palace dwarves reached up, tweaked at a basket and said in their very accent, "At home, of course, we use them for tableware. The gravy has to be ate off the cloth, of course . . ."

A roar of laughter followed the pair down the street, but they advisedly took no notice. This was not the time for brawls with the citizenry. The dwarf, wearing the basket as a hat, went on chatting to the amused little crowd.

Flags draped in black were climbing the poles round the great square. The palazzi hung out black-ribboned banners in due response. Stones and dirt were flung at the shut Palazzo Bandini, and a ballad-monger sang "Leandro's Lament," a maudlin confession, across the street:

> *And so repulsed*
> *By righteous chastity*
> *In vicious lust*
> *And cruel enmity*

> *I struck, O had my hand*
> *In palsy first been numb!*
> *And purple purple streams*
> *Now from her side did come . . .*

Here some officer of the Duke's, from either impatience or an informed taste, moved him on.

The morning advanced. The Lady Donati's chaplain performed an exorcism on the haunted chamber, to the great comfort of the steward's family. They all refused to assist, whether from fear of possession or terror of seeing the spirit they could not say.

The messages with di Torre's Council seal were received at the gates. Bandini and his escort came up with Il Lupo and his advancing mercenaries on the heathland not far from Duke Ludovico's border. The Cardinal Pontano presented the condolences of the Holy Father to Duke Ludovico; he had noticed, but did not mention, that blood was again being scrubbed from the Palace doors and threshold. He offered his own condolences to the Duke Ippolyto and assured him that all resentment at his family's bereavement must be assuaged by the very adequate reparation about to be made by the young Bandini.

He was not aware that the priest who had come to confess the young Bandini was being kept waiting because Piero, and Piero's keys, could not be found, and although Piero knew where other keys were kept, nobody else did. While the priest, calling through the judas in the cell door, attempted to rouse the sleeper, messengers were flying in search of the seneschal, the Duke's steward, the Duke's secretary and anyone else who might be held to know where keys were.

"Old Piero must've been on a hell of a toot," said the second jailer.

Leandro, recovering from the hysteria occasioned by Sigismondo's operations with sonorous Latin as he paced the room, sat in the chimney corner by the replenished brazier and, as the door shut, was locked and powerfully splashed with water, he listened to the last of the exorcism and spooned the soup which Sigismondo had also brought; and he realised, as he ate his way through the vegetables and bread with which the soup was furnished, that the morning was advancing. It made him pause. Sigismondo had come in, finger to sculptured lip, and had smiled benevolently, but his head had still that disturbing resemblance to an executioner's. Leandro felt that, in conjunction with the approaching noon, it quite put him off food. He contemplated the bowl and saw that the soup was almost gone, and wondered that he had so little sensibility. Cheerful sounds of cleaning came from the floor below, and from the street, shouting, chases, the crack and thud of thrown stones, a scream or two, more shouting, a rush of horses, orders being given; and behind all of it, the dull murmur of a crowd.

Perhaps an hour later, when the street had become quiet and the crowd louder, the lock clicked and Sigismondo entered. He was in the black boots, hose and jerkin in which Leandro had first seen him, though he also wore one loose black robe and carried another. He wore no shirt, which made him appear both more muscular and also more ruffianly.

"If you wear this and keep hooded, you may watch from the roof loggia," he said, and held out the robe. "The house is empty of servants; they've all gone to see you die."

Through the house Leandro went, treading the rough brownish marble of the upper stairs, finding his way by guess. He heard a door clang shut below. He came out at last under the tiles on an open gallery, to find Cosima sitting beside a comfortable, handsome woman who greeted him warmly as her guest. Behind them, eating something from an earthenware jar, was the scruffy little man whose appearance suggested attendance on horses rather than ladies. A cheerful one-eared dog, grubby and curly, came bustling to investigate him.

"Sit here," said Cosima di Torre. "There's a perfect view of the scaffold."

They could see the upper part of the square, the face of the new Palace and the Cathedral, the side of the old castle. The baroque façades facing them had each a balcony across the *piano nobile*. On the Palace balcony, benches and velvet chairs had been placed, and some of the Duke's guard stood there. The Cathedral balcony was filling with clerics. Minor members of the Court had emerged into the sunlight from the apartment behind the balcony, like those too early for a party. Two came out on the apron that was the scaffold, looked at the garrotting post and made exaggerated gestures of horror. Leandro wrapped his borrowed cloak more tightly round him and wished he owned a less active imagination, one which would not so persistently confront him with images of himself in the stages of being slowly strangled.

"I've never seen an execution," Cosima remarked, "and now I'm not going to." He thought she need not have sounded so regretful.

The Lady Donati was busy netting. "I don't go any more. When you've seen one, you've seen them all." She offered them marzipan.

More of the Court appeared. The Lady Violante, sumptuously enfolded in black velvet dagged with gold, stood talking. The crowd suddenly booed, and she turned and, from her posture, was doing the same: up from below had come the executioner, masked and brawny, and his assistant, slight and with golden hair on his neck under the leather cap. He unrolled a black bundle and laid out an array of instruments.

"I'm glad Hubert's arrangement with the Duke's headsman came off all right," remarked the Lady Donati.

"That's *Sigismondo?*" Cosima all but squealed.

The Duke Ludovico and his brother-in-law, Duke Ippolyto, appeared in the long windows. White and green banners flared out beneath the trumpets, and a fanfare sounded. There was cheering in the crowd, but also an underburden of discontent, a subterranean tremor. The Lord Paolo joined them and this time there came enthusiastic cheers. The royal party sat, the Duke signalled, and the assistant went to call the accused.

People craned to be the first to see, so that the whole crowd seemed to lean forward.

A man in the Duke's livery appeared from below. He approached the balcony, knelt, and spoke to the Duke, who leant to hear him. A note of speculation swept through the crowd.

"Bit late," Benno said. "Looks like they've only just found you've gone missing."

"They'll have found Piero," Cosima said. "It must have been a perfectly revolting surprise."

Sigismondo stood gravely waiting, arms folded. He did not move in the slightest. Crouched over the instruments, Angelo waited, the breeze stirring the golden fronds on his neck.

The Lord Paolo leant to speak to his brother, and then advanced. He raised his arms, and the crowd slowly obeyed him. He looked round the great piazza, at the crowded windows, the side streets where armed men seemed to be pressing in through the crowds there like dark tributaries to a lake. Finally his voice rang out.

"People of Rocca! The wretched boy accused of this terrible murder is not here . . ."

An outbreak of indignation was hushed among the crowd as Paolo again raised his arms.

"But I tell you that the true murderer *is* here, is present in this place. The vile deed robbed you and all of us of a kind and loved benefactress. I cannot tell you with what unwillingness I speak or how I grieve, but I saw her die and can no longer hold my tongue. There, there is her murderer—*her husband*—"

His outflung hand pointed.

21. "MY SON, WHAT HAVE YOU DONE?"

A roar came from the crowd, an animal howl. The Duke was on his feet and had advanced. Duke Ippolyto, sword drawn, ran forward, overtook him and turned, sword arm back for a thrust. A swirl of black velvet had followed him, and Violante's hands fastened on his sword arm. He swung round, lost his balance and thudded to the boards, Violante falling on him kicking and shouting, her grasp relentless as he tried to free himself and rise. The Duke had turned and gone into the Palace, with Paolo after him. Sigismondo and Angelo leapt the struggling royal scuffle that had hampered Paolo and pursued, Sigismondo's guise cleaving a way before him as if he used the axe he now suddenly carried, his grip near its head.

The Duke, entering the gallery behind the balcony, found not the sea green and white of his guards, but his brother's slate blue and sulphur livery, on men who closed on him as if on a criminal; but he was armed, and not only with his sword. One man fell back on meeting his imperious eyes. He ran their leader through and fled on up the room, a confused pursuit at his heels. Without pausing, he sliced the cord holding the door-curtain, which closed on the foremost man behind him. Others thrust by, until the man in the curtain convulsively pulled it all down. Paolo and two of his guards had got through; two agile black-clad men leapt over this second confusion and gained on the chase.

A vertiginous flight of rose marble led down on the right. One of Paolo's men lost his footing and brilliantly overtook the Duke, but not in any position to apprehend him. The Duke also shed his cloak on the stairs, a vast hazard of fur and purple which slithered after him. Sigismondo leapt it and landed soft on the reviving guard at the foot. Angelo followed him. Behind them streamed a trail of courtiers, a mêlée of guards in the two colours who at least knew whom to fight, and at the stairfoot all these were joined by a covey of dwarves who brought down a dozen of them before anyone knew. The rest fell over these.

The Duke had gone ahead into the Cathedral.

His running feet startled the priests round the Duchess' bier; his drawn sword startled them more. Tebaldo struggled to stand at the prie-Dieu in a side chapel. The priests scattered, shouting interdictions. The Duke paused by the catafalque, lowering his blade as if he believed that here no one would attack him. He breathed hard. As Paolo approached he called in stupefaction, "Why did you say that? Brother—"

For answer, Paolo attacked.

Having said what he had said, there was no option open to him but that. He could hear the massive shout in the square. The shout was for the Duke and not for him. He had heard it when he stood on the scaffold and Ippolyto's blow was foiled. The mercenaries surging from the side streets had not roared *Paolo* as they were paid to do. It rang in his ears now: "Duca, Duca! Lu-do-vi-co!"

They fought. As they circled and swung and parried, priests, one with a processional cross, hovered around them, moving as they moved, trying to get up courage to run in and part them. A pair of shadows stalked beyond. The Duchess lay in her black velvet, remote and pale. A tall gilt candle-holder, touched by a working elbow, rocked, swayed and crashed. Angelo had been poised with his knife; he jinked and altered aim, altered it again as they circled. Wax spread on the floor, cooling at once. The Duke's boot stamped, slipped, and he was down, his sword sliding away across the marble. A priest ran in, but Paolo stood over his brother, sword raised.

"Father!"

Tebaldo, incredulous, came limping across the floor. Paolo sprang up. In that instant his sword hand was nailed to the Duchess' coffin by a thrown knife.

The Duke rolled clear. Paolo wrenched out the knife, dripping blood, and turned on his brother, who, seizing Paolo's sword from the floor, ran him through the neck as Sigismondo's axe clove his spine.

Paolo toppled across the coffin, gripped the far edge and fell. His blood ran over the pearl-sewn dress, the velvet pall. As a priest tried to right the tilting coffin, the body rose up. Paolo and the dead Duchess fell to the floor. Pearls bowled among the watchers' feet, some leaving little red trails, some like tears.

They arrived then, priests from the Cathedral balcony, embouching from the tower stairs. The Cardinal Pontano, as he came, gave directions, pointing. Two priests hurried ahead, passing the catafalque and the ghastly tableau with amazed stares and swift crossing, but not halting until they reached the altar. There, one removed the Host and hurried away with it. The other lowered and extinguished the lamp that was burning. The Cathedral must be reconsecrated.

The Duke stood, his gaze on Paolo's sprawled figure. Sigismondo did not move. Still masked, he leant on the long handle of his bloodstained axe, a headsman who had dared to desecrate this place in the sight of all. The Cardinal came forward; priests flooded round the group but kept their distance as from a plague.

The Duke's guards held crossed pikes at the foot of the Palace stairs against the press of people there. Outside there was a trampling on the steps of the Cathedral beyond the great doors, and the clamour of the crowd, cries and screams, and the steady undertone of "Duca! Duca!"

The Duke's sword shifted at a spasm of his arm, and blood slid from it.

"My son, what have you done?"

The Duke did not answer or stir until the Cardinal put a hand on his shoulder and repeated the question. Then he turned his head as if in a dream.

"He tried to kill me. Paolo! Who loved me."

"No, Your Grace." The headsman, sonorous in that echoing space, answered. "He conspired to overthrow you and rule Rocca in your stead. He did not love you."

Cardinal Pontano's face was normally dour and now grim. "It is not to be believed. Have you proof of it?"

Sigismondo stripped the mask from his face and said, "I can prove it."

"Let the relics of Saint Agnes be brought," said the Cardinal. "Any speech now must be upon oath."

A shout from the door drew their eyes as the Duke Ippolyto and the Lady Violante were allowed past the guard. He still held a drawn sword, the lady still gripped his arm; she wore a small grimace like a feral cat. They halted at the sight—the Duke and the bodies tumbled before him. The Duchess lay, eyes still closed but mouth ajar as if in protest. Her husband's brother lay across her body in the gathering pool of his blood, his cloth of gold sleeves and her velvet skirts innocently drinking it in.

"Mother of God!"

The Cardinal now held out in both hands a flat box that gleamed with a crust of rubies and diamonds.

"Your Grace: the blessed relics of Saint Agnes will be your witness. If you are clear of this blood, call on God on the bones of His holy saint."

The Duke stooped to lay his sword on the stones, then he pulled off his glove and laid his hand on the golden box.

"I swear, before God and His saint, and as I hope for redemption, that I am not guilty of my wife's blood. Of my brother's death I am guilty. Why he would have killed me I do not yet understand."

Sigismondo moved again, and his deep voice sounded. "With Your Grace's leave and that of His Eminence: Rocca must be assured that its rightful Duke lives and the traitor is dead."

"Traitor . . ."

There was a whimper. Tebaldo was helping himself along by the bier, his face agonised, his stare fixed on his father's body. He took a step away from the bier and fell on his knees, putting a hand to the floor as he reached the other to his father's hand limp in its blood. His choked voice was the sound of animal mourning.

Violante left Duke Ippolyto and ran to Tebaldo. "No, no. Come with me. Father, I'll vouch for him. Let him come with me."

At this appeal to his power, the Duke seemed to wake. The habit of authority returned. "He is released into your custody. His guilt or innocence will be examined. Sigismondo, take"— he pointed to his brother's body—"take him out there and let the people see. We shall appear ourselves here on the Cathedral balcony. Once this uproar is calmed we can begin an immediate inquest into this terrible matter."

Ippolyto helped Violante to lead her cousin aside. A page in slate blue and yellow crept forward, trembling, to lend his arm to the boy. The two Dukes and the Cardinal swept away towards the turret stair, and Sigismondo took up Paolo's body—Tebaldo turning his head for a last desperate gaze. The priests were left to their task of restoring the Duchess to the catafalque and preparing to carry it to the Palace chapel as fast as possible from this unhallowed ground; and at last an old priest came out in a sacking apron, with bucket and cloth, to clean the terrible stain away.

22. AFTER THE DEVIL, THE DEAD MAN

"Dear God, what is happening?" Cosima cried.

The crowd was shouting—they had answered Paolo's speech with the shout; it had started from the edges and the side alleys—"Duca! Duca! Lu-do-vi-co!"

"Why do they shout for the Duke?" the Lady Donati asked. "Do they want to kill him?"

"Who was Sigismondo chasing?" Leandro asked. "Whose side is he on? I thought he was the Duke's man."

The crowd, at first bewildered, had taken up the shout with vigour. They had surged up the steps to the closed door of the Cathedral.

"Benno, lean out at the corner there and look down our alley. Was that Barley I saw on the roan?"

"Barley," Benno affirmed. Biondello, who had reacted badly to looking at the drop to the street, rammed his face into the recesses of Benno's shirt

Leandro rivetted his attention on those unresponsive ornamental façades, the Palace, the Cathedral, that hid his fate. He imagined Sigismondo failing, himself hunted down. He found he was grasping Cosima's hand too hard, and as he apologised they looked into each other's eyes for a moment. A rush of thoughts dazed him. Cosima *di Torre* . . . Sigismondo said the feud's a fake . . . She's lovely, she's brave . . . married in the cell . . . but it's a fake . . . danger . . . marriage . . . What's to become of us? What's Sigismondo *doing*?

"Oh!" cried Cosima, "look!"

The trumpets were being raised; the dignitaries emerged on the Cathedral balcony, the Duke—even from here startlingly pale—the Cardinal beside him, the Duke Ippolyto and a crowd of clerics. A file of men in green and white came out on the Palace balcony. Two of them shifted the scattered benches and chairs, then joined the line. The crowd's noise dropped in anticipation of an event, and Sigismondo appeared masked in the Palace doorway, Paolo's body in his arms. The crowd seemed to take one breath. He crossed the balcony onto the scaffold and laid the body down on the straw. He nodded to the drummers below, who, all but caught out by the signal after so long, started raggedly but picked up into their steady rattling beat. Angelo appeared, carrying the axe across both hands, and came forward. The crowd swayed with internal dissensions, but their noise was lost in the shuddering of the drums.

Sigismondo took the axe and struck before they knew he would do it. He stooped, and as he rose the drums stopped. His left hand held Paolo's head by the hair, and his voice rang out, measured and very loud, so that it came clearly to those on the loggia.

"Behold the head of a traitor."

Although the response of the crowd was undecided, overwhelmingly from the outskirts came the cry of "Duca!" Sigismondo raised both arms; although the dead face of Paolo confronted them with a sluggish drip of blood, they slowly obeyed the signal and the shouts died into an expectant quiet.

"A traitor to his Duke; falsely accusing his own brother; giving the Duke's alms in his own name to corrupt your hearts; falsely brewing hatred among you; falsely buying powerful men by abducting their children; a traitor who at last drew sword on the Duke, his brother, and would have killed him. May all traitors have such an end!"

The crashing roar of the Duke's name responded. Anyone who might be inclined to disbelieve now had the sense to keep his ideas to himself. Among those who did not shout was a man whose child, hoisted on his shoulders for a good view, had been sick on his head at sight of Paolo's. The crowd turned towards the Duke on the Cathedral balcony, and threw up their caps and cheered. The Duke acknowledged this expression of their confidence, and bore it for all of four minutes. Then he withdrew.

The Duke sat in robes of sable and burgundy, silent at the centre of the Council table, pale and haggard against his high collar, the dark carving of the chair of state, and behind that the dark arras, where a different kind of judgement was being enacted. Paris, lolling against a tree trunk, offered the golden apple to Venus, her voluptuous back modestly turned towards the Council chamber, while Minerva and Juno resentfully resumed their draperies. Sigismondo, facing the table in his own black clothes, which seemed to melt into the shadows, may have mused that the subject of the tapestry, being the exercise of power in bribery and corruption, had some relevance to what was before this Court today.

The Cardinal, his robes bright as blood where the light caught them, sat on the Duke's right. On his left, Duke Ippolyto with a dark troubled face gazed towards the high windows and twitched at the ribbons of his sleeve. He had come for an execution and his sister's funeral. So far, although an execution had in sort taken place, he had a sense that his sister's honour, and therefore his own, was to be in question.

"Whom are we to hear first?" The Duke's voice at its best was seldom less than harsh. It was near its worst now.

"By your leave, the Lady Cecilia, Her Grace's mistress of the robes."

The Duke nodded, and Sigismondo went to rap at the door and usher in the Lady Cecilia, who appeared there. She came forward, her black brocade stiffly brushing the floor, her golden hair in a net of silver and pearls, to sit on the tapestry-covered stool facing them. In spite of her skill at maquillage, swollen eyes bore their witness to her distress and, perhaps, fear. Sigismondo stood beside her. The Duke stirred, sighed and spoke as if constrained to, as though, like his brother-in-law, he was reluctant to know what must now be known.

"Sigismondo, you have leave to question."

Acknowledging this, Sigismondo turned to the lady.

"Had Her Grace arranged to meet someone during your wedding feast?"

"Her Grace would not do such a thing."

He turned to the tribunal and said, "It would be best if the Lady Cecilia were to answer on oath."

The relics of Saint Agnes were no doubt locked again in their chapel. The Cardinal lifted the chain of his pectoral cross over his head and leant to lay the crucifix on the table's far side. "Come, daughter. We are here for the truth."

She rose, but faltered. Sigismondo's hand under her arm took her the few paces to the table, where she laid her hand on the crucifix and repeated the oath as the Cardinal dictated it. The Duke's eyes watched her; his thoughts were not to be fathomed. The oath would force a truth from her that he could not want to hear.

She took her place once more. The aqueous shimmer of the pearls on her bodice showed that she breathed fast and shallowly.

"Had Her Grace," came the inexorable question, "arranged to meet someone during your wedding feast?"

The lady's answer was almost too faint to hear, but it was "Yes."

"Was this an assignation of love?"

"Yes."

"Who was it whom she had arranged to meet?"

"I—she's dead, my lords. Does it need . . . ?"

The Duke, at his harshest, said, "Answer!" and she obeyed almost below her breath. "The Lord Paolo."

The Duke withdrew his attention from her and looked at the pattern of the carpet on the table. He seemed to withdraw more than that. He had known from Sigismondo that there had been a lover, and he was now facing the deeper betrayal.

Ippolyto suddenly asked, "Was this the only time? Had they met so before?"

"She . . . I . . . Your Grace knows I was her friend, her best friend since we were girls at your father's court—"

"Had she lovers *then?*"

"No! No, His Grace knows she was pure virgin on her marriage. I meant, I meant that I loved her."

"So did I. For the pity of God, will you answer the question?"

"She had met him so before."

"Were there others?"

The Lady Cecilia closed her mouth and shook her head. It might have been denial of other lovers or denial of any answer. Sigismondo's question was soft and almost negligent. "By Your Grace's leave—was Leandro Bandini one?"

"Never! That? Hardly out of boyhood!"

After a second's silence she put her hand over her mouth. It was clear that she saw what she had admitted.

"Enough." The Duke's hand was clenched on the table. He had been staring at the cloth as though he tried to find a meaning in the pattern, but now he shot a look of bleak distaste at her. "Woman: take care that I never see you again."

Sigismondo took her to the door. She walked as if in her sleep, and when they reached the door he had to guide her through it. As he shut the door the Duke said, "What more must we hear?"

"Cousin." The Duke Ippolyto spoke. "Truth may not be sweet, but it must be found."

"Shall we know it, when it's found? I thought, all my life, that my brother was Truth's own self." The Duke subsided into silence, moving his fingers in the pile of the cloth.

Sigismondo moved, his heel sharp on the marble, and said, "The Lady Cecilia spoke of the arranging of an assignation, Your Grace. The Wild Man was to spoil the dress by kicking the wine over so that Her Grace should have reason to retire."

The Duke's head came up. "Leandro Bandini was in my brother's pay! So, all along, he knew he was to be rescued and the blame thrown on me. Where is he skulking? I will banish every Bandini in Rocca."

"Your Grace, I have the Wild Man here." He opened the door.

The Duke sat forward. The Cardinal even put a hand to his cross as, outlined by the light from the anteroom, stood a shaggy figure dark as the Devil himself. It came forward to stand before the tribunal and, at a word from Sigismondo, took off its head as neatly as any executioner. Long golden hair shone in the sunlight of early evening, around a face Piero della Francesca would have delighted to paint. The devil was an angel disguised. Without knowing it, the three men looking at him were already disposed to believe this heavenly messenger.

"This was the Wild Man, Your Grace, who danced at the Lady Cecilia's wedding feast. Hired by Niccolo the festaiuolo, he was paid also by one of Lord Paolo's men to kick over the wine-cup."

"So he worked for my brother, did he?" The Duke's tone was ominous, and Sigismondo interposed.

"He did not know that, Your Grace. He was told it was for a jest and, when he protested that the Duchess would be angry at the ruin of her dress, he was told she was party to the jest."

"Where did the skin for Bandini come from? It could not be the same."

"There were several in the festaiuolo's store. He told me he cannot always protect them from theft, and the Lord Paolo's men were very helpful over the entertainments." Sigismondo was assisting Angelo out of the skin, and now he stood, clothed in blue, in that chamber hung with dark tapestry and draped in black, more than ever a creature of the sky. The Cardinal addressed him.

"Tell us what happened that night."

Angelo told, succinctly, the light a halo in his hair, how he had danced, spilt the drink, been chased out, had changed his clothes, been paid, and had seen his paymaster burn the bundle of the skin and then follow him off of the Palace grounds. "I tried to throw him off, but he followed. I ran, but he gained on me. I don't know this town. He brought me down, and so I fought and killed him."

There was no flicker on Sigismondo's face to say this was not the tale he had heard, that Angelo, knowing he was followed, had lain in wait and knifed his pursuer without valediction. Such embroideries as this made the incident more forgivable to earthly justice.

"How are we to know that the man was Paolo's?"

"I can't tell, sir," said the angel, humbly. "He wore no badge or livery; as we fought, though, this chain came off his neck. It may be it's known to someone."

He pulled from his pocket, and put down on the table, a thin double-twist silvergilt chain, broken, with a curious *memento mori* pendant of a small ivory skull with deep-set ruby eyes.

The Duke said in a voice without feeling, "One of my brother's most constant attendants wears one such. Giannini, Giacomino, something of that sound. They are all in custody. It can be seen if he is missing."

"So, you have found the dancer."

Sigismondo said, "Do my lords wish to question him more?" and as they made no answer the Duke waved dismissal. Angelo withdrew his celestial presence. The little skull lay on the cloth beside the Cardinal's crucifix.

"We have, my lords, one man who cannot speak because he is dead. Another whose story is necessary at this juncture is also dead. It may be, however, that His Grace has the power to resurrect him."

"Have a care, my son," said the Cardinal smoothly.

"Were he alive, my lords, this witness would be a dead man." The Duke frowned, but his quick glance at Sigismondo showed a face serious and considerate. The play on words certainly was not an effort to joke on a subject so grave. "He would be hanged for theft, and his witness is such that he would tremble for his life, did he live, at the telling of it."

"This doubly dead man can be revived?" the Duke Ippolyto enquired.

"I see that, if he lived, he would require a pardon for theft and an assurance of indemnity for what he might speak." The Duke, however stunned by grief he might be, was as quick of apprehension as ever. He regarded Sigismondo with an unfathomable blue stare. "A pardon for theft is not a heavy matter, but if he speaks the truth and trembles to tell it, against whom does he speak? Ourself? My innocence has been in question. The truth can only clear it. Why does this dead man tremble?"

"Your Grace, he speaks against the dead."

After a moment the Duke Ippolyto said, "All of us here now know that my sister was an adulteress. This witness could scarcely defame her."

"By digging out the mud, we shall come to clear water," said the Cardinal.

"Let us hear your dead man, Sigismondo. Truth should be worth a pardon. If I do not promise him his life, what then?"

"If Your Grace will not promise it, he may not have it." Sigismondo bowed and spread deprecating hands. "He cannot live."

"In the wars in Germany you saved my life," said the Duke, "and you have served me well now; or I tell you, you should not bargain with me. He shall have his life. Let him come."

Sigismondo bowed once more, not a courtier's bow, but a back bent in response to a concession not willingly granted. He went to the door and disappeared beyond it.

The Cardinal remarked, "The reconsecration of the Cathedral requires some days. I would suggest that the obsequies of the late Duchess take place in the Palace chapel."

"If that satisfies Her Grace's brother."

"God works all for the best." Ippolyto sighed. "Diminished pomp is more to my mind, as things stand."

The door and curtain opened. Sigismondo was standing aside to admit a hesitant and desperately anxious dwarf.

After the Devil, the dead man.

23. NO ONE IS WHAT THEY SEEM.

Under the scrubby beard Poggio had industriously started to grow as a disguise, he was sweating heavily, and all the lines of his face, round eyes and a mouth Nature had designed to turn happily upward, looked stretched by fear. His hands knotted themselves together before him.

The Duke regarded him for a long moment and then spoke.

"You have our pardon, Poggio, for your theft." His voice sharpened. "Now earn it."

"Tell His Grace how you came to hear what passed in Her Grace's chamber the night of her death."

Plaiting and unplaiting his fingers, Poggio told. He explained his need for the Duchess' favour and how he had hidden in the inner room while the waiting-women were there. He was pitiably embarrassed over the extreme necessity for tact over what he had heard, but Sigismondo's questions, unemphatic, insistent, got the truth: he had been on the very point of emerging to speak to the Duchess when he heard her greet someone. The newcomer had spoken softly but was a man. Poggio feared to make a sound by shutting the jib door, and so he had unavoidably heard. They had made love. He could—though he tried not to hear—distinguish two voices, at least, two . . . He foundered at this point and Sigismondo suggested "the sounds of two persons"—yes, the sounds of two people, until at last one of them had given an odd cry, a strange, short cry; then, there was silence. After a moment, someone, breathing hard, had crossed the matting of the floor. Yes, he had heard more. At ease over this part, although puzzled, he said he had heard curtains drawn, then a brief scuffling and a sound as if something had been thrown on the bed. Then the curtains again, and silence.

The silence, made deeper by the rattle of fireworks, had gone on until he thought it safe to venture out. The Duchess lay there, her hand over the side of the bed. He thought she slept and he began to creep past her. He knew he could not approach her now, in case she might guess he knew of her lover. He never thought it could be the Duke, as they were so hurried and spoke so low. He looked up to check that she slept and saw the knife. It stuck—

"His Grace saw the knife," Sigismondo interrupted. "What did you do, when you knew she was dead?"

Poggio looked up anxiously at Sigismondo, transferred his gaze to the Duke and said, "I took her ring and I ran." For this, at least, he had a pardon.

The Duke brooded. Duke Ippolyto studied Poggio's face as if to estimate his truth—Poggio licked his lips and fortunately decided not to smile at him. The Cardinal stroked the cross that still lay on the table.

"You heard nothing after this—cry—and the noise of something being thrown on the bed?" The Duke had gone unerringly to the heart of the matter. He had been listening to witnesses for a good many years, and omissions of truth may have become apparent to his ear. Now he watched Poggio, who was unwise enough to put on an expression of childlike innocence.

"What I have said, Your Grace. No more."

"No one could have entered after that without your hearing?"

Poggio, relieved that he could answer this in complete sincerity, did so. He had not been asked if anyone actually *had* come in, so he had no need to mention the Lady Violante. His private devotion to her and his desire to keep her out of any possible trouble with her father would not have stood up to even the threat of torture, but so far none had been made, and his trust in Sigismondo was profound.

"Do you swear on the Cross that the witness you have given is true?"

Poggio ducked respectfully as the Cardinal moved the crucifix towards him. The sun that had shone on Angelo's hair was now lower. It struck rainbow sparks from the diamonds and rubies embedded in the gold, eclipsed by Poggio's hand as he laid it on the figure and swore.

The Duke spoke.

"Go. You have our pardon, but not our leave to be in Rocca. By the third day from now, your pardon fails and your life with it if you are found here."

Poggio's scramble for the door indicated that he was starting his exile on the double.

When the door was shut after him, the Duke called for wine, as if to help them swallow all that they had heard that afternoon. Sigismondo conveyed the message and brought the wine when it came, the golden tray with three jewelled cups, the flagon of gold and crystal. The Duke moved to the long window that overlooked the square, and opened the casement for a view uninterrupted by the Rocca arms in burgundy and ochre stained glass. The sound of crowds outside, which had been so aggressively loud in the Cathedral, had dwindled all the time since, and now, instead of a turbulent sea of heads with a spume of arms, the great empty shore of stone was left, with only a few knots of people. The largest tidewrack was round the scaffold where were still displayed the head and body of their Duke's brother, the lately loved and charitable traitor. This group seemed to be silent, and as members of it moved away they were replaced by others as silent. Children were lifted up for a better look, but when one was held out to touch the bloody hair, one of the Duke's men on the scaffold fended the child's hand away with a nudge of his halberd's butt. The Duke's eyes had lingered, but now his regard ranged to the outskirts of the square, decorated by lounging archers. They stood or sat and leant on walls.

"Sigismondo."

"Your Grace." He was nearby. The Duke's quick turn of the head showed he had thought him to be across the room.

"Those men?"

"They were the men who started the cry of *Duca!*"

"Are we to hear why?"

"All is open to Your Grace."

The Duke regarded him for a moment and then gave a quick nod. Turning, he swung back to the table as if he would now, at once, bring this enquiry to a conclusion.

"So, my lords. We are to believe, from what we have heard, that my brother paid an entertainer to make pretext for the Duchess to lie with him in secret while I and the Court watched the fireworks; that then he murdered her. The dwarf seems to have heard my brother put Leandro Bandini on the bed. Why did the boy not struggle? Why was he not there when she was found?"

"Because he did struggle, Your Grace. Drugged by the mulled wine offered him by Lord Paolo's man—who wore, he recalled, a chain with a little skull on it"—they all glanced at the necklace that still lay where Angelo had left it—"Leandro Bandini had not quite succumbed when he was brought to Her Grace's chamber to be hidden there. The blow on the brow did indeed come from either her mirror or the candlestick found on the floor, but she did not inflict it. He was knocked unconscious and hidden under the curtains on the far side of the bed, on the floor, before Her Grace came up from the feast."

"She did not see him."

"He lay between the bed and the curtains, Your Grace. Lord

Paolo, after he had done what was planned," and Sigismondo's even tone made nothing significant in the words, "had only to drag him out and put him on the bed. He was not quite as unconscious as they may have thought, as he had some memory, when I spoke to him that night, of the Duchess lying there. In his horror, he tried to come to his senses more fully. It seems he struggled to move, perhaps to draw away from Her Grace, and rolled off the bed into the oblivion where he was found. I saw that the curtains were pulled taut on that side as if something held them to the floor."

The Duke laughed, an unattractive sound. "So my brother was right to proclaim him innocent. If I had found him where he was meant to lie, I would have his blood on my hands." He looked down at them speculatively. Then, turning to Ippolyto, he asked, "Are you satisfied?"

"I have no more to ask. She brought her own death, Cousin, deceived as everyone was by that serpent."

Ippolyto held out his own hands, fine-boned, wiry, to clasp those of the Duke, who, looking at him closely and seeing in his eyes those amber-brown depths that had once delighted him in Ippolyto's sister, drew him into an embrace to disguise his desire never to see him again. The Cardinal smiled that such great men were at peace, and resumed his great cross again, the weight slithering to rest on the scarlet watered silk. Sigismondo had disappeared beyond the door curtain, and the low vibration of his tones could just be heard.

"Tomorrow we shall see the Duchess buried. Tonight, let us dine together in celebration of our renewed alliance."

The Cardinal improved the occasion, lifting his hand in blessing. "Amity is pleasing to God, my sons. May you flourish in such harmony." Rustling out, the Church took precedence over the temporal powers, and benevolently proffered a ring towards Sigismondo, who knelt to kiss it.

One temporal power, after seeing the other out, remained

and beckoned. Sigismondo closed the door and returned. The Duke leant against the table in the last of the evening sun.

"You were to tell me, Sigismondo, your final secrets. To whom do I owe my duchy?"

"Like so many sovereigns, Your Grace: to mercenaries."

"Those men round the square, the men who cried *Duca* and took the crowd with them?"

"The same. They, in conjunction with your marshal, are in control. Those who were paid by the Lord Paolo now no longer dare to speak."

"Mercenaries don't act on promises. They were paid. Who paid them?" The Duke reached out and closed a hand on the black velvet sleeve. The face attentive to his was strangely reassuring; hooked nose; thick-lashed eyes, dark and intent; the mouth with the sensually curved upper lip full above the restraint of the lower one, a mouth for secrets, a mouth that now smiled with deep amusement.

"Your Grace: Bandini. Ugo Bandini paid the mercenaries."

The Duke, willing enough by now to believe Sigismondo, leant back and stared into the smiling eyes. "*Bandini*. When I was about to have his son executed? God's teeth, what's his reason?"

"Loyalty, Your Grace. He had been approached by Duke Francesco to pay the mercenaries in his name; and he, on gaining the city, would free his son; but instead, Bandini paid them to shout *Duca Ludovico*. If they had shouted *Duca Paolo*, as was their original order . . ." Sigismondo paused and hummed, with foreboding of what might have been.

"I would be dead. Even if Paolo had died too, Rocca would have been held for Francesco. I owe Bandini my life, then." He gripped his lower lip between thumb and forefinger and mused, then shot out a finger and prodded the broad chest. "You. You know more than you've yet told me. How did that boy escape from my dungeons? It seems to me that his delivery from death predated by a few hours this loyal gesture of his father's. Would you say that?" Prodding Sigismondo's chest repeatedly, he began to laugh.

"Impossible to deceive Your Grace."

"And where is the boy? The innocent boy? Are you going to tell me that, you villain?"

"Why, Your Grace—he and his father will be among the first to congratulate you."

The Duke's laughter had more than a touch of hysteria in it.

"I forbade them the Palace, tried to take the life of one of them, and now I am to embrace them as my saviours! Has the world any more surprises for me today? No one is what they seem. Next you'll be telling me that *di Torre* is hand-in-glove with the Bandini to uphold me in Rocca!"

24. THE PROMISE OF VENUS

It was a problem in tact. The festaiuolo, ready packed to go home to Florence, unpacked everything and sat with a flask of inspiration and a ragged bundle of old pageant notes, cobbling up and casting a spectacle which celebrated the triumph of Justice and Right without personifying Wrong. He looked regretfully at Envy's iron teeth in their little rush basket—wholly relevant to the late traitor, but impossible to use. And that dancer who had caused so much trouble had presented himself again for employment, with the reasonable remark that nobody had seen his face last time . . . and it was too true that there was a lack of full-sized skilful dancers, although a plethora of small people expected to be used—and no help to be got as before from these useful men of the Lord Paolo's.

The Duke's marshal, dealing with the useful men, found those who were willing, and likely, to die before implicating the Lord Paolo in anything but excessive philanthropy and a disinterested concern for justice; and those who were willing, and zealous, in implicating the Lord Paolo, their colleagues, friends, enemies, officers and grandmothers in corruption, perfidy, sodomy and treason. The marshal did manage to establish that old Matteo di Torre, whose encounter with a dish of scallops had set off the feud, had certainly been sitting next to Ugo Bandini, but on his right had been the Lord Paolo. Hindsight is a marvellous clarifier of situations.

Sigismondo, escorting Leandro openly through the streets to his father's house, delivered him at the door to an incoherent Ugo with the words *"Tutum patris te limine sistam,"* which reprise of the *sortes Virgilianae* did not strike either of them at the time;

nor that in this promise of Venus to Aeneas, the Goddess of Love had assumed one of her more interesting disguises in the person of Sigismondo. Ugo embraced his son, embraced Sigismondo, re-embraced Leandro, and led them both in under the Titans, who seemed today almost easily to support the Bandini arms. In the comparative privacy of his library, Bandini, after a Herculean effort at breaking his son's ribs in another embrace, wept and thanked Sigismondo and then, in a belated hurry, the saints and the Trinity. He would have given Sigismondo half his wealth, he exclaimed, had he not disbursed it too recently to Il Lupo and his band. What was left, although it was negligible, was all at Sigismondo's service. Sigismondo obligingly said that his satisfaction lay in restoring Leandro to, so literally he might have added, his father's bosom. Ugo thereupon took off a massy gold chain, of a design amazingly complex, with plaques of enamelled allegorical beasts and lumps of jewellery, and put it on Sigismondo, across whose shoulders and chest it looked remarkably at home.

The feast a few days after the Duchess' interment was private and unostentatious. The Duke had expected Ippolyto to leave after the funeral, but he stayed and went hunting with the Lady Violante, so the feast had to include him. The Bandini and di Torre representatives were invited.

Cosima, not at all enjoying being back at home, was particularly bored at the prospect of dining yet again with her aunt when everyone was at the Palace. Her aunt had done nothing but ask questions ever since her return, exactly as if she suspected that Cosima had in fact spent a night alone with two men. She wondered what was to happen to her and if anything ever would. There was no likelihood of seeing Leandro again, and now he knew that she was a di Torre he would not think about her at all. It was true that Sigismondo had called the feud a false one, but feelings did not so quickly alter; that is, men's feelings. What would he have said to her that night, when

Sigismondo stopped him from coming towards her? By now, of course, he would have had time to reflect how very unfittingly she had behaved. He'd taken it for granted that she must be a common girl hired by his father.

At least Sigismondo would not tell the Duke that her father and Bandini were prepared to be traitors. She need not fear that, but if her father ever found out what she, his sequestered and modest daughter, had really done, he would think a convent, in earnest, the only place for her. At least if he ever married her to someone she would have a married woman's freedom and might actually see Leandro again. It would be much better if she could only stop thinking about him.

The elderly waiting-woman her father had supplied in place of poor Sascha came squawking in. "There's no time to sit dreaming! Quick, quick! Your best dress. Come along, m'lady. Let's have that gown off you."

"Why—"

"Your father's orders! What sort of thing is 'Why?', eh?"

Confused, Cosima pulled laces undone.

Il Lupo, with a handsome present from the Duke and a skinful of wine, with the help of Sigismondo-Martin and Barley, rode off a little carefully, scarred and saturnine, at the head of his men, towards a promising war in the south. His men had picked up a Roccan ballad about Paolo the Bastard, and it dwindled into the distance now in the warm spring evening air.

When the evening came and the feast was prepared, several problems had been resolved. The festaiuolo Niccolo had found a way in which Evil, so unfortunately individualised in the late Lord Paolo, could be happily diversified into the Seven Deadly Sins, which also offered an opportunity for Envy's iron teeth.

Faith, Hope and Charity were to triumph over the sins, and an angel with a flaming sword would finally banish them from the soil of Rocca. The three Virtues had been recruited from local talent, and it was to be hoped that no courtier and in particular no churchman was an habitúe of the house where they worked; they might be taken exception to as Virtues. The festaiuolo's own virtue had been under critical strain when the opulent, ravishing Madam had pulled him off his bench in a sporting effort to be cast as Charity.

Only very few were aware of the adultery of the late Duchess, and the festaiuolo was luckily unaware that the Duke might discover an extra significance in the caperings of Lechery.

A fine effect was to be the flaming sword wielded by the angel at the finish. He had decided to use the dancer who had made such a hash of the Wild Man, since it was a pity to waste such a face. Certainly there was a risk, if the angel drank too much this time as well, of his setting fire to the Vices with the burning tow on the sword. There had been moments, rehearsing Gluttony, who had thought it repeatedly amusing to shift his false belly round to his backside, that Niccolo's heart had yearned after this satisfying spectacle.

Problems had been solved by people more important than Niccolo. Duke Ippolyto and the Lady Violante, with identical reasons for wishing to appear at their best while yet obliged to maintain the convention of mourning—one for an adulterous sister and the other for a detested stepmother—each decided to lighten the mourning. Duke Ippolyto changed to a burgundy so dense that it quite, at first glance, deceived the eye as nearly black and then seemed to burn in its depths. He was about to enter negotiations through Cardinal Pontano for a dispensation to marry his brother-in-law's daughter, for since he first thumped down on the scaffold beneath her and they had struggled for mastery of his sword arm, he found the idea of a very different kind of struggle with her wholly enticing. The

Lady Violante was selecting deepest purple to set off her white skin and blonde hair. Turning over the jewels spread out on the table by her lady, she made a face at the mourning jewels of jet and pearls, and picked up a diamond and pearl cross, magnificent on her breast. Her lady had seen it somewhere before but did not recall that this had been on the bosom of the Duchess Maria, the gentle lady who had brought up Violante as her own.

While these weighty questions were under consideration still, the Duke sent for the heads of the two factions and their children. He received them in his library, and alone. Cosima appeared as a parcel of white silk lawn, but when in respect to the Duke she took off her veil, all four men had a distinct impression of moonlight emerging from cloud. Cosima herself did not look up, and so her view of the proceedings was of an expanse of floor, two long gowns of velvet, brocade, Flanders weave and silk braid, the seated Duke with an embroidered shoe beneath a swathe of furred cloak, and Leandro's legs. She did not take in the start of the interview.

Her father and Bandini were not so fortunate. They had to bear the concentrated and for a long moment silent attention of the Duke.

"On your knees."

The uncompromising words brought all four of them instantly down; the stiff older joints were as fast as the limber young. Cosima felt cold. With the optimism of her years she had believed in Sigismondo and supposed all was well. But he was not here, and the Duke's face was chill.

"We sent for you to know that we have heard all that you planned against our person and our state, all that a timely intervention thwarted you in doing."

His eyes—how frightening blue eyes were—turned on her father.

"You, by disobeying us and seeking to deceive us, put your

daughter into the hands of our enemies, and to save her from the consequences of your misdeed you were prepared to open the gates of your city to those who would kill your Duke—you, a member of our Council whose particular duty and whose first thought should be how to uphold the state. You would have put Rocca under Castelnuova's domination."

Jacopo seemed about to speak, but the Duke had turned his face from him.

"You, Bandini, were ready to betray us, to give half your fortune to those whom you knew sought the ruin of Rocca. You, Leandro, disobeyed our ban. In your vanity, you imagined our daughter would make an assignation with you." Leandro, his head bent, became crimson. *Indeed*, thought Cosima. "You flouted our ban in coming to the Palace. Your folly forced your father's hand.

"You, Cosima . . ." She was startled. What had she done wrong, who thought herself wronged? ". . . You lent yourself to your father's deceit, aiding him in setting aside our command. You obeyed him and not the father of your city.

"All of you are guilty: disloyal, treacherous. You may blame one who manipulated you—I tell you the weakness in our state which he used was caused by your feud. No traitor could flourish without the chances which your disaffection, your disregard of your true duty, gave to him."

There was silence. No one lifted eyes or head.

"You two fathers: where do you expect your children's duty to lie? To their friends, their pastimes, their quarrels? Or to you?"

Di Torre, Bandini muttered, blurted an assent: "To us."

"So do I expect your duty."

Bandini this time was about to protest his future devotion when the Duke's harsh voice silenced him.

"One traitor, dear to me, now hangs in chains from the city

wall." Cosima remembered the maids' dreadful account of the tar-covered body in its chains.

"You are less dear to me. What do you look for?"

Dear God! Cosima was trembling. She saw, through tears, her father throw himself flat down, arms towards the Duke.

"I implore your mercy."

Bandini went down on his face. Cosima thought, frantic, *Should I, too? My dress . . .* She was putting her hands to the floor all the same, seeing Leandro do so, when the Duke said, "Up, up," and her father and Bandini pushed themselves to their knees again. The Duke's hand gestured them to their feet.

"You will carry out my former decree. You will betroth your children to each other now, here in our presence."

Cosima's eyes met Leandro's. She saw his dazed smile and felt herself smiling, tentatively; then, remembering modesty, she blushed and looked down. It was becoming quite a habit, marrying Leandro.

The Duke had been talking about fines, about her dowry. Now he said, "Your grandchildren shall share your blood," and Cosima blushed again.

The Duke's handclap summoned a page. All had been arranged, for the Duke had only to nod to him. They waited in silence. She did not dare to look up in case Leandro was still watching her. The doors opened to admit the Cardinal himself, and after him a priest carrying his stole, which he kissed and put on.

In the prison Leandro's hand had been clammy. Now it was warm. The Cardinal's stole lay over their clasped fingers, rough gold threads embroidered like the borders of a missal with vines and flowers. She must have said what she was supposed to say. A betrothal was not usually as formal as this, but the Duke was clearly leaving no chance for the families to rescind it. Now the unthinkable, di Torre himself embracing Ugo Bandini, exchanging the kiss of peace. Watching, Cosima became aware of another watcher, in the shadows by the door, clasping an elbow and rubbing his lips with a forefinger. He was slightly smiling.

At the feast that night, Leandro was thoughtful and hardly conscious that everyone at the tables was regarding him in the light of a fascinating ex-corpse, who instead of sitting there looking handsome in brocade might have been wearing tar and chains, like Lord Paolo—whom people had recently discovered that they had never really trusted. They thought the pretty little di Torre girl looked radiant, though of course on her first appearance in public, now she was betrothed and could show her face, she was properly shy and did not venture a word. She had been in a convent, it was said, captured by the Duke Francesco's men, but all delays had been in vain: the enemies were to marry, after all. People professed themselves not deceived by the apparent friendliness of old di Torre and Bandini. Feuds were not buried like that without a few bodies being buried beforehand. No one could remember which classical myth told of two warring families compelled to marry, all the males with all the females, who were pledged to murder their husbands to prevent consummation, but someone had the pleasing idea that Cosima di Torre looked radiant because she was planning to take a knife to her marriage bed and show Leandro Bandini how the Duchess ought to have dealt with him.

Leandro was, in fact, wondering if the marriage ceremony, which the Duke had announced he would honour with his presence, would now take place in the Cathedral. He had been among the silent crowd in the great square today, watching Cardinal Pontano conduct the long and complicated final stages of reconsecrating the Cathedral; they watched him blessing the outer walls with salt and water. The great doors had remained closed since the Duke's brother was cut down in the chancel.

The Cardinal had knocked thrice on these doors with his staff while the choir recited, "Lift up your gates, ye Princes, and be lift up, ye everlasting doors, that the King of Glory may come in." The voice inside the doors could not clearly be heard asking "Who is this King of Glory?" but the Cardinal's reply came with firm triumph: "The Lord of Hosts, He is the King of Glory." Leandro had reflected then that on the temporal plane, too, the Lord who commanded the hosts was the one with the final say in things. He had listened to the Cardinal's thrice-repeated "*Aperite!*" which at last was obeyed; the doors slowly groaned open on the darkness beyond. The tall scarlet figure had stooped to trace a cross with his staff on the threshold and to bid all phantoms flee the sign; two black birds, startled by the sudden chanting of the choir, burst into flight from some perch on the Cathedral front and the crowd with gleeful horror called them phantoms; Leandro had the idea that they might indeed be the shades of the guilty Duchess and her wicked lover, vanishing with a clapping of wings over the roofs. He heard again the echoing cry of the Cardinal as he stepped into the empty Cathedral: "Peace be on this House!"

Leandro looked at his father and saw him raise his cup to his future daughter-in-law. Peace be on all houses.

Sigismondo was at the end of the table, perfectly placed to survey everyone and to be seen. He was wearing, besides the Bandini chain, a splendid collar of faceted links from which hung a pendant jewel. It was obvious that he had been greatly instrumental for the present happy safety of the state and everyone would have liked to know how.

Benno spoke from behind Sigismondo, but with his mouth full, so that he had to repeat it, leaning over his master's shoulder. "I've been wondering about that nun you tied up. What d'you suppose will have happened to her?"

"That will depend on her Mother Superior."

Benno took a flagon officiously from the hands of the approaching server and filled Sigismondo's cup to the brim. Sigismondo drank deep, Benno holding on to the flagon until he could pour again.

"I fancy it will all come out how little she left the world behind when she entered the cloister. She was too used to power to give it up."

The server got hold of the flagon and bore it away.

"My lady says you told her the nun was a Bandini, but I never heard of no Bandini taking the veil in Castelnuova."

"I didn't tell her it was a Bandini. She was suggesting we should confide in her; I asked what she would say if I told her the nun was a Bandini. To ask her for help would have been indiscreet, as she's Lord Paolo's mother."

Benno's face lit with pure pleasure. "Was she then? The old Duke's bed-warmer." He was struck in the back by a platter carried past, and bumped into Sigismondo's chair. He clung on to it to support him in his surprise. "Now I come to think of it, of course she turned nun when he died. So she was working to make her *son* Duke."

"Mothers are like that. Remember Poggio's mother—she'd do anything for her son. Dangerous things, mothers."

Benno squatted beside Sigismondo, the better to carry on the conversation amid the din of the feast, and was given a drumstick pulled from the fowl on his master's plate. He asked, obscured, "How'd you know she was Lord Paolo's mother?"

"You might have known for yourself if you'd got a good look at her in the stables. Her son and grandson have the same eyes."

"Sort of sad look, you mean? Wonder what'll happen to the young one, then. I mean, life didn't hand him a good deal from the start."

"It seems the Lady Violante has taken charge of him. I dare say when she marries," and Sigismondo glanced at the blonde head near the Duke Ippolyto's shoulder, "that she will take him with her. He'd be happier away from here—as happy as he's able to be."

Benno cogitated, which gave him an expression of complacent idiocy. "You can do what you like now the Duke is so grateful to you, can't you?"

"No. The gratitude of princes is limiting. You must be there to display it. Princes need it to be seen that deeds done for their advantage are rewarded."

Benno was silent, sucking the joint of the drumstick. The music broke out very plangently as a new course was brought in, and he had to wait to be heard. Then he said, "I suppose you're saying that this is my last feast for a while."

Sigismondo smiled and drank his wine. "What makes you think I'm going to take you with me?"

Benno pointed the drumstick. "Two reasons. One, I can look witless, so people say things in front of me they wouldn't say in front of anyone else. Two—"

"Even if they know I employ you?"

"Two, if they know you employ me, they think you must have a soft heart." Benno belched. "And that gets them dead."

Sigismondo offered him another drumstick. "Eat while you may. We leave tomorrow."